The Rise of Isarn

The Dark Artifacts – Book 2

By

T. R. Edwards

Table of Contents

Clan of the
Iron Mountains

Brahne ✦

The House of
CORVUS

Rhyke ✦   Dullahan ✦

The Freehold of
STANROCC

The
Granite ✦
Hall

✦

Isle of
VAIN

Kingdom of

SKELDUS

Sirion ✦

The Tribe of
DOCGA

A Map of Fyrian and Beyond

Chapter 1: The Beginning of the End

"It is over." Draegan felt a wave of relief wash over him and he loosened his grip on the sword. Exhaustion dulled his thoughts as he stared at the floor. "Vangen is dead," Draegan whispered as he stood motionless in the quiet study. He blinked at hearing his own words, as if waking from a dream. "And yet I live." He touched the clasp at his neck and looked down at his chest where the sword had pierced him, finding no damage to himself or his clothing. "This is beyond reason."

It had been an hour since sunrise and Draegan hadn't moved from where he stood when he drove the black flames of Carnis Fornax through his brother's chest and into his own. The blade still burned greedily as he held the cold grip of the sword in his hand, its ethereal fire causing the shadows of the heaps of books to dance on the opposite wall. The green fire of Vangen's *ferian* spell had died earlier, leaving nothing but ash where his brother's body had lain.

"If I am to believe his last words, then Vangen killed the members of the Council in cold blood, and delivered one Dark Artifact each into the hands of the other four kingdoms." He shook his head. "And through all his deceit and foul sorcery he would blame me for his terrible actions. Vangen's mercenary Ravens must even now be spreading rumors of my treason against the Empire, blaming the murders of the Council members as well as his own death on me. He has invited war to the very doorstep of our kingdom."

Draegan bowed his head over the ashes of his brother's corpse and watched flecks of dust float gently in the sunlight that streamed through the sooty window. He took a breath and looked up. His wheeling thoughts snapped to attention. "Gron," he said anxiously as he extinguished the flame of his brother's sword. With a hurried gesture he tucked the hilt into his belt. Draegan walked quickly to the center of the study, which was the only place where the flagstones of the floor lay uncluttered by books and papers. Trying a few simple spells with little success at first, he eventually happened upon the one that opened the hidden staircase beneath the floor tiles that he had ascended only hours ago. He cast an illumination spell as he descended the staircase that spiraled down into the catacombs beneath Dullahan. After what seemed an eternity of walking downward, he once again felt the lingering dampness of the stale air.

At the bottom of the staircase he cast the ball of light from his spell high into the air, illuminating the shadowy space. Above him a dimly lit, barrel-vaulted chamber soared several stories upward and into the bedrock of the castle. In front of Draegan the chamber ran into the darkness, intersected at ninety degree angles by hundreds of smaller vaulted chambers. Thousands of small alcoves were carved in the walls, each containing countless dismembered bodies whose arms and legs spilled over the sides of the niches.

Draegan walked toward the far end of the chamber where the light of his spell revealed a mass of rubble that sealed the far end of the tunnel. Beneath the giant slabs of stone and hunks of support columns, the pallid white flesh of the Beast of the Blade shone in the dim light. The creature shrieked as Draegan approached, and the multitude of arms and legs that protruded from the rubble flailed in the wavering light of the spell. He stared at the abomination in silence. Though it felt like an age had passed since he and his Graywalkers had fought this creature it had been only a few hours. Draegan drew a short breath and held it in anticipation. Pushing aside the memory of Gron, buried on the other side and betrayed by Ceredyn, Draegan allowed some small hope to enter his heart that he could somehow get past the creature and the pile of rock to save his trapped comrade.

Draegan stopped a few feet from the beast and crouched to the ground. Drawing a rune in the stone dust on the floor he let his trapped breath escape in a rushed whisper. "Graywalkers, to me." He waited a moment and after getting no response, he bowed his head, now swimming with despair. "So I have lost Gron too," Draegan growled through clenched teeth as he slammed his fist into the rune. "Will I have everyone taken from me before this ends?" He clenched his fist and rose with a resolve building in his heart. "Then I will make sure they will not have died in vain," he said and grasped the sword at his belt. Black fire jetted from the hilt making a darkly shimmering blade where there had been none moments before. The beast shrieked and rolled its hundreds of eyes in terror as it gnashed its teeth in protest. A bilious fluid leaked from its many mouths and burned its pale skin as the caustic spit trickled down its soft white body. The creature began frantically grasping at the stones that held it prisoner and tore at its own flesh as Draegan approached.

"I can feel it hunger," Draegan said as he looked at the blade. The chamber cooled as the voracious flames leapt and moved ever closer to the beast. The creature panicked, and using what little strength remained, began to pull and heave at the stones that buried it, twisting and breaking several of its limbs in its desperation. Draegan shook his head in sorrow. "Vangen was a cruel master to have trapped so many souls in such a piteous creature as you, Beast, but I will end your suffering." He raised the blade high above his head the black fire casting an unearthly pallor through the chamber. "Now sleep."

An instant later the blade was buried up to the hilt in the creature. For a moment, its mouths howled in agony and its body trembled as the black fire coursed from the grip and jetted across the flesh of the creature. Draegan felt a surge of power rush through him as the hundreds of souls that lived within the dying beast were pulled into the greedy blade. Draegan's eyes widened. "Incredible," he said as he drew the blade from the withering carcass before him and regarded the black fire. He stood mesmerized as he gazed into the flames of the blade. He felt its hunger course through his own body as whispers of power echoed in his mind. Suddenly the rubble that had trapped the beast shifted and slid. Draegan jumped out of the way of the landslide and cast the blade to the ground, dodging a rolling chunk of support column that would have crushed him.

"I feel you corrupting me, twisting me and reshaping me in your dark image. I came here to help a friend and instead have taken the lives of hundreds of Vangen's innocent victims." He picked up the blade in disgust and extinguished the flame with one motion. "I must steel myself against you," he said as he tucked the hilt back into his belt and headed down the tunnel toward the spiraling stairs that wound their way up and into the bedrock of the castle. "And I must begin anew to save Fyrian."

Chapter 2: The Eye

"There must be answers here," Draegan said as he rifled through the sheaves of papers and pushed aside the books on Vangen's lectern. "Though with these thousands of books and codices scattered about, finding them will prove more difficult than sorting through the vaults beneath Vatn.

He slumped into Vangen's chair and folded his hands across his chest. "When I sought the Artifacts before, it was with the aid of my Graywalkers. I must once again hunt the Artifacts, taking them back from the other Kingdoms, but this time I must go alone. And those who now hold them will no doubt find it most difficult to relinquish them to me though it is for their greater good." He leaned forward and tried opening the drawers in the desk, looking for any inspiration. On the ground by the chair sat a leather-bound tome that looked much newer than the tattered antiques strewn about the study.

"This is what he was writing in when I entered," Draegan said as he lifted the heavy volume and laid it on the desk with a resounding thud. The thick leather cover was tooled with thousands of arcane marks, only a few of which Draegan could read. "The tongue of Iss," he said and drew a sharp breath. "Vangen was more fluent than I thought. Now I too will have to master it in order to make sense of all his work," he said glancing around the dusty study. He opened the cover and was met with a loose slip of parchment scrawled in Vangen's child-like hand. "At least this is written in a language I can read, although his penmanship may prove my undoing."

"I have connected the eye to the dark energy surrounding the Artifacts," Draegan read aloud. "It should be a simple matter of manipulating my thoughts to make the eye conjure the necessary images." Draegan crumpled the paper and moved his other hand unconsciously to his hairline. "So that's how he did it. He pushed the images of the Artifacts into my head through the eye of Islak," he said, rubbing his temple absent-mindedly. He thought for a moment and walked to the window. He brushed his hand over the panes and cleared some of the soot. The noon sun, so long absent from the study, fell on the myriad books that lay strewn on the floor. Draegan watched the dust filter through the sunbeam. "I have been in the presence of all but one of the Artifacts and felt their evil. If I have knowledge of the Artifacts, and the eye is linked to them, perhaps I can force it to show me where they are now."

With renewed vigor, Draegan spent the rest of the evening reading from the assortment of tomes and folios that lay just within arm's reach of the desk. Shortly past midnight he came upon the notes Vangen had written explaining how to manipulate the eye of Islak. Hours later, after a few failed attempts, Draegan yelled and grabbed his head as he curled up in pain. The familiar swirling chaos in the eye parted and showed him a bow sitting on a table in a great wooden hall built of living trees, the branches intertwining into the stones of the soaring structure.

"The bow known as the Dark Ichor sits in the Conclave Temple in Sirion." He stood and straightened his cloak. "Then I ride for the Tribe of Docga."

Draegan picked his way through the heaps of books as he moved toward the wood and iron door opposite the desk. As he placed his hand on the door, the iron bands glowed briefly and then cooled to the touch before he heard the mechanisms inside the door click and begin to stir. Heavy bolts withdrew into the wall and the door swung easily open. "It seems the magic in the door obeys me now," Draegan said as he gathered his cloak and stepped into the darkened hall.

He moved silently down the hall and through the darkened corridors until he came to the entrance to his old room. He paused for a moment and collected himself. It had been more than a year since he had been to his chambers and Issa had been alive to greet him. How much had changed since then. He pushed the door open expectantly, cast an illumination spell and was shocked by the chaos he saw. He had left his room in a state of disorder, but since that time someone had visited turning the clutter to chaos. "Vangen," he said as he looked around. His bed was ripped to pieces and feathers covered the hundreds of books that were torn and tossed about his room. Stones from the fireplace had been removed and all his furniture had been smashed.

"What was he looking for?" Draegan wondered. He spotted a Night's Watch uniform partially obscured by books and shredded parchment. He changed into the new clothing and rummaged through the debris until he found an empty pack. "I'll need food."

The castle was still asleep and Draegan easily slipped unnoticed as he made his way to the store rooms near the kitchen. He passed the massive stone doors of the Council Chamber and thought again of Vangen's betrayal. "My kingdom is leaderless. I dare not show myself or stand before my people. They think me a traitor. War will be upon us soon unless I can reclaim the four remaining Dark Artifacts, but I have no way of convincing my people that it is Vangen who deceived them and that my current actions are the only path to peace." He placed a gloved hand on the figures carved into the door, feeling the smooth stone through the leather. He looked up and saw the Sages leading their armies into battle against the armies of Iss. "For now, I must leave Fyrian and my people to their own fate. I trust they will hold together while I once again hunt the Dark Artifacts. May the Sages guide them, and hasten me in my quest."

Nearing the kitchen he slowed as he heard people moving about, getting ready for the day. He overheard pieces of conversation as the cooks prepared.

"It's all rumors, anyway. I knew the boy for ten years and he'd never do that. I don't care what they're all saying."

"Believe what you will, but the lad killed the Council and his own brother. Lucky for us Vangen got the Artifacts out of here before he could use them against us. Old Atrox must be rolling over in his grave to see what's become of his golden boy." There was a pause as some pans banged together. "I'm taking my family south, don't want to be anywhere near Dullahan anymore. I hear part of the army is defecting north over the Iron Mountains. There's not much left to keep me here."

"You must be crazy. Dullahan's the safest place you can be right now. We've got walls and gates and guards. Besides, if all this nonsense is true, the countryside is the first place that gets it. If any of the other kingdoms are foolish enough to attack us now that we've no King, they'll pillage the lands on their march here. In war people are tripping over themselves to get behind high walls, and there aren't many walls higher than ours. Besides, Draegan's long gone by now and the whole Empire is out hunting him, if it makes you feel better. Though I don't know why. He couldn't have done it. I just won't believe it."

Draegan flushed with anger. He considered stepping into the kitchen to defend his honor, but decided it was more prudent to make his way into the store room, gather some supplies in his pack and exit through the hidden door in the back of the closet that led to the gatehouse near the inner courtyard.

Draegan shut the hidden door behind him quietly and moved down the dark corridor. A little over two years ago he had entered Dullahan through the same hall and encountered Vangen leaving. If he had known then the depths of his brother's madness or the treacherous things Vangen would convince him to do, he would have ended him then and there. Draegan shook the fantasy from his mind and focused on the present task at hand. He needed to leave Dullahan undetected and make his way to the Greater Serpion River that bordered the Vilkas Forest in Docga. From there he would head to the Conclave Temple in Sirion and claim the Dark Ichor, though he trembled at the thought of holding the fearsome weapon again.

Skirting the inner courtyard he made his way to the drainage gate and, pressing the locking mechanism, released the grate. Listening to the rush of water as the sewage was diverted down another drain, he slid himself into the damp tunnel and secured the grate behind him. Walking a few feet into the darkness he felt along the cold, wet stones until he found the mark carved in the rock. Touching it, a soft green glow emanated from the seal and began to travel along the mortar joints in the stone, casting a dim light through the tunnel. Draegan made his way under the width of the inner wall into the outer courtyard. At the other end of the sewage drain he extinguished the illumination spell and unlatched the grate above him while sliding it onto the cobble stones of the empty courtyard. He waited and listened to two guards walking the wall above him.

"He was one of the best swordsmen in the Empire. I wouldn't want to fight him, especially now that he's given himself over to the dark arts."

"That's exactly why we have to stop him. If we leave and go north with everyone else, then no one will stand against him. Our families are here. Our lives are here. This is our country and I refuse to run without a fight."

"Well I wish you luck, since it'll just be you here patrolling these walls by next week. I'm taking my family and heading north. You're a fool to stay."

Draegan waited for the voices to recede as the guards continued their patrol along the top of the inner wall. When he could no longer hear them he exited the sewer and replaced the grate, feeling the metal catch, silently locking it in place. He reached his hand through the bars and pulled the ring, listening to the low rumble of the sewage water rush back into the tunnel. He crouched near the massive wall and considered his next move.

"How quickly the hearts of men change. They are as inconstant as the wind. If only they knew the truth." Draegan shook his head. "I haven't the time for this. I need to find the Artifacts quickly and I can't take a horse from the stables through the Eastern Gate without rousing half the castle. I'll have to shadow walk through the portcullis."

Draegan took a slip of parchment from his pack and drew the shadow walking rune in blood which he took from a small cut he made on his forearm. He slipped across the courtyard and reached the shadows of the guard tower unseen. Passing the paper through the bars of the gate he touched his palm to the wall of the tower and let the darkness swallow him as the ground began to heave. A moment later he was beyond the gate. He listened for any alarm. A cold wind picked up and dissipated the black mist that surrounded him. The colonnade of braziers that lined the King's Road guttered in the breeze as Draegan watched the steam of his breath and put his glove back on. "Winter has come. The murder of Vangen and the Council will have the King's Road heavily patrolled. I'll have to move through the country. A *staminis* spell will do."

He made the *staminis* mark on his throat and was off in the faint light of the false dawn, heading south and east through the rolling farmland to the Greater Serpion River and the Vilkas beyond.

Chapter 3: Desolation

Draegan ran for hours eastward into the sun, staying off of the roads and moving in what little cover he was afforded by the rolling farmlands near Dullahan. The sun gave a rosy glow to the frost covered fields, though as he moved through the pastures he saw little life stirring in the few barns and houses he passed. No chimneys gave sign of breakfast cooking and no barns stood open to let their occupants roam in the pastures. By aid of the *staminis* spell he continued sprinting through the empty fields for some time until at last on the horizon, he spied a small wisp of smoke and curiosity drove him to head directly for it.

Once Draegan arrived at the barn he broke his spell and circled around it, keeping an eye on the house as he gulped down the cold morning air in ragged breaths and slowed his racing heart. He heard no signs of livestock in the barn and moved closer to the house, trying to peer through the window for a better look as he positioned himself near the cellar entrance.

"You looking for me?" the old man asked as he walked up behind Draegan.

Draegan tensed and his hand shot for the hilt of sword, and then relaxed. "Yes, though you gave me a start," Draegan said as he turned to face the old farmer. The farmer stopped and stared at Draegan for a moment before he shook his head. "Do you know me?" Draegan asked.

"Aye, I know you. You're Leon's boy. Saw you win a few tournaments, years ago." He paused and looked around. "Though I don't see your dark army anywhere." He stuck his hands in his pockets. "Do it quickly or don't do it at all. I've got a farm to keep. Such as it is."

Draegan held up his hands defensively. "I'm not going to kill you, sir. And as you see, I have no dark army. Those are lies spread by Vangen. It is true that I'm gathering the Dark Artifacts, but I do it to destroy them. I have no designs to use them against my countrymen." He looked at the barn and turned to the farmer. "If you have a horse you are willing to part with, it would give me and all good men of Fyrian great aid." Draegan reached behind him and into a pocket and produced four gold coins. "This is more than fair."

The old man scoffed. "What would I do with gold? Look around. I'm the only one left out here. Everyone else has fled. I got no family left alive so I got nowhere to go. Might as well get buried here rather then get buried somewhere foreign."

"I had noticed on my journey here. What caused this exodus?"

"Your reavers, boy. Over the past year we've seen enough people go missing in the night, seen enough livestock slaughtered, and seen enough hamlets burned. People eventually get the idea to move." The farmer spat on the hard packed ground in the shadow of the barn and hunched his shoulders as another cold wind blew across the fields.

"Vangen's reavers, sir, not mine." Draegan said through his clenched jaw, trying to control his anger. "I knew his evil extended to the other kingdoms, but I thought he might have had enough grace to spare his own people."

"Had?" the farmer asked, lifting his head to look at Draegan and squinting.

"There is truth to the rumor that Vangen is dead. I admit that it was by my hand, though what you hear of the Council and my dark army are all lies." He looked toward the barn. "I tarry to long. I must recover the Dark Artifacts or it will all be for naught, and

Fyrian will be plunged into war once again." Draegan looked at the farmer. "If you have a horse, I will pay you dearly for it."

"She's in the barn. Almost as old as me though," the farmer said as he motioned for Draegan to follow him. "I don't know where you're headed but she won't get you very far."

Draegan thanked the man who had little trouble accepting the gold when it was offered again. The farmer saddled the old nag while Draegan inspected his new mount with dismay. Minutes later he was gone, riding through the fields and searching for a road to pick up on his journey east. He rode for an hour before he found a foot path that led to a dirt road. The sun was high in the sky and the rolling hills of the farmland gave way to the great basin valley in the southeast of Skeldus that gave the kingdom so much of its wealth. Here the soil was rich and crops grew with ease. Temperatures were mild and rain plentiful enough, save for winter, to ensure Skeldus never suffered famine. But as Draegan looked across the landscape he saw the fields lying fallow and what few buildings stood were burned and partially collapsed. There was no indication the laborers had turned the remains of the fall harvest into the earth or sowed any winter wheat. He saw only desolation covered in a white sheen of hoar frost.

"The reavers," Draegan said as he pushed down the road and headed into the great basin. Everywhere he looked houses were abandoned and destroyed. Plows were left overturned in fields that showed no signs of life.

"He's poisoned the ground so nothing will grow," Draegan said and clenched the reigns of his horse as he spurred her onward down the road. An hour of riding later Draegan spotted three figures on the horizon riding toward him. He decided it would look suspicious to move off the road and strike across the fields as they had likely already seen him. He pulled his hood up and rode toward them.

"A Night's Watchman this far south?" the rider shouted when they were within a few hundred feet of each other. "I thought you lot stayed behind the walls and left the dirty work to us."

Draegan saw they were dressed in the colors of the standing army of Skeldus, though they were covered in dust and their garments were in need of repair. Draegan waved and answered the men. "The Emperor lets us off the leash from time to time, mostly to clean up after you lot." The others grinned and rode toward him.

"War is coming friend," the lead rider said. He was older than the other two riders and bore the mark of a sergeant on his collar, though it was nearly faded beyond recognition. "What drives you so far south on your own? This land is dead. Almost as dead as that nag you're riding."

"I would ask the same of you," Draegan said as he looked at the other two riders who pulled up beside their friend and eyed Draegan warily.

The soldier grinned, his leathery skin nearly cracking as his thin lips parted, showing more silver than teeth. He patted the satchel that hung from his mount. "The reavers don't leave much life where they go, but unlike us they don't have an appetite for the finer things." Draegan heard a metallic noise coming from the bag and instantly understood.

"So you ride through the countryside relieving the dead of their valuables?" he asked. "And what good will that do you when the war comes?"

"Well they don't need 'em no more, and we'll be long gone by the time anybody marches on Skeldus," the lead soldier answered as the other two smiled at each other.

"Indeed you will," Draegan growled as he reached to his belt.

The riders in the back were still smiling at each other when the lead rider's face drained of color. "It's Draegan!" he shouted and yanked his reigns to turn his mount and flee. In an instant Draegan had drawn his fiery blade and plunged it through the man's chest. He felt a rush of cold turn his blood to ice as the rider's soul was pulled into the weapon. The other two fumbled to draw their blades while their mounts panicked at the sight of the black fire, keeping their riders off balance.

Draegan cut down the second rider while the third managed to gain control of his horse and flee. Draegan whispered a word in his mount's ear and she took off like a bolt after the third rider. Draegan closed the distance and effortlessly cut the man down from behind. He grabbed the reigns of the other horse and slowed both down to a stop. He dismounted and left his old nag standing in the barren field as he walked the other back to the road. By the time he finished moving his packs to the soldier's horse, his old nag had started to make its ponderous way back toward the old farmer's land.

"Thank you for your service old girl." He dug his heels into his fresh mount and pushed toward the Vilkas in the east as the sun began to set behind him, casting a long shadow before him.

Chapter 4: The Crossing

Draegan rode for two nights and as many days before he reached the Greater Serpion River. He encountered no one on the road and saw no other signs of life as he traveled in silence, the hooves of his horse churning through the hard packed earth and its labored breathing his only distraction from the devastation he saw all around him. He slept in the saddle, punishing himself as much as his mount, reasoning that his current path was the only way to correct his failure to stop Vangen sooner.

He had pushed his horse hard, almost to the breaking point, trying to cover as much distance as quickly as possible. Near the banks of the river the horse could give no more. Draegan dismounted and immediately the beast collapsed amid the smooth, frost covered rocks that lined the shore. "You have done well," Draegan said as he untied his pack and removed the horse's saddle. The horse rose on shaky legs and stood for some time, staring at the frigid waters as great clouds of its breath drifted over the smooth water. Draegan watched steam rise from the animal as it shambled to the edge of the water and took a long drink before turning back the way it had come.

Draegan saw the silhouette of the Vilkas Forest on the far side of the Greater Serpion, its golds and fiery oranges muted in the pre-light of dawn. In some places the trees had shed their leaves altogether, signaling the turning of the season.

"I'm sure the Rannulfr have erected barriers and placed seals all over the wood. I doubt the best woodsmen and mages in all of Docga have left me any easy ingress into their Kingdom," Draegan said as he tied his boots and gloves to his pack and stepped into the icy waters. He took a sharp breath as the water soaked him through. "I wish there were another way, but I'll have to take my chances."

The Greater Serpion was wide and calm where he crossed, though the current was enough to carry him several miles downstream by the time he had pushed over. The eastern bank of the Serpion had a smaller shore with a much steeper grade that rose several feet above Draegan's head. He sat beneath a tangled mass of overhanging roots and laid out his clothes to dry while he conjured a smokeless fire with some wood he found nearby. He checked for seals but found none. Pulling some hardtack from his pack, he watched the frost melt on the reeds growing by the shore as the sun rose above the horizon, the long shadows of the trees stretching across the leaden waters of the Serpion. Behind him the few birds that endured the colder climes of the northern reaches of Docga awoke and began chattering.

Draegan slipped his boots back on and thought of Gron's betrayal at the hands of Ceredyn. Hate rose within him. "I trusted Ceredyn. And he slew Gron in cold blood and took the Artifacts…" Draegan's body was suddenly racked with pain as the eye of Islak burst to life, sending flashes of light through his mind. Visions of the World Render and two men fighting for it swirled in the tumult. A cloud of black mist shrouded the scene, wiping it from his mind as quickly as it came before the vapors parted and he saw several shadowy forms bent inquisitively over the Black Horn. As the pain died down he was left again with a clear image of a great black bow resting on a table in a grand meeting hall made of living trees.

"Simply thinking of the Artifacts brings them into my mind." He drew a deep breath of cold morning air and rubbed his temples. "I must find a way to get to the Conclave unnoticed. Sirion is a much smaller city compared to Dullahan, and I do not have knowledge of any hidden routes of entry. I'll have to make heavy use of my cloak, although first I must make it through the Vilkas without incident," Draegan said as he rose. He shook off the last vestiges of pain still lingering in his head and scrambled up the bank, slipping into the undergrowth.

"I suppose I control the eye now," he mused as he scanned the tree line for any threatening shapes. "I'll have to keep my thoughts in check so I don't cause the eye to flare to life again." Draegan moved as carefully as he could through the brush, remembering what he had learned as a boy when he studied with the hunt masters in Docga, and the few things Aran had taught him when he was last here, moving south through the Vilkas to the Black Temple beyond the Wolf's Teeth Mountains.

He looked around for the type of shrub Aran had used when they first put ashore on the western limit of Docga and noticed some growing near a stand of poplars. Crushing the leaves just as Aran had, he smeared the oils over his skin in the hope that its scent would keep the Rannulfr from picking up his trail. "I would not have men of Aran's caliber pursuing me."

Draegan decided it was best to move cautiously and use the *staminis* spell only when he was close to the city of Sirion in case he needed a final push to shake his pursuers or needed to charge the gates and make his way to the Conclave Temple in the city's interior.

He slept little and ate less, walking swiftly for days and through most of the nights. He used the fragments of the stars that shone through the thick forest canopy as a guide, and left as few signs of his movement as possible for any trackers to follow. Draegan made no seals or barriers for fear the Rannulfr would sense the magic and be drawn to him. As the sun set behind him on the third day of his journey, in order to get a better view of the land, he climbed an old oak that still held many of its leaves despite the turn of seasons. As he picked his way to the upper branches he saw the eternal watch fire of Manath the Hunter burning at the top of a hill a few miles southeast of him. In the fading light he could make out the wall of Sirion as it rose from the forest, the only evidence of man's presence in this sylvan wilderness that stretched as far as he could see.

Draegan was about to climb down and head for the wall when he heard a rustling beneath him. Peering through the leaves he saw a human form crouched near the trunk of the oak. The man was dressed in a simple leather jerkin and breeches with a bow slung over his shoulder. His hand rested on the handle of his hunting knife as he bent down and looked at the disturbed leaves near the roots of the tree. Draegan's chest tightened as he watched the Rannulfr push the leaves aside and touch the trunk of the tree, noticing a boot scuff he'd carelessly made when he ascended earlier. Looking up the man's face tightened as he saw a shadowy mass fall from the branches. Draegan plunged his dirk in the Rannulfr's neck and used the dead man's body to break his fall. Draegan lay still atop the corpse, holding his breath and listening for signs of other Rannulfr nearby.

"I hope he was alone." Draegan rose, cleaned his blade and sheathed it in his boot. "Rannulfr hunting parties are not known to let prey slip through their grasp, and if he was a scout, others will follow when he doesn't report back." He sat the corpse against the tree to give the impression the man was merely resting before he cast the *staminis* spell and headed for Sirion. The sun had set and the forest had turned black within minutes, swallowing Draegan in shadow as he ran east.

***

As the forest thinned Draegan picked up a footpath that eventually became a road as he neared the capital city of Sirion. He broke the spell and fell in with a large group of stragglers, mostly woodsmen and a few hunters who were returning home before the gates locked for the night. He said nothing and no one seemed to pay him any heed. Only a few talked, mostly complaining of the scarcity of game and the unseasonable cold.

Draegan passed the gate tower with little scrutiny. To disguise the fact he wore the garb of the Night Watch, he pulled the Shadow Walker cloak tight about him and kept to the center of the group as much as possible. The dark cloak seemed to swallow him and what little light the guard's torches cast as the group passed under the archway was muted as it fell upon him.

"All in for the night," the guard yelled up to the two men above. As the stragglers made their way up the cobblestone road Draegan heard a click followed by the sound of chains rattling. A resounding thud told him the portcullis had descended for the night. "That will make leaving more difficult than I'd hoped. Perhaps I should wait for dawn," he wondered as he broke from the group and slipped down a side road and into an alley. A dog sniffing at some garbage started when it saw him and ran away.

The small alley was comprised of the backs of simple shops that had their storefronts facing the main road. All were closed until dawn. A few of the second stories of the buildings had candles in the window, indicating the shop owners and their families were upstairs and settled in for the night.

Draegan scaled what seemed to be an empty leather merchant's shop, judging by the look and smell of the refuse piled near the rear door, and made his way onto the tiled roof. He could see the watch fire of Manath burning in the center of the city near the Conclave Temple. Seeing the city from this vantage point reminded Draegan of when he and Vangen were first brought here to the Tribe of Docga to be presented to the hunt masters as part of their education. As much as he was awed by the magnitude of Dullahan, having only been in King Leon's custody for less than a year, he was equally stunned when he arrived in Sirion and first saw the Conclave Temple.

The city of Sirion was built upon a hillock that gave a sweeping view of the Vilkas Forest. Atop it sat the temple, a living structure formed from the ancient trees that grew on the hill. The legend of Sirion's founding spoke of how Sage Docga bent the massive trees and wove their branches together to form the Conclave for his people. The building had few traditional walls and birds and other wildlife passed in and out. During the day dappled light filtered through the rooftop canopy, yet Sage Docga's skill with magic was such that three thousand years later, the Conclave still permitted no rain to enter the hall.

Snapping himself from his reverie, Draegan dropped down from the roof and landed as softly as a cat on the cobbles of the alley. Having a better view of the layout of the city and marking in his mind a convoluted path to the temple that would keep him in alleys and shadow, he turned and made his way toward the Conclave, pulling his cloak tight and his step light.

Chapter 5: The Dark Ichor Returns

"It is too evil a thing to bend to our good intentions. We cannot profit through its use," Tior said as he addressed Eldra and Keda, the two highest ranking members of the Conclave. He stood and stepped away from the table where the others sat, still staring at the great dark bow on the table before them. "It reeks of poison and hate, and I would sooner have it swallowed in the Southern Sea than debate any longer."

"And yet what other options lay before us?" he asked, smoothing his hunting tunic and casting a wary glance over his shoulder at the bow. He pulled his long black hair tight and bound it behind his head before turning back to face the other two who sat at the table. "The Dark Ichor has been with us barely a week and already I feel it clouding my better judgment. How do we know the rumors are true?"

Eldra Lykos stood and addressed Tior in the great hall. "Our Rannulfr are incorruptible," she said. "When our spies returned five days ago with news that Draegan had executed Tysta along with the rest of the Council at Dullahan it was a shock to us all. But here lies incontrovertible proof." She gestured toward the bow. "Vangen managed to relieve Draegan of a few of the Artifacts and sent them to the other four kingdoms to be used as a boon before he was murdered by his brother. Draegan will come looking for this, accompanied by his dark army, and we are in no position to offer resistance unless we take the initiative and make use of this small hope."

Tior straightened his thin frame and stood to his full height as he approached the table. He leaned over the other two. "When you chose me as the Master of the Hunt after news of Tysta's assassination, the responsibility to protect the Tribe of Docga became my burden." He looked at Eldra with his clear gray eyes. "I cannot in good conscience make use of this 'small hope', as you call it, without loosing a plague upon all of Athar and ending the greater hope of peace. The weapon is evil through and through."

Keda coughed and waved at Tior. "We were right to choose him as the Master of the Hunt. He sees with eyes unclouded and his intentions are pure. But you are right, Eldra. Draegan will come for the Dark Ichor in time. And he will come with his shadow warriors of Iss and ravage our lands. Already the southern and eastern reaches of Skeldus have fallen to his power. The great basin that fed Leon's Kingdom lies fallow and there is little left of its people. Without the continued aid of Skeldus, the other three kingdoms will soon feel the pangs of hunger and will march on Dullahan, even if the Artifacts they possess do not compel them to do so sooner. War is again imminent. And we have yet to regain our full strength from the War for Unity. We will suffer greatly at Draegan's hands when he crosses the Serpion and comes for our unspoiled resources."

"Then what would you council, Keda?" Eldra said. "Are we to give up the one thing that can stand against a force so powerful? Would you have Docga lie down in supplication and hope that Draegan proves a merciful master?"

Keda coughed again and furrowed his brow. "I believe in peace, and this Artifact removes all chance of it as long as we possess it. Tior was right. This bow must not be in our possession when Draegan arrives in our wood with his legions of reavers. We must rid ourselves of it and in doing so hope that his wrath passes over our kingdom and spares us the carnage that his forces would have unleashed upon our land."

A clear voice rang out from the shadows near the Conclave entrance.

"Keda gives good council, although you are wrong in assuming I need an army to take what is mine," Draegan said as he stepped from the darkness and into the light of the Conclave temple. "But you are right in saying that I will spare you my wrath if you give me the bow."

Chapter 6: The Flight to Dullahan

"Stand down Usurper." Tior spun to face Draegan while his hand slipped to the hunting knife in his belt. "Your dark arts will gain you no advantage here. Vangen has made it known how to stop your Shadow Walking, and this Conclave is protected with ancient seals from Sage Docga himself should you try your dark magic." Eldra wove her hands together as Keda traced a symbol in the air which caught fire and vanished in an instant. Tior continued. "You are trapped. Give yourself over to justice and pay for your crimes."

"Usurper?" Draegan asked curiously as he slowly approached the table, keeping Tior to his left and approaching the other two who were rising slowly from their chairs. "Crimes? When did preserving peace become a crime? Taking the throne from Vangen was simple justice. You have been gravely misled. He slew his father, King Atrox, and it was Vangen, not I who betrayed and killed Tysta and the members of the Council. I only seek these Artifacts in order to remove their threat from our Empire and restore the peace Vangen disturbed. I heard Keda and Tior agree with my reasoning, so I urge you to follow their advice. Allow me to bear away the heavy burden of the Dark Ichor."

"It is difficult to believe the words of a man who dons the Shadow Walker and even now makes ready to wield Carnis Fornax against his fellow countrymen," Tior said as he came to a stop between the table and Draegan. "Your words are belied by your actions, Draegan. Perhaps if you gave up your sword and cloak we would find it easier to listen."

"We have no time for debate, Tior," Draegan said as he tucked his thumbs into his belt, near the hilt of Carnis Fornax. "The Dark Artifacts are once again loose in Fyrian. The twenty year peace you and my father fought for is ending as we speak. My kingdoms make to fall upon one another. I act only to prevent this and in so doing I must once again take back these weapons and lock them away from the world of men, for you see how easily they corrupt and twist even the most noble of hearts and righteous of intentions."

Keda stood in front of Eldra and folded his arms across his chest. "Perhaps it us who should keeps these things from you, child. Your conceit is truly grand, if you think yourself Emperor of Fyrian. We would not have a traitor and murder as our ruler."

"How thoroughly Vangen has poisoned you against me. You cannot reason while the Artifacts are nearby," Draegan said. He bowed his head and sighed. "Hope is lost while the Artifacts live. You give me no other choice."

Draegan launched himself at Tior. In one fluid motion he grabbed Tior's wrist as the older man moved to unsheathe his hunting knife. Planting his feet and shifting his weight, Draegan tossed Tior over his shoulder. The elder man's sinewy frame crashed hard into a thick oaken chair. Without pausing Draegan turned and pulled the hilt of Carnis Fornax from his belt and ran his hand over the missing blade as black flame erupted from the gaping mouth carved in the hilt.

Keda held out his hands to shield Eldra as Draegan closed the distance to the table in two bounds. He feinted at the old man causing him to stumble back. In one swift movement Draegan grabbed the bow as he jumped over the table. He shouldered the weapon, and using the massive council table as a temporary shield, Draegan ducked to the ground and placed his palm on the cold stones of the Conclave floor as he whispered the words of the Shadow Walking spell. He felt the ground pitch up and wheel, but rather than the familiar black mist enshrouding him, he screamed in pain as he was stung by a thousand cuts that covered his body.

"You cannot use your dark arts in this hallowed ground," Tior said as he stood, pulling a splinter of wood from his shoulder. A small trickle of blood ran down his cheek from a cut above his eye. "There is no escape, save through us." Tior turned to the others as Draegan rose, wincing as he tried to shake the off the pain from his failed spell. "Keda and Eldra, raise the alarm. Bring the Rannulfr here." The two moved as quickly toward the doors of the temple as their elderly frames would allow.

Draegan shook his head and regained his composure as Tior circled him, hunting knife drawn. "I can still use my feet," Draegan said as he burst toward the door. Tior sprinted after him, closing the distance in short order and slashing wildly at Draegan with his knife. Draegan ducked and threw himself into Tior, sending both sprawling to the ground near the doors of the temple, sword and knife alike clattering to the floor. Now weaponless, the two men struggled to gain advantage until Draegan pulled a dirk from his boot and lodged it Tior's throat.

"You will fail," Tior said faintly, trying to staunch the flow of blood that bubbled from his neck. "All of Athar will hunt you."

"I know," Draegan said as he picked himself from the floor. "I will not stand against them. I merely seek the Artifacts." He walked to the doors and peered down the steps into the darkness as Keda and Eldra stood, shaken, watching Tior bleed upon the stone floor. "I wish it hadn't ended this way, Tior," Draegan said as he bent to pick his burning blade from the stone floor, its black flames licking hungrily toward Tior's crumpled body. "But these foul instruments serve no master but evil. They cannot be used for good, no matter how noble the intent of the wielder. They must be hidden away from the Fyrian." He turned and made for the stairs that led out down the hill and into the streets of Sirion.

Draegan felt a shock run through his body moments before he fell down the flight of marble stairs and out onto the street. At this late hour the city of Sirion slept and no one heard Draegan's scream as he reached behind him and pulled out the hunting knife that was buried in his shoulder. In the light of the twin braziers that burned at the foot of the temple stairs he saw a sickly green sheen mixed with his blood on the blade. "Poisoned." He looked up at the soft glow emanating from the entrance of the Conclave and saw Tior collapsed at the entrance.

"A parting gift from my old Hunt Master," Draegan whispered. He rose and let the knife clatter to the ground. Already his vision began to swim. "The limits of their seal can't possibly have reached beyond the city. A *staminis* spell will get me to the woods faster," he said as he drew the mark on his neck with the blood on his glove. He felt a rush of heat course through his body as he raced down the street toward the Greater Serpion River in the west.

All the main roads in Sirion flowed radially toward the Conclave Temple where the watch fire of Manath burned day and night. These main thoroughfares were connected by smaller streets that spread from the Conclave in concentric rings. Draegan looked into the night sky, and finding the flickering light of the Tear of Helian in the west, he made quick work of navigating through the empty streets and pressed toward the city limits, only the sound of his boots scraping the cobbles and his labored breathing disturbing the quiet. He could feel his joints groaning and his muscles aching from the poison, but the *staminis* spell gave him the fortitude to push through the pain. In less than an hour he was at the great wall that rose from the Vilkas forest and encircled the city of Sirion.

Ahead of him the iron portcullis of the gate tower was drawn shut and four guards took aim from the top of the wall with their short bows. "The two elders must have raised the alarm," Draegan said as arrows whistled by him. He hesitated for a moment, and then ran directly at the gate, trying to get underneath their vantage point. He dove the last few feet and crashed into the portcullis, separating his shoulder. Drawing Carnis Fornax he rent the iron as if it were straw and tumbled headlong down the road, trying to get out of range of the guard's bows as quickly as possible.

Behind him he could hear the men shouting in frustration as fires were lit along the wall and the city came to life. A few hundred yards beyond the wall, on the pavers of the road that led to the gate, Draegan collapsed against a brazier, nearly spilling its burning contents. His vision began to cloud and his ears were filled with a high-pitched whine. Taking some of the blood from the wound on his shoulder he removed his glove and slapped his palm on the rough ground.

Bolts flew past him as he crouched, slamming into the earth near him and flinging shards of stone and dirt in his face as he closed his eyes. He felt the world contract as a dark mist swallowed him. An instant later he was gone and his pursuers' arrows flew ineffectually through the black haze left in Draegan's wake.

***

Draegan fell in a heap on the floor of Vangen's study. The musty smell of moldering books overpowered him. He tried to use a stack of tomes to raise himself, but fell over again. Dragging his body to the desk, he picked himself up and dumped his sword and bow on the cluttered surface. Behind the desk in a curio partially covered in maps and half obscured by yet more piles of books he saw the faint morning light illuminate a shelf heavy with vials and miniature amphorae.

"There has to be something in there," he said as he crashed into the curio, shattering the glass. He wiped the sweat from his eyes, clumsily grabbed a handful of vials and slumped against the wall. "These are either all poison meant for Vangen's enemies, or all antidotes to prevent himself from being a victim of the same."

Draegan removed the stopper from the first vial and was overpowered by a sickly sweet smell. "That has to be poison," he said and uncorked another vial with his teeth, his arm having gone numb. "This smells worse than the salves the acolytes used in the infirmary. If it smells this bad it has to be good medicine," he said and drained the entire vial.

He retched and dropped the vial to the ground, then wiped the spittle from his mouth. Already he could feel the thick liquid sliding down his throat as it slowed his body, making him desperate for sleep. Draegan pushed aside a tower of books to make room on the floor. He looked up at the small window admitting the first rays of dawn. "Has it only been six days since this began? It feels like a lifetime ago since I slew Vangen…" He trailed off as his body went limp on the floor. His thoughts churned as sleep took him.

Chapter 7: The Secret of the Sword

Draegan awoke with a start in a puddle of his own emesis, loose sheets of parchment adhered to his face. He struggled to his hands and knees, feeling every muscle strain as he did so, and then vomited again. Wiping his mouth he stood using the desk for support and looked toward the small window. Through the one clean streak where he had wiped away the layers of soot he saw the harvest moon rising above the walls of Dullahan .

"Three days," he said sinking into the chair and wincing in pain. "I almost feel worse than I did before I took the medicine." He cradled his throbbing head as he leaned forward on the desk and tried to make sense of the runes tooled into the leather cover of Vangen's handwritten book. "The Salvation of Athar," he mumbled. He snapped to attention and looked at the tome his brother had left him. "How was I able to read the language of Iss so easily?" He looked again at the runes and where once he saw meaningless symbols he found he could now make sense of them. "Is this the eye's magic or is something else at work here?"

Draegan opened the book and carefully turned the heavy stock of the pages. Every bit of space on the parchment was littered with symbols and runes. He could discern no obvious pattern to Vangen's frenzied writing, as some pages were written with runes running vertically while others had the text careening at odd angles. No matter the layout of the page, the text was heavily footnoted, crossed out in places and rewritten in many others. Intricate diagrams filled every available space not already crammed with words and glyphs. "It's a two thousand page notebook of a madman." Draegan rubbed his temples and shuddered, a wave of cold passing through him as he stared at the tome. "But where do I begin?"

He was quickly flipping through the pages, when his attention was caught by what appeared to be a rendering of Carnis Fornax. He read the words hastily written next to it. "This reaper of souls has the power to collect the very essence of a life and hold it in stasis. Some unfathomable magic keeps the soul trapped, in effect preserving it and granting it a sort of immortality. Though the body perishes, should one be able to later extract a soul from the blade, that soul could gain another opportunity at life. To be reborn will be the motivating factor for my continued research on this magnificent Artifact." Draegan shuddered against a chill, though no wind stirred in the study.

"I dare not believe it," Draegan said and folded his arms as he stared at the runes, reading them again and again until the words blurred in his mind. "Could Vangen still be alive? Trapped in this blade?" He pushed aside the sheaves of paper covering the hilt and stared at it warily before rising and walking to the window. He saw fewer watch fires on the walls than he expected considering the late hour. Dullahan was being deserted. War was coming, and his already limited time to recover the other three Artifacts was waning. "But if there exists a possibility of Vangen returning…" he trailed off and returned to the desk. "Before I killed him he had constructed a heavily modified *ferian* spell using the entirety of the room to contain the marking. What could have been his intent?" Draegan turned the book to the first page and sat down in the heavy chair. He leaned over the thick tome and cracked his knuckles. "I must solve this riddle."

For the next several days and nights Draegan read the book as his body healed from the wound in his shoulder and continued to empty itself of the Hunt Master's toxin. He left the study only once, to poach food from the store room, and to make a shadow walking rune on the wall behind the barrels of flour, for future use. On the third day he came across Vangen's first written account of how he pulled souls from the sword. He read on with equal parts disgust and fascination as Vangen described how he mastered the process of removing souls and implanting them into corpses. He saw the depths to which Vangen had sunk in order to possess such power. That evening as he read further, the text became hurried and Vangen's hand grew excited. Deciphering the words with some difficulty, Draegan made out several references to the land of Iss.

"Impossible," he said as he looked up and stared blankly at the morning rays peeking through the window. "He dwells in the shadow realm of Iss, as do all slain by Carnis Fornax." Draegan looked at the hilt of the Artifact on the desk, its carven figures wrought with such fidelity they seemed to almost breathe with life as he stared.

"So this Artifact, Carnis Fornax, traps the soul of its victim by some ancient dark magic. If I am to believe this madness Vangen wrote, he used the *ferian* spell to split his soul in two as the sword struck him, with half of his soul being taken by Carnis Fornax and the other swept to the shadow realm of Iss." Draegan smashed his fist on the tome. "He thought to go beyond my grasp, but underestimated my resolve. I will hunt him to the ends of Athar and beyond. If he lives in the shadow realm, then I will see that he dies there as well."

Draegan finished reading the rest of Vangen's notes and by evening had begun to craft a plan. With the Artifacts loose in the Empire, war was inevitable. But with Vangen still alive and able to return at any moment, Draegan feared this was the greater threat. He had vowed to end Vangen and would make good on his oath.

He took the Dark Ichor, along with his pack, sword and cloak and opened the passage in the study floor that led to the catacombs. He descended the stairs and disappeared into the darkness.

Chapter 8: The Portal

Draegan placed the great bow in one of the innumerable alcoves that lined the walls of the catacombs. Covering it with a rotting wool blanket he pulled from atop a decomposing body, he returned to the center of the great vault where he had placed his pack.

"I can do little to stem the growing tide of war. Even if I were to collect the Artifacts and bring them here, I would only bring the consolidated hate of the other four kingdoms to bear on my people." He opened a carafe of viscous oil and, dipping his fingers into the fluid, began tracing a large circle on the flagstone floor of the catacombs. "I have seen what evil Vangen brought against his own countrymen in the Great Basin of Skeldus, and I would have him suffer for his crimes." Draegan squatted and began carving glyphs around the perimeter of the circle in the tongue of Iss. "He betrayed me, killed his mother and father, deceived the Empire and took my own parents, Gron, and Aran from me through his dark schemes and lust for power." Draegan finished the last rune and stood to look at his work. "And he took Issa from me," he said and ground his teeth as a hateful rage flashed through him.

He pulled the hilt of Carnis Fornax from his belt and waved his hand over the gaping maw carved in the cross guard. The black fire surged from the grip and crackled in the quiet damp air of the catacombs. It strained against Draegan's grasp, trying desperately to find a life and escape the circle within which Draegan stood.

"In using the Dark Artifacts and casting this blood magic I profane myself and bring shame to my family and kingdom. But my purpose is true. I do not seek to absolve myself of my sin, only to bring Vangen to justice. He is still a greater threat in the land of Iss than any Artifact here in Athar. And to stop his madness I have but one choice. I must kill him again."

Draegan bowed his head in the circle of runes and began chanting. The oil began to glow a deep crimson as the symbols flared to life. He continued chanting, feeling a sickness swell within him. His head swam as he continued, and the eye of Islak came alive with unrestrained fury, sending bolts of pain through his body. The circle burst into flames but Draegan stood firm as he continued his spell. The fire intensified and Draegan swooned in the heat, but never stopped his conjuring.

The fiery blade of Carnis Fornax flared in anger and tugged frantically, trying to wrench itself from Draegan's grip. He took the sword and plunged it into the center of the seal. Instantly the fire of the circle turned black. The flames rose higher and climbed his body, though he no longer felt any heat or pain from the fire. Draegan sustained his chanting as the flames engulfed him.

As quickly as it began, the fire extinguished without a trace of smoke. The circle and runes glowed briefly and dissipated into the flagstones. Draegan had vanished.

Chapter 9: The Awakening

Isirah stood silently before the doors of the great vault and sighed. Though he was sixty five years old, his hair was still jet black and cropped close. The white and scarlet robe he wore was crisp and bright, not showing any signs of wear though he had donned it every day for the last forty years. It was cut in a similar style to the humble and plain white robes of the acolytes of Vatn. Although it had two slits on either side from the hem to the waist to allow for more movement, the voluminous garment nevertheless barely managed to contain Isirah's massive physique. He had grown softer with age, but his frame still carried the promise of great strength, and the casual way he stood before the vault belied his sharp reflexes.

"How long do you intend to make me wait," Isirah said, his deep voice echoing through the hall. He paused as he heard shuffling footsteps grow nearer.

"As long as it takes me to get here," Ieros said, stopping to catch his breath before the towering iron doors. "Shutting down the library and making the journey across the open sea in little more than a leaky bathtub is no small feat for anyone, let alone a man on the precipice of one hundred." Ieros righted himself and drew a deep breath. "It would do you good to learn some patience, young man."

Isirah frowned. "May we begin?"

"Yes, yes. For someone who cares little for these things, you seem to be in quite a hurry."

"I wish to return to my fire and my books," Isirah said and pushed the sleeves of his vestment above his elbows, revealing thick cords of muscle twining up his forearms. Ieros hobbled forward and placed his frail hands on the cold iron of the doors. The instant Ieros touched the doors a red light glowed from the seal carved in the portal and trickled outward, following a series of channels etched in the iron. In moments the door appeared to be consumed in a scarlet light. The locks clicked and several bolts retracted with audible clunks, allowing the doors to swing inward silently.

Isirah grimaced. "You were right, Ieros."

Ieros pushed past him and entered the small round room into which the doors led. On the far wall, a tall thin banner hung, woven in rich scarlet with a white seal embroidered in the center. In front of the banner, atop a four foot tall plain white pedestal of marble, two masterfully forged daggers lay on a thick scarlet cloth.

"Do you see them glow, Isirah," Ieros asked with child-like awe as he approached the pedestal. "Bhel and Asai have awakened after thousands of years of sleep. What you saw in the scrying pool was no idle vision. The bonds that shackle Iss are breaking."

"And what of it, Ieros? We've known this day would come. It's only a shame I am still alive to see it." Isirah entered the small room and stood next to Ieros, towering over the elderly man's bent frame. "I had hoped to leave this world long before the shadow returned."

"Your duty is to the Clade, Isirah, and you are honor-bound to carry out your tasks. The awakening of the twin blades can have no effect on your obligations. In fact they lend it more urgency." Ieros looked up at Isirah. "You must train the boy."

Isirah set his jaw, snorted, and exited the chamber. On the threshold of the great doors he stopped. "Training the boy is futile. As we speak Iss throws off its fetters and Athar is once again plagued by the Dark Artifacts. War will devour everything and send us all to the grave." He looked over his shoulder at Ieros. "Training the boy in the mysteries of the Clade would serve no purpose other than to prepare him to stand warden over this hollow tomb, clean its halls and tend the fire until the last life on Athar is ended. Then he too will join the legions of dead."

Ieros looked at the faint blue light emanating from long blades of the daggers. He saw the Sundering of Athar etched with perfect fidelity on the blade of Asai and studied the depiction of the Fall of the Sages rendered expertly on Asai's sister blade, Bhel. He reached his hand toward the blades but then withdrew it and turned to face Isirah.

"The child must be trained. He must bear these daggers, the Vaghat, and take the oaths as you and I have. The Clade has been unbroken for three thousand years and I will not have it perish due to your self-pity and malcontent."

They stared at each other in silence until Isirah dropped his heavy shoulders. "Bring him here, old man. I will train him." Isirah stepped back into the small room and put his thick hand on Ieros's frail shoulder. "And I will do a better job of it than you did for me."

Ieros smiled and shuffled down the hall to make his way back to the nursery on the Isle of Vatn.

Chapter 10: Beyond the Gate

Draegan looked about as the black flames that surrounded him diminished. Beneath his feet an image of the seal he had drawn on the floor of the catacombs glowed momentarily and faded away.

His senses returned with a slow awakening, as if reentering his own consciousness. Above him a ruddy glow lit a desolate landscape. Dark clouds roiled in the sky, but there was no sign of sun or moon or stars. Draegan cast no shadow on the soft, black ash covering the ground. Stretching before him he saw nothing but flat, lifeless plains, perfectly level and devoid of any structure, natural or man-made. At his feet the fine black powder lay a few inches deep, stirring slightly from Draegan's cloak as he turned to scan the horizon. In every direction the uniform, black ground stretched to the vermillion horizon. He felt no breeze, despite the agitated sky, nor heard any noises that would indicate life.

"This land is dead in every direction, an empty shell. If I am truly in the land of Iss, than I must decipher a way to find Vangen." Draegan cast a *topos* spell and was overwhelmed when he felt the land continue in every direction, a perfectly even dead space covered in ash. "I suppose I have little choice in this barren place but to move. Staying here gains me nothing."

As soon as Draegan stepped from the charred ring of his seal he was set upon by shadows and mist that dove from the sky and flew straight at him, dissolving as they passed harmlessly through him. He threw up his hand to shield his face instinctively and drew his blade. He swung wildly as the shadowy forms assailed him from all sides. The flaming sword passed as ineffectually through the wraiths as they did through him. "What manner of creature is this?" he said as he shielded his face and began running, still swinging at the black vaporous forms that hounded him.

Draegan ran for what felt like hours, though he did not weary. The wraiths worried him, keeping him off balance and off course as he moved. They disturbed his vision as well, though they seemed unable to harm him.

"If this is the best the shadow realm can offer, perhaps I overestimated the threat of Iss," Draegan said as he continued running forward. He pushed onward constantly trying to find some landmark or object to head toward. Hours later he saw no difference in his surroundings. The land continued to stretch endlessly before him, melting into the crimson horizon. "Is there no sun in this cursed land?" Draegan asked as he swung his blade at the circling wraiths. "It should be day or night. Some change must have happened during these hours I've been running."

He stopped and let the powdery ash settle on his boots. Peering through the swirling haze of wraiths he still saw no change in his environs. "Have I covered no ground? I feel like I've been running for hours, though I do not tire," Draegan said moments before he convulsed and dropped to his knees. The eye of Islak sent waves of pain through his body. Amid the swirling chaos in his head he saw a mountain range rising above the plains, but it was obscured seconds later. As the pain subsided, Draegan stood and sheathed his sword while the shadowy apparitions continued to break around him like mist.

"So there is an end to this loathsome desert of ash and shadow." He looked around in every direction and was met with the same spectacle, and endless waste of ash beneath the bloody sky. "But where are these mountains the eye has just revealed to me?" He cast a *topos* spell and felt a subtle variation a great distance away and to his right. He ran through the swirling shadows and once again headed for the burning horizon.

Draegan pushed onward relentlessly, continually hounded by wraiths. He neither tired nor grew hungry. There was no change in the crimson sky, and he had lost all sense of time. He looked up into the seething mass of wraiths and noticed they were flying higher above him and diving at him less often. As he took sight of the horizon again he saw a slight deviation in the perfectly flat ground. "I have found them," he said and redoubled his effort toward the mountains.

Draegan watched the mountains grow larger as he made his way across the ashen desert. Though he had lost all sense of day and night, he felt that it had been many more days of running before he could make out the features of the range. He never wearied nor hungered, but pressed continually onward. The wraiths had left him some time ago, though when, he could not say. Eventually he made it to the foothills of the mountain range and stopped near a gray boulder.

"I see nothing living here either," he said as he scrambled to the top of the rock to gain a better vantage point. "I hope the view at the top of these mountains holds a change in scenery."

Beyond the foothills, sheer cliffs of dark rock soared into the crimson sky. As he wended his way through the hills, the size of the mountains became apparent. Now they towered above him, almost completely blotting out the sky. "This will prove more difficult than the Frozen Maw. This range is nearly three times their height." Yet Draegan had no trouble making his way to the summit. He climbed without stopping, but as he never tired it was solely a matter of choosing the right path and being sure of his footing at every step.

Draegan pulled himself off the flank of the slope and into a col where he paused and looked below. He saw the black ash desert stretch beyond the limit of his sight, still and silent beneath the ever crimson sky. The clouds that churned in the sky continually moved but he never felt even the slightest breeze. He squinted to try and make out any shapes or movement on the horizon but he saw none. "I guess the wraiths have given up." Draegan shifted his pack and began ascending the face of the next peak.

Draegan was nearly a mile above the desert when he clambered over the brink of the mountain. He dumped his pack on the rocks and stood. Beneath him the mountains plunged downward for thousands of feet before they ended abruptly in the largest basin he had ever seen. It sunk lower than the desert he had just left, but where the desert was a dead and empty space, at the far end of the basin a great walled fortress the size of a city rose from the earth. Shaped like a pentagon, the massive walls of heavy stone wedded to black iron were thick enough that the King's Road could have fit neatly atop them. Great channels were dug into the basin floor, radiating from the fortress like the spokes of a wheel. Viscous magma labored down them and into the structure through barred grates in the outer wall. Fires burned behind the wall and black smoke rose above the cruel guard towers spaced along the top. Beneath him he could make out what appeared to be birds wheeling lazily above the heights of the city-fortress, flying in and out of the black smoke. Inside the outer wall there was another wall of the same shape, nested within but rising even higher. From each of its five corners red towers rose above the smoke like bloody claws grasping at the sky. In the center of the fortress a great obelisk of bright red steel towered above the entire city, floating above the height of the inner wall. Four great chains bound it at each corner and kept it anchored. Above the obelisk a terrible storm raged. Lightning flashed and deafening thunder cracked, though Draegan saw no rain. As he gazed into the valley from this great height he felt a rumbling in the ground. The rocks at his feet shifted slightly and he bent over to steady himself. When the tremor passed he stood and again beheld the spectacle of the iron fortress below.

Draegan was gazing at the fortress in stunned silence when the eye of Islak flared to life. Clutching at his face he doubled over and tried to keep from pitching over the edge of the cliff. In the chaos of his mind he saw legions of armored soldiers shouting up at a figure sitting in a blood-red throne. He watched Vangen rise from his seat and smile.

Chapter 11: The Red Keep

"He lives," Draegan said. He grabbed his pack from the ground and secured it to his back. "But not for long." He scrambled as quickly as he could down the sheer cliff face, finding easy hand holds as he descended into the great basin beneath him. He picked his way hurriedly through the cracks and crevices of the great cliff, slipping several times and losing his grip more than once, but each time he was saved from plummeting to his doom. After many hours of pushing himself to his limits, he made his way to the base of the mountain unharmed.

Here the ground was composed of a reddish hard-packed earth and a thick rust colored dust blanketed everything. There was no sign of life outside of the fortress-city's terrifying walls. No plant grew and no wind stirred in the empty basin. But Draegan could hear the roar of flames behind the great wall, even from this distance. Smoke continued to issue forth from unseen chimneys and the dark birds he had glimpsed before wheeled lazily through it, appearing and disappearing in the dark plumes. Every so often one would shriek and dive, only to circle up later and continue its lazy route.

"What nightmare is this place?" Draegan asked. "I have come from the silent, dead wastes filled with shadowy apparitions, to a valley filled with flame and terrors lurking behind the walls of a fortress that reeks of evil." He adjusted his pack and looked around for any possible alternative route to save him from marching directly at the front gate. "I suppose I shall seek an audience with Vangen directly, as I have few options."

Picking his way through the red rocks and staying clear of the channels of magma that flowed laboriously toward the fortress, Draegan made his way across the basin floor. The heat was overpowering, and though he felt little thirst, he instinctively drank, carelessly emptying his water skin before he was halfway to the fortress. He was within what appeared to be a few miles of the main gate, though he began questioning his ability to judge distance. The walls soared before him. He struggled to comprehend how they could be built so high. Nothing like this existed on Athar. He had never seen iron bands wedded to stone in such a cruel fashion. Constructing something of this magnitude must have required forges larger than any in Fyrian and an army of laborers that never tired.

The fires behind the walls suddenly ceased and the billowing smoke dissipated into the red sky. The great birds shrieked and rose higher until at last they turned and flew over him toward the great mountain Draegan had just descended, their shadows flickering across the rust colored earth. He was watching their angular silhouettes vanish beyond the edge of his sight when he heard a great pounding from behind the gate. The magma in the channels began to drain, leaving smoldering pools of lava in the stone lined grooves that ran through the basin floor. Before him the titanic gates of the fortress groaned and began to part.

The great black spikes retracted into the iron doors, moved by an unseen internal mechanism. With an ear-splitting screech the gates swung ponderously inward. Draegan watched as figures began to issue forth from the opening. He scrambled across a now empty channel, still burning hot from the magma, and crouched behind a group of boulders.

Twisted human-like forms came running from the gate on all fours. They wore no clothes and had no hair, their skin burnt and blistered. The creatures gnashed their teeth and howled as they passed. The beasts were covered in ill-fitting plates of iron that beat against them as they half ran and half crawled toward the mountain he had just come from. "Do they give chase to the birds, or are they searching for me?" Draegan wondered as he watched hundreds of them move past him and head for the base of the mountains. Slipping further behind the rocks, he peered out the other side.

The rhythmic pounding that had begun earlier grew louder as it was joined by the sound of metal clashing with metal. "I know that sound. Shields and armor." Draegan's eyes widened as he saw more iron-clad figures issuing forth two legions wide from the now fully opened gate. These creatures were armored in full plate and marched with a drilled precision, unlike the wild beasts that had gone before them. All were armed and some carried great red banners that hung lifelessly in the dead air of the valley. He watched them march straight for the mountains, the pounding of their steps shaking the ground and disturbing the rust colored dust that covered the boulders he hid behind.

For hours Draegan watched the army march forth until they finally vanished into the haze of red dust at the far end of the basin and the pounding receded to a low rumble. "Impossible," he said. "How do they keep so many behind those walls?" Not giving him time to ponder, the gates began to groan once again, closing with the same ponderous speed with which they had opened. Draegan tensed as he watched the doors close. "I have little time and no other opportunity."

Draegan carved a shadow walking rune on the back side of the boulder, then bolted from behind the rocks and tore across the basin at full speed toward the gate. "If they have archers, I'll soon find out," he said as he neared the gigantic walls. Draegan looked up to scan the walls for movement when he was within a few hundred yards of the gate. He saw nothing but the black smoke that had once again begun to rise up into the crimson sky and obscure the inner wall. To his left and right the magma flowed into the fortress again, the rising heat causing the walls to shimmer.

When he was within a hundred yards of the gate the great iron spikes sprang out, each large enough to easily impale an ox. "I must be quick," he said and dashed through the iron doors. Draegan dove the last few feet and checked himself when he heard the gate slam close behind him. He looked around and saw that the fortress was completely deserted. A great stone road as wide as the gate led straight ahead to a raised portcullis in the inner wall. To his left and right rows of massive forges glowed as the magma flowed into them and smoke poured from their stacks, but he heard no sound of iron being shaped.

"It is more of a factory and less of a fortress. And all of it empty." He moved cautiously forward, expecting to be challenged, but he made his way to the inner wall uncontested. He paused for a moment beneath the portcullis, eyeing the massive spikes. "It can't be this easy," he said and dashed through the inner gate as quickly as he could.

Draegan stopped short when he saw the base of the obelisk, floating several stories above the courtyard. The bottom was a perfect square, a hundred yards wide in each direction and forged of a deep scarlet material that shone like steel. Great chains anchored it at each corner, holding it fast. No ornamentation or marks marred the perfectly smooth surface. His eye followed it up as it stretched above the blood red towers and seemed to vanish in the sky. At its very top it angled in sharply, capping itself with a smooth pyramid. Just beyond the top of the floating pillar a swirling mass of black clouds rumbled while lightning occasionally struck the blood red shard.

"As there is no sewer in the Red Keep, I left the front doors open to make things easier for you," said a voice.

Draegan tore his eyes from the obelisk and looked straight ahead at the source of the voice. Directly beneath the obelisk a familiar figure rose from a red throne that sat atop a raised dais. It descended the steps toward Draegan.

"It is good to see you again, brother."

Chapter 12: The Name

"Today your training begins in earnest, boy," Isirah said as he pushed his simple chair back from the small wooden table, the harsh scrape of the oak against the flagstones filling the empty hall. The giant man stepped in front of the fire that hissed and spat in the great hearth behind him, casting a monstrous shadow over the boy who stood several feet in front of him. "For these ten years you have obeyed and studied the rote teachings of Vatn under Ieros. But now he has walked the Western Path as do all who serve the Clade." Isirah clasped his hands behind his back and looked down in reverence. The boy knelt on the stones of the great hall in front of the fire, his eyes downcast, dressed in the plain white robe of an acolyte of Vatn.

"You have also served me faithfully here in the Halls and I have found you worthy of training. Today you shall be named and written into the Silfren Klados along with all those who have served the Clade before you." Isirah paused and waited for the boy to look up at him. "Mark well your name. You shall be called Isarn, named for the Holy Iron, and you will be forged in the crucible of the Clade. You will be hammered and shaped for one purpose, the single purpose for which the Clade has existed these three thousand years. You will bear the Vaghat and you shall avenge the Elder Gods of Light at long last." Isirah brought his hands before him and motioned for the boy to stand. "Rise, Isarn, and accept the holy obligations of the Clade."

The boy stood at attention and looked directly at Isirah. "I will prove worthy."

"You must Isarn, for these are desperate times. The Vaghat awakens from its three thousand year slumber, which can mean only one thing. The shadow of Iss will be upon us before long." Isirah looked down at the boy who held his gaze. "You don't understand my words now, but you soon shall. Come, follow me."

Isirah turned and exited the hall through a side door with Isarn following close behind. "There are still parts of this enclave you have yet to discover. This building stretches beneath the whole of the island and beyond, into the very waters that separate us from Vatn. In time you will know every part, but for now we stop here."

Isirah placed his hand on a small oak door banded in iron. In the center was the seal of the Clade, similar to that of Vatn, but where the seal of Vatn had twined hands atop the shield, this sigil contained crossed daggers. As Isirah touched the seal it glowed blue and the door clicked before swinging open. Isirah took a step and stopped, his massive frame blocking the doorway. He grumbled to himself and entered the room. When Isarn stepped over the threshold he was stunned to see a great circular hall rising many stories above his head and lined from floor to ceiling with books. Balconies and staircases connected the upper reaches with the ground. In the center of the floor a single book rested open upon a pedestal draped in thick black velvet.

"The Silfren Klados," Isirah said as he approached the book. "The Silver Book of the Clade contains the true account of Athar, and it is ours to protect. None know its secrets save us, and they must not, for the truth would ruin the world. This is where your name will be written, and you will swear by this book to protect the secrets of the Clade."

"I will prove worthy," Isarn said as Isirah took a small knife from his robe and pricked Isarn's finger.

"Touch the page there," Isirah said, pointing at the book. Isarn winced as he touched his bloody finger to the page and instantly the parchment drank the scarlet drop into its fibers. Isarn watched in awe as the blood spread and turned into red letters that spelled his name. "Isarn," he said aloud. He looked and saw Isirah's red name above his and Ieros's above Isirah's. On the opposite page at the top he saw a name written in black. "Who is Greydin Vir the Accursed?"

Isirah grimaced and tucked his hands into his robes as he read Greydin's name aloud. "Listen well Isarn, for now you must learn the true history of Athar and the Founding of the Clade."

"As an acolyte of Vatn you have read the Chronicle of Fire and can recount how the Elder Gods of Light and Dark descended to Athar from the heavens and warred for rule of our future home. Being equally matched, neither side could force a victory though they clashed in brutal combat for eons. In time they sought to settle their eternal struggle by proxy and so they created man, a flawed but noble creature whom they used as pawns to continue their struggle. The Elder Gods each chose a champion from among the masses and imbued these crusaders with a portion of their might and wisdom. They taught their champions the secrets of magic and the mysteries of creation and destruction. Over time these warriors became the six Sages of Light and the six Blades of Darkness, each aligning himself with the god that chose him or her. The six Blades banded together and inhabited the land we called Iss. The Sages formed their kingdoms in the land we call Fyrian. They built armies and warred, the Sages of Light against the Blades of Darkness.

"The War for Athar," Isarn said under his breath.

"Yes, the War for Athar. For ten thousand years they battled, slaughtering entire armies with their terrible might. For each champion had long ago been gifted a token of their god's esteem that augmented their already considerable power. The Sages of Light received what we call the Talismans of Light and the Blades of Darkness were given the Dark Artifacts. These powerful weapons equalized the two forces, such that neither could gain advantage in battle, just as the Elder Gods had fought to a stalemate thousands of years earlier. Three thousand years ago the Sages of Light put aside their petty differences and merged their armies together to ride against the Blades in one terrible, final battle. The Sages proved victorious and felled the Blades, sending their broken armies back to the shadows of Iss. It was then that the Sages claimed the Dark Artifacts as symbols of their triumph and returned to Dullahan to divide the spoils of their victory.

"The Failed Council at Dullahan?" Isarn asked, looking at the Silfren Klados as Isirah paged through it. "Ieros has spoken of it many times. He claims this is when victory was taken from the light."

"And he was right to say so," Isirah said. "For at the council the noble intentions of the Sages were corrupted by the Artifacts. The Elder Gods of Darkness, bitter at the defeat of their chosen Blades by the Sages of Light, imbued the Artifacts with their rancor and the Sages became defiled as they handled their spoils of victory. While the six Sages debated how best to divide their newly won weapons in the great Council Room at Dullahan their talks became increasingly hostile as they succumbed to the corrupting influence of the Artifacts. What began as a celebration of victory and a new order for peace in Athar escalated to near violence as the Sages sought to gain power over of one another."

Isirah closed the Silfren Klados and turned from the book to face Isarn. "It was here that Sage Vatn the Pure saw the deception and alerted the other Sages to the power of the Artifacts, but her warnings went unheeded. They saw her censure as an attempt to deceive them and thereby gain the Artifacts for herself. Seeing that she could not persuade the other Sages from giving up the Dark Artifacts she left with her followers and broke from the Council. Sage Vatn the Pure took the Dark Ichor with her to the Isle of Vatn where she and her people disavowed the outside world and tried to build a kingdom of peace and prayer."

"Why did she bring the Dark Ichor with her? Would she not condemn herself and her followers by keeping the Artifact?"

Isirah nodded and clasped his hands behind him. "This is where the histories diverge. This is where those in Fyrian understand one teaching and those on Vatn believe another. But here, Isarn, is the truth," he said turning and pointing at the Silfren Klados on the pedestal. "Here is the secret that has stayed buried for three thousand years in this living tomb, protected by the Clade. And this is why Greydin Vir's name is written in black. Today you shall know the truth and today you shall bear the curse of the Clade."

"I will prove worthy," Isarn said as he knelt on the floor at Isirah's feet and bowed his head with raised arms. Isirah reached forward and grasped Isarn's hands at the wrist, his own arms extending beyond his robe, revealing two bands of arcane symbols tattooed around each wrist. "You are named and now you are marked. You are ready to bear the Vaghat and the curse of Greydin Vir." Isirah released Isarn and straightened himself. Isarn rose and looked down at his hands. Where Isirah had held him were two black bands of the same runes wound around his wrists like shackles.

"Pay heed to this tale, Isarn, for it is the truth that separates you from the rest of those in the Fyrian Empire and even your brothers and sisters in Vatn." Isirah smoothed the folds in his robe and continued.

"When Sage Vatn the Pure left the Council at Dullahan she and her followers departed the land of Fyrian and crossed the Endless Deep where they found a large uninhabited island. There they built the White Temple at the headwaters of the river known as the Falling Light and terraced the mountain for their gardens. They spent their days in peaceful prayer and meditation while Fyrian was consumed with hate and a lust for power."

"But all was not well in their kingdom in the sea, for Vatn's Chief Council and First High Abbot, Greydin Vir watched in growing apprehension as the five kingdoms once again balanced on the precipice of war, so soon after defeating the armies of Iss. Greydin urged Sage Vatn to give up her isolation and broker peace with the other Sages in a desperate attempt to solidify the fragile peace and prevent more bloodshed. Vatn refused. Greydin was powerless to help his former friends and those he had fought alongside as they succumbed to the madness of the Dark Artifacts. He pleaded with Vatn to at least divest themselves of the Dark Ichor that they kept in the vaults beneath the White Temple, knowing that it would inevitably lead those in Fyrian to their door. Again, she refused to heed Greydin's advice and he withdrew his council and became distant."

"Greydin sought to help those in Fyrian but knew not how. If he could not broker peace with the five kingdoms, and if he could not rid the Isle of Vatn of the Dark Ichor, he was at least determined to protect those who dwelled in peace on the island. So in secret he began to train himself on a small island off the coast of Vatn in a unique style of combat and meditation he had devised from his own experience fighting at the side of the Sages in the War for Athar. He wished to perfect this new style of fighting and train other like-minded priests so that they would be prepared for the war when it eventually threatened their shores." Isirah held up his massive hands toward the domed ceiling of the library. "This enclave he built is where we live now, Isarn, in the Halls of the Clade that he founded three thousand years past."

Isirah looked up at the soaring towers of books and intricate latticework of ladders and spans that connected the library in an iron and stone web. He grunted in approval and returned his attention to the young charge before him. "It was only ten years after Sage Vatn had left the Council of Dullahan when five great ships arrived in Vatn, each bearing a Sage. They came to the White Temple to speak with Vatn and asked her help in brokering peace between them. Greydin was relieved that the Sages had sought to walk the path of peace, but Vatn refused to treat with them, having renounced the outside world. She spoke with them once and only briefly, pleading for them to lay down their arms completely, disband their armies and join her on Vatn. The Sages balked at such a request and showed their true intent when they threatened to raze her island unless she gave them the Dark Ichor." Isirah looked directly at Isarn. "This is the true evil of the Artifacts, for they were able to completely defile the hearts of the Sages."

"Sage Vatn was outraged and demanded that the other Sages leave her island immediately. It was then that Sage Corvus used his Dark Artifact, the Shadow Walker to steal into the White Temple's dormitories and take Vatn's twin children, Dalus and Dalthyd. The Sages retreated and taking the children with them put out to sea in their ships. While at anchor just off the shore they again asked for the Dark Artifact that Sage Vatn kept in her vaults, threatening to kill her children if she didn't comply."

Isarn stared dumbfounded at Isirah. "I can't believe the Sages could act so wickedly."

"The Artifacts had control of their minds and hearts," Isirah said, shaking his head. He paused before continuing.

"For days Vatn deliberated and sought council from her advisors. She was despondent at the prospect of losing her children, but dared not give the other Sages the bow. Eventually Greydin, her Chief Council, convinced her to allow him to attempt to retrieve her children in secret. He used his mastery of magic to steal aboard Corvus's ship, but rather than rescue them, he killed the twins, knowing that while they lived, Vatn could always be manipulated by the Sages."

"Upon hearing the news, Vatn poisoned herself in her grief, but not before telling Greydin that Dalus and Dalthyd were his children by her and cursing him with her last breath. Overcome with despair as he watched Vatn die before him and distraught at the heinous act he had committed, Greydin prayed to Helian for deliverance from his wicked deed. That night the sky burned red and stars fell from the heavens as the Elder Gods themselves wept. Great tremors tore through Athar and the land of Iss was sunk into the sea and the scattered armies of the Blades of Darkness were cast across the void and into the shadow realm."

"The Sundering of Athar," Isarn said, staring wide-eyed at Isirah.

"The next morning the Sages left the isle in anger after discovering Greydin's betrayal, promising to return with their armies and burn the island to the ground. In the short time left to the priests, before the Sages returned with their armies, Greydin, as the new head of the order, taught many students in his secret art. He began crafting a magical weapon of great power, for he knew the five Sages would show them no quarter in the ensuing war. Forged from a fallen star, Greydin crafted twin daggers that bristled with otherworldly energy. These are Bhel, the flame of life, and Asai, the frost of death. Together they are known as the Vaghat, the vow of Greydin, for it was in his prayer that Greydin asked for deliverance from his sin and with these daggers fallen from the heavens he would atone for his transgression."

"When the armies of Fyrian returned months later they met with fierce opposition, led by Greydin, who seemed unstoppable in battle. Greydin realized that though his handful of disciples were better warriors than those of the Sage's armies, their numbers were too few to withstand an extended siege. Greydin offered himself and the Dark Ichor to the Sages if they could best him in single combat. In their pride and arrogance the Sages agreed. This was when Greydin Vir proved his worth, for he slew each of the Sages using only the twin daggers Bhel and Asai. Despite their near god-like mastery of magic, none could withstand Greydin's assault and he sent their armies home, broken and defeated. This is known as the Fall of the Sages in the history books in Fyrian and on Vatn, though you see now that it is only a fraction of the truth."

"What became of Greydin?"

"When the dust had settled and the acolytes buried their dead, Greydin established a new order of warrior priests on Vatn known as the Clade. He placed his chief disciple Islak at their head. Our teachings come from him. The armies of the five kingdoms returned home and began to war internally to replace their fallen Sages, falling upon each other in their weakness. Though he had defeated the Sages, it was a hollow victory, for the Dark Artifacts still lived in Athar, poisoning those who wielded them. So, in secret, Greydin took the Dark Ichor and left Vatn, never to return. He was lost to history, though he lives on in the Clade, for Islak continued the traditions begun by Greydin here on this small island. Over many generations and thousands of years, as the five nations warred among themselves and the need for the Clade lessened, the High Abbot of Vatn reduced the power and number of the Clade until it eventually became a relic, all but forgotten. Four hundred years ago the Clade was officially abolished by the High Abbot, though we have continued our existence in secret. The Clade now consists solely of a master and disciple. None on the Isle know of our existence and we are erased from all their histories."

Isarn thought for a moment. "How could one man with no Talismans or Artifacts be powerful enough to defeat five Sages? They were the most powerful beings on Athar aside from the Elder Gods."

"This is the training of the Clade and the secret of Greydin which you will learn. In time I will show you how to kill a god."

Chapter 13: The Decision

Draegan charged Vangen who descended the steps slowly, his face twisted in a mocking smile. In one fluid motion Draegan ignited the black fire of Carnis Fornax and swung violently at Vangen's throat. The blade passed cleanly through him, as if Vangen were nothing more than air. The ferocious force of Draegan's swing pulled him off balance, and he nearly stumbled to the ground. He caught himself, wheeled about again and sprung at his brother again, bringing the sword down in a vicious arc at Vangen's face. Again the blade passed through him as if he were not there.

"You waste our time, brother," Vangen said, stopping to look at Draegan. "I have much to accomplish and neither you nor your blade can stop me." He looked down at Draegan who was picking himself up off of the stairs and preparing for another strike. "Save your strength. I am immortal."

Draegan drove the black flame directly through Vangen's heart and watched as it pierced clean through, the icy black flame crackling in the still air. His brother merely smiled and shrugged.

"It gains us little to keep at this game, Draegan. Put the sword away."

Draegan pulled the sword back and watched the flame flicker for a moment, before flaring back to life. "What trickery is this? I feel the blade search for you but it seems lost, as if it cannot see you, though you stand right here."

Vangen smiled and held out his hands. "If I had not written precise instructions in that book I doubt you ever would have made it here Draegan. You are being outshined by your blade. How is it that your sword can solve the riddle, yet still you struggle?" Vangen looked at Draegan and continued. "I am not entirely here, brother, because what you see before you is only half of my soul. The other still lives in Carnis Fornax when you wrenched it from me during our last encounter."

Draegan lowered his blade and circled Vangen who shook his head. "When you killed me in my study in Dullahan, I split my soul in two pieces. One entered your blade and the other was sent here by craft of my *ferian* spell. As long as the two halves remain separate, I remain immortal."

Draegan gripped his sword and backed away from Vangen. "Then I shall simply give it back to you, that I may take satisfaction in killing you again."

Vangen laughed. "But here is your plight," he said raising his arms and looking about. "We exist, immortal, in this shadow land, banished beyond time, death, and even the reach of the Elder Gods. When you opened a portal to this realm it required great sacrifice. You drew the seal and gave it life with the souls trapped in Carnis Fornax. This is how you came to this place. You paid the toll for crossing the void with the souls of the fallen, rather than your own." Vangen turned and began slowly ascending the steps back to his throne.

"To leave would require a similar sacrifice, though only a single soul is necessary to open the gate from the shadow lands back to Athar." He paused and looked over his shoulder at Draegan. "You only have one soul left in that blade of yours, and I believe it is mine. Give it to me and the door opens."

"You will never have it Vangen," Draegan shouted. "We will both be trapped in this deathless world until the heavens crash to the earth beneath us before I would aid you."

"Crash to the earth they will, for the shadow realm is dying Draegan, and you have no one to blame but yourself." Vangen sat in his seat beneath the suspended mass of red iron and folded his hands. "When you collected the Artifacts you unwittingly began to unweave the great seal that kept these two realms separate. What you do not know is that when the Elder Gods of Light tore the land of Iss from Athar and exiled it here to this void they did so in great haste. Their spell was not without flaws and promised to collapse in a few thousand years. Long ago someone came upon this truth and by craft of this great mage he sealed the land of Iss in the void. This unknown champion of Athar used the shadowy life force of the Elder Gods of Darkness that inhabited the Dark Artifacts to bind this realm, keeping Iss apart from Athar and securing the seal. When you removed the Artifacts from their temples and towers you unbound the seal. Now the Shadow Lands of Iss are tearing apart as we speak."

"And what would I care for the fate of this empty land?"

Vangen smashed his fist into the arm of his throne. "How little you have learned. How troublesome it is to plant even the smallest seed of wisdom in your barren mind." Vangen took a breath and calmed himself. "This realm is held in stasis, imprisoned within a spell that is unraveling. When the bonds are broken, Iss will return to Athar in a cataclysm that will render all who dwell there dead."

Draegan ground his teeth and balled his hand into a fist, about to speak when Vangen cut him off.

"I am the only hope for Athar, Draegan. Only I can save these two realms from mutual destruction as the spell that keeps these worlds apart unwinds. I will open a portal and unite the twin lands once again, making Athar whole and complete as it was before the Elder Gods of Light sentenced us to our eventual doom in their ill-conceived wrath."

Draegan shot his arm at Vangen, pointing accusingly at him. "Always you place some larger threat before me, staying your death by playing upon my sympathies for the greater good. I will be misled no longer, brother. This day you will die."

Vangen laughed. "Oh how quickly your love for your people becomes clouded by your hate for me. Do you not recall that as we speak four of the Dark Artifacts are loose in Fyrian? Do you not recall how even now the people make for war? Do you not recall how your kingdom of Skeldus is nothing more than an empty shell, hollow and barren and without leadership? What will they say of the usurper Draegan who fled when the kingdoms swept into Skeldus and raped and pillaged their way to Dullahan? What will the history books write of the cowardice of a false king who stood idly by as the Four Gates were overrun?"

"You lie as always Vangen," Draegan said as he brandished the flaming blade at him from the base of the stairs. Vangen sat in his red throne and folded his hands. "You seek to deceive and mislead," Draegan continued. "I know not the truth of your words when you speak of the doom of Athar by Iss, but I do know that you must die if those who live in Athar have any hope of peace."

Vangen shook his head. "How little you have understood. I will not seek to convince you, only to impress upon you a sense of urgency no matter your choice. But know that you have few choices, Draegan. You may release my soul, making this form you see before you whole, and then kill me, trapping me in the blade. But you will also be trapped here with me, unable to help those in Athar, for there are no other souls in this land that can be used to open passage home. Fyrian will plunge into civil war while Iss unravels and rejoins its twin, utterly destroying both realms in the process."

Vangen leaned forward and smiled. "Or you can release my soul from the blade and use it to open the gate, return home to your people and your quest for the Dark Artifacts and all those noble intentions that cause such tension in your soft heart."

"But you would still be trapped here." Draegan stopped on the stairs and eyed his brother. "There is no profit for you."

"Indeed?" Vangen asked. "Look around you. Do you not see this Keep? Did you not see my army pouring out from its gates? Do you not see this obelisk I sit beneath and the storm that rages above it? There are five more fortresses like this scattered throughout the shadow lands, each one inhabited by the soul of a Blade of Darkness, and each one soon under my control. I will command the unliving forces that inhabit each Keep and send them into the Ashen Wastes to gather the shades that you so recently encountered. The shades are instrumental in my opening of the Grand Gate."

Draegan stood a few steps below the throne and stared at Vangen. He looked up at the roiling mass of energy that crackled about the top of the obelisk. "What is this gate?"

"When you acquired the Artifacts you broke several of the seals that keep this shadow land of Iss separate from Athar. The barrier between Iss and Athar is weakening. Once my armies acquire enough shades to feed my spell I will use their energy to completely unweave the seals, open a massive portal to Athar and draw through it this shadow land. I will make Athar whole once again and restore the balance that was upset three thousand years ago. And when Athar is stable once more, I will march my legions through the gate and devour the world. I care not if I rule from a throne here or in Athar, as long as I rule."

"The Fyrian Empire will stand against you."

"They will fall, Draegan, for the armies of Iss are truly deathless. And I am more powerful than a god here, able to give life and take it as it pleases me. Life and death bend to my command in this realm. Soon all of creation will. All except you Draegan. You and that magnificent pin you wear."

Draegan's hand snapped to his neck as he grabbed the clasp.

"I see you still have yet to understand. Then I shall have to be explicit. You wear the Great Aegis, gifted to Sage Skeldus the Unbreakable ten thousand years ago by the Elder God Cear, called the Guardian in the South. You cannot be killed in battle when you wear it. It is the only reason the shades in the Ashen Wastes did not rend you limb from limb, and it is the only reason you are able to stand before me. My power is such that I could take the life from your body as easily as I breathe, but for that simple pin."

Vangen stood and pointed at Draegan. "That was my birthright! Father had no right to give it to your father Havek. Had he only known that it was no mere trinket, but a Talisman of Light and had he known how to awaken its power I doubt he would have given it away so carelessly. But by this cruel twist of fate it ended up in your possession, awakened." Vangen shook his head. "Yet I bear no grudge, for I have moved beyond your concept of life and death and done so through my own power. I do not rely on some mere bauble as do you."

"I wear a Talisman of Light," Draegan said. "The Great Aegis."

The ground trembled, causing the chains holding the obelisk to snap and tighten before they slackened again. "Time grows short, Draegan. The seal between our worlds breaks. What will you do? What will be your choice? Do you stay here, trapped with me and watch as this world becomes unhinged and crashes into an Athar embroiled in bloodshed? Or will you release my soul and return home to a world on the brink of war, in a vain attempt to save them from themselves before my forces arrive and march upon you?"

There was a long silence as the brothers locked eyes. "The people of Fyrian are innocent Vangen," Draegan said at last, pointing at his brother. "I do not run from you now nor will I ever.

You shall have your life only because I will it. I will return to this place and when I do I will put an end to you with my own hands."

"So you run home to your crumbling Empire," Vangen said and snapped his fingers. "It is like outthinking a child," he muttered to himself. "Look there," he said and pointed behind Draegan. "At the base of the dais is the spell to open the portal. All you need do is plunge your sword into the seal and give me back my soul. Then you are free to walk in Athar again and prepare for my imminent arrival."

Draegan walked down the stairs and stood in the center of the seal. "Make peace with yourself, Vangen, for your time is indeed short," he said and drove his flaming blade into the center of the circle. Immediately the seal burst into flames that turned from red to black. Carnis Fornax shuddered in Draegan's hand, as if it was trying to free itself from his grasp. The flames rose higher and nearly engulfed him. "I will return, Vangen," he said as he disappeared into the black fire.

The flames died out and the seal glowed briefly on the ground before it dissipated, leaving no trace of its existence. Vangen sat in his throne and looked thoughtfully at the empty space where his brother had just stood.

"I hope you do, Draegan, for my plan requires it."

Chapter 14: A Wrinkle

Draegan took a gulp of air and nearly collapsed. The flames of the spell died at his feet, leaving him in utter darkness. "The catacombs," he choked out before catching himself as he stumbled into the damp stones of the wall. He cast an illumination spell and his guess was confirmed in the sickly green light emanating from the orb over his head.

"They have always reeked of death and decay, but never like this." Draegan saw the pile of rubble in the distance had shifted and fallen even more, unblocking the opposite half of the vault. He thought to climb over it, but remembered seeing Gron's body writhing on the ground as Ceredyn stood over him, and decided to not punish himself further. "The Dark Ichor," he said and ran across the chamber to the alcoves.

He found the bow exactly where he had placed it, covered by the wool blanket. He slung it over his shoulder and felt a wave of anger as he recalled Vangen's words. "So he is alive in Iss and makes ready to send his armies here. He has played his hand well, for there is no reason left in the Empire and I will receive no aid or compassion here. I am despised and hated. None will listen to the truth as long as the Artifacts poison their minds, which will make Vangen's task that much easier when he opens the Grand Gate. My only hope is to gather the remaining three Artifacts and hope to use them to stand against Vangen when he returns."

Draegan ran to the end of the catacombs and ascended the spiral staircase that led up to the study. As he pushed open the flagstone door that sealed the study from the stairs he was overpowered by the smell of moldering books and stale air. "I suppose it's good that no curious hands have managed to find a way to open Vangen's door." He looked around the room and saw it still in a state of disarray, with books piled haphazardly over every available square inch of floor, and charts and maps indiscriminately hung from the walls, several half-fallen from their fastenings. A layer of dust had blanketed the space as well.

He placed the bow on a lectern behind the heavy desk and sat in the worn chair. "Where to begin," he said, overwhelmed by the number of books and papers that lay scattered before him. "I must seek the other Artifacts through the Eye of Islak," he said and bowed his head as thought of Gron and Aran. He tried to recall an image of the Black Tower when he heard shouting outside.

Looking out the small window he saw the Night Watch barracks on fire in the courtyard below. He looked up and down the walls but saw no guard raising an alarm. Part of the barrack's roof collapsed sending ash and embers swirling into the air as three figures tumbled out of the door. They were wearing the mark of Stanrocc on their armor. "What is this?" Draegan said as he pulled his cloak about him and placed his hand on the wall. He saw the morning light filtering through the window begin to blur as he became swallowed in a black haze.

Draegan stood and hit his head on the alcove near the door to his bed chamber. "How many times before I remember how small this space is," he said and rubbed the back of his head. Checking his belt for his sword, he took off down the hall and made for the rear stairs. He encountered no one as he raced through the castle and across the inner courtyard to the Night Watch barracks. As he rounded the near wall of the building he saw thick, gray smoke billowing into the clear blue sky. He looked down and saw the same three figures still standing in a semi-circle outside of the barracks and smiling.

"What business has Stanrocc here?" Draegan asked as he walked toward the men. "Raise an alarm and make yourselves useful. Clear out the court." He looked at their garb and noted their disheveled state. They appeared to be common foot soldiers of Stanrocc, but they made no move to obey him.

"Clear out the court, old man?" the smaller one in the front said as Draegan neared them. "Maybe you should do the clearing out, no?" he said and pulled a long knife from his belt.

"Guards," Draegan shouted as his hand slipped to his belt. His voice echoed in the courtyard. The crackling of the fire was the only noise he heard as he strode toward the men.

"There haven't been guards here in a long time, old man," the soldier with the knife said as he eyed Draegan hungrily. "Not for twenty years. Though stragglers like you show up every now and again to see what's left to pick over." He switched the knife to his other hand. "But if we'd a known you was hiding out back we'd have killed you first before we burned you with the rest of the lot," he said and gestured toward the burning barracks. The other two men began to fan out and flank Draegan.

"I will kill you last, so you may have the good fortune of telling me what madness is going on," Draegan said as the three laughed and drew their blades. Draegan slowly pulled the hilt from his belt and held it upright before him.

"You might want to put a blade in that rusty handle before you go playing with soldiers of the Red Hand," the small one said. "Makes talking tough a lot easier if you have something to back it up with."

"Indeed," Draegan said and tightened his grip on the hilt. The black flames of Carnis Fornax erupted from the hilt and crackled to life. Draegan felt the air around him chill as the fire searched for life. A hunger moved through him as the blade half pulled Draegan closer to the three.

"He's a Raven," one of the soldiers said and sprinted toward the outer wall. In a flash Draegan had cut him down, moving at inhuman speed. Turning on his heel he sprinted to the other man and pierced him through, removing the blade and walking toward the smaller soldier before the other's corpse collapsed in a heap on the ground.

The last soldier sheathed his blade and raised his hands as Draegan walked calmly toward him. "I don't want no trouble, sir," he said and flinched as the fire of the sword snapped and stretched toward him. "I didn't know you was a mage of Corvus."

"I am Draegan, King of Skeldus and Emperor of Fyrian, sergeant," Draegan said as he looked over the man trembling before him. The man looked up, aghast.

"Draegan? You can't be, he's gone. Twenty years ago, he left," the man stammered as he tried to look at Draegan while shielding his face from the hungry flame of his blade.

"I see you have a fear of fire," Draegan said. He flicked his wrist and instantly the flame was gone. Draegan tucked the hilt in his belt and looked at the man. "Begin at the beginning and go slowly. Tell me what is happening here in Dullahan and in the Empire."

"Empire? There isn't one," the sergeant said. "Not since I was five years old. My father said Draegan killed Vangen twenty years ago and fled the land. No one knows where. So the other four kingdoms swooped into Skeldus to carve up pieces for themselves. They been at war with each other since. Nothing left in Skeldus though to fight over. So now they kill each other."

Draegan's eyes grew wide. "Twenty years I walked the Wastes," he said. "I can't believe it." He turned to the soldier. "Tell me who rules the four Kingdoms."

"Erdrik Cor is the Red Hand of the Freehold of Stanrocc. Kelthus Artel is the head of the House of Corvus and Tor Valdin is the War Chief in the Iron Mountains."

"What of Docga? What of Tior?"

"Tior?" the man asked. "Never heard of him. "Docga doesn't exist. It fell to Stanrocc. We invaded after they lost their Artifact. Erdrik never found it, but he burnt the kingdom to the ground looking. Nothing left in Docga but ashes."

"This is madness, some trick of Vangen's," Draegan said looking around at the state of the city-castle. The inner walls were crumbling and in need of repair. Gates hung open on broken hinges. Behind him the fire in the barracks billowed black smoke as it lost its fuel and died down.

The sergeant watched Draegan scan the entirety of the grounds, confusion showing plainly on his face. "There ain't no one here," the sergeant said. "It's a cursed place, Dullahan. Only ones who come are those desperate enough to look for scraps."

"Then why are you and your men here?"

"We broke from our force heading north over the Iron Mountains," the sergeant said looking down. "We're tired of fighting. There's no living to be made outside the army though, so our only option was to run here."

"So you deserted and thought you'd make a living persecuting the wretched victims of your wars." Draegan looked squarely at the man. "If what you say is the truth I will spare you from my blade."

"It is sir, I swear it," the soldier said and clasped his hands in front of him, looking hopefully up at Draegan.

Draegan nodded and reached down toward the sergeant. He quickly stepped behind the man and cupped his hands under the man's chin, bent him backward over his knee, and snapped his neck in one fluid motion. "But that will not spare you from justice." He let the body slip from his fingers and thud to the ground. Draegan walked toward the swirling smoke pouring from the barracks.

"As much as I am loathe to think of the traitor, I believe Ceredyn taught me a useful spell for suffocating flames. If only I could recall…," Draegan said as he placed his hands on the warm stones of the building. As he did the roof collapsed completely, sending ash and smoke pouring out the windows and doors. Draegan stepped back and watched the smoldering ruins for a few moments. "I don't think that was it, but it seems to have had the same effect."

He looked around the courtyard and saw the desperate state of his castle. Though the inner wall was mostly intact, the stables had been stripped bare. He circled back behind the barracks and saw the same held true of the forge. Nails and iron stakes had been pulled from the wood, collapsing every shed that lined the wall. Even the scrap metal had been taken. Draegan pulled his cloak tight about him and passed through the mouth of the Lion of the West and into the outer court. Though the massive lion's head still stood, the outer wall was in shambles. The market stalls were broken and burnt. Charred remains of soldiers littered the square, so badly burnt he couldn't tell to which kingdoms they belonged.

"Dullahan has fallen. My kingdom is gutted." He returned to the inner court, wishing to see no more of the devastation. He entered the castle through the splintered oaken doors of the guard house. The inside of the castle told a different story. There were no signs of destruction or violence. The halls and rooms were simply abandoned and devoid of anything not built into the castle's walls. He went to the kitchen and found it empty. The store room was the same, though the Shadow Walking rune he had made on the ground was gouged and scratched with what appeared to be knife marks. "Unusable, now," he said and left for his bed chamber. "Why has the castle proper been spared? Do they believe it to be cursed?"

Draegan entered his old room and saw it as unkempt as he had left it a few days ago, though when he stepped in front the mirror attached to Issa's bureau he was greeted with an unfamiliar face. He stopped and stared at the older man that gazed back at him. Gray streaks colored his once jet black hair. His face was thinner, and lines shown around his eyes. Draegan paused. "The man spoke true," he stammered. "Twenty years have indeed passed."

Overcome, he dropped to his knees and smashed his fists on the floor. "I have lost everything. Vangen is beyond me and my Empire has crumbled." He drew a deep breath. "I have failed utterly."

Draegan sat motionless and collected his thoughts. He remembered his friends, Gron and Aran, and Ceredyn's betrayal. He recalled how Vangen had used him and deceived him so completely. He thought of the last time he'd seen Issa, lying in bed. His head swimming with rage and regret, Draegan stood and left the bed chamber. In a daze he stumbled down the hall to Vangen's study. The door opened as he approached and he saw how similar the study mirrored his own chamber, with books and papers and scrolls heaped carelessly on every available surface.

"He has taken everything from me. My wife, my friends, my honor, and my faith. I swear by the Elder Gods of Light and those of Darkness I will see him dead."

Draegan entered the study and shut the door behind him. Snapping his fingers he ignited a small candle on the desk and seated himself in the heavily worn, oversized chair. Pushing the scrolls and papers that littered the surface of the desk to the floor, he took Vangen's book and opened it to the beginning. He hung his head inches from the thick parchment and read through the day and night, finishing the tome by evening of the next day. Having read every note, discerned every rune, and unraveled every glyph, Draegan closed the book and stared blankly at the study door. He now had a complete understanding of the power and hate that burned within his brother.

"The scope of his power rivals that of the Sages. He is powerful enough and mad enough to open a portal from Iss to this world. And when he comes with his legions, Athar cannot stand against him." Draegan glared at the tome that lay before him on the desk and thought back to his failed encounter with Vangen in the shadow realm. "But he needs time to open the gate, and as I am now sorely aware time flows differently in that realm. There may be a chance to stop him, but I have to move quickly."

Draegan spent the rest of the night scratching down notes and reading through various scrolls and books that were mentioned in Vangen's book. By the time the first rays of dawn shone through the small soot stained window in the study, Draegan had made his pack and collected several small books in another satchel. He rose, and slinging both over his shoulder he snapped his fingers. The flagstones in the floor glowed green and began sliding slowly open, revealing the staircase to the catacombs.

"Islak's eye has shown me what I need. Dullahan and the Empire will suffer more before I'm done, but I must regain the other three Artifacts and return to the shadow lands to face Vangen. If there is any chance at peace then I must stop him before he has time to open the Grand Gate." He looked down the winding stairs into the darkness. "And my only chance is to use all six Artifacts against him."

Draegan slipped down the stairs and descended into the gloom. He heard the groaning of the flagstone as it closed behind him, and then a thud as it fell into place, plunging him into complete darkness as he descended into the catacombs.

Chapter 15: The Burning Shadow

Vangen descended the steps from his throne. He held out his hand as he walked, lightly touching one of the four massive chains that bound the floating splinter of blood red metal that rose above him. A thrumming echoed through the whole of the valley. Vangen turned to look over his shoulder.

"Calm yourself Pyr, it will all be over soon. You have little reason, and less to gain, from struggling against my prison, for soon your soul will be joined with mine and once again you will walk in Athar."

The ruddy metal of the obelisk begin to pulse with a deep red light. The red metal gave way to a translucent, crystalline material and within the giant hovering structure, Vangen watched a black vapor swirl madly as if driven by some violent wind. As the black mist crashed into the interior walls of the obelisk, a booming echoing resounded through the Red Keep. Then the dark cloud within the giant crystal shard congealed for a moment, giving Vangen a brief glimpse of an outline, almost human in form, before it was carried off.

"Enough of your complaints, Pyr. Your hate has blinded you to the opportunity I present to you and all your brothers. You should be thankful, for without me you would be trapped forever in this waste, ruling an empty kingdom that begins to tear apart at the seams. I give you a greater purpose. In me you will have life again." The chaotic black cloud slammed again into the face of the obelisk. "And yet you remain ungrateful at this small inconvenience."

Vangen raised his hand dismissively and the obelisk turned from crystal back to a blood red metal.

"But I am thankful for you army Pyr. Even now we march through the Ashen Wastes to join Dalken Tor to our cause. And I will be there when we parlay at his gate, for I would not wish the same struggle upon him as I put you through. I hope he has the good sense to aid me without engaging in the wasteful histrionics you displayed. We have little time before Draegan returns with my Artifacts."

The obelisk thundered at Vangen's words, shaking the very walls of the Red Keep. Vangen laughed and walked through the empty fortress and out onto the desolate plains of the valley. He saw the lava flowing through the channels and raised his eyes to gaze at the leaden clouds churning through the crimson sky. He snapped his fingers and vanished, a small cloud of rust colored dust hanging in the still air where he stood moments before.

***

"This looks oddly similar to what I recall of the Rookery," Vangen said as he faced the black iron wall molded into the cliff face. He stood before his army, hands on his hips as he looked around him. Behind him his forces were spread out, a legion deep and hundreds of legions wide, covering the valley floor in a sea of red iron plate. Lances and pikes bristled above their ranks and banners hung lifeless in the dead air as the soldiers stood perfectly still, awaiting their master's command. The great birds that wheeled above the foundries in the Red Keep now soared above the army, piercing the still, silent air at intervals with their shrieks.

Vangen stood in a large basin. It was similar to the one that held the Red Keep, though the far wall of this basin was ringed in soaring cliffs into which a large metal plate hundreds of yards in width and height was sunk so that it lay flat with the rock face of the wall. There was no break in the metal wall, save for one large gate which stood open. No light crept past the gaping entrance so that it was impossible to see deeper into the cliff face.

"I call upon the Blade of Darkness known as Dalken Tor, the Burning Shadow, Lord of the Night and Bane of Sage Helian to come and treat with Vangen Atrox, your humble servant," Vangen shouted into the dead air of the valley as he bowed slightly. He waited and watched the clouds churn as the carrion birds rose in lazy circles above him.

A blast of cold wind rushed from the open portal in the cliff wall. It snapped Vangen's cloak and shrouded his army in dust from the basin floor. An icy voice echoed through the valley seeming to come from every direction at once.

"You are known to me, Vangen Atrox. I know what you have done to my brother Pyr the Red Scourge," the voice hissed.

"Then you know my purpose is for our mutual benefit, Dalken Tor. I ask only that you listen to reason. I give you and all your brothers another chance at life. We will walk upon Athar again and through me, we will rule it completely."

Another blast of icy wind howled from the gate, knocking over several of the first ranks of soldiers behind Vangen.

"The Blades of Darkness serve the Hands of Darkness alone, those who you call the Elder Gods. It is foolish impudence to attempt to bend us to your will. I know not how you deceived my brother into bondage but I will prove your doom."

Vangen laughed. "You do not see my vision either, Shadow Walker. So be it. I will chain you as I did the Red Scourge. I shall chain you all in time."

Vangen raised his right hand above his head and the legions of soldiers behind him snapped to attention, metal scraping against metal in a harsh burst of sound that filled the valley. The birds dove and shrieked, hungry for war.

Before Vangen could drop his hand to signal his troops to charge through the opening in the metal wall, a great black shadow poured through the gate and rose up like a tidal wave hundreds of feet over the valley. Vangen stood still, watching the shadow as it shifted form, rising higher and higher blotting out the crimson sky.

"A cheap trick," Vangen spat, keeping his hand raised over his head. "You waste my time Dalken, and time is limited even in this deathless place." He squatted to the ground keeping his right hand raised and placing the palm of his left hand flat on the dirt of the basin floor. He gritted his teeth and set his jaw. Speaking a single word his eyes turned white as they rolled into his head. Beads of perspiration rose on his forehead as veins began to swell at his temple. He trembled for an instant, and then exhaled.

Before him the shadow began to contract, twisting and writhing as it was pulled against its will into itself, folding and twisting into a smaller and smaller form. Vangen rose slowly, trying to keep his balance. He stepped back from the spot where he knelt as the ground began to shake. From the barren black dirt of the valley floor the tip of a great obelisk broke through the ground, sending debris scattering and rising slowly as Vangen continued to step back, his right hand still held high. The black iron obelisk continued its violent birth from the splintering ground, shaking and cracking the whole valley as it rose into the air. The swirling shadow began to contort in a futile effort to try and escape the pull of the obelisk. Within moments a massive obelisk similar to the one that hovered above the Red Keep, but of black iron, had risen from the floor into the sky and floated gently, borne on some subtle current. Within it the form of Dalken Tor surged against the sides of his prison.

"You proved much easier than your brother, Dalken Tor," Vangen said in a hoarse shout. "You should not have wasted your opening gambit trying to awe me with your power. Take a lesson from Pyr and attack." Vangen wiped the sweat from his brow and caught his breath. "Now I will send my forces through your fortress and join your army to mine."

Vangen let his right hand drop and the legions of red iron clad soldiers behind him roared to life and seethed forward, the valley floor thundering with their footfalls as they rushed the open mouth of the metal wall carved in the cliff face and poured into it like a blood red tide. From the gaping hole in the cliff face thousands upon thousands of gray clad soldiers rushed to meet Vangen's forces. They moved silently across the battlefield, like wraiths. Their armor made no noise and no war cries echoed to meet the rushing red onslaught. When the vanguards clashed it was if thunder split the valley. Bodies poured over one another as pikes and swords carved into their victims with ruthless abandon. The clashing forces churned like a raging river, the echoes of their weapons and armor ringing through the basin.

Vangen took his eyes from the carnage and smiled as he watched the great black birds circle the floating obelisk. "You will need to move swiftly Draegan, if you hope to match me."

The cold air shocked Draegan's senses as he stepped out from the fetid, humid drainage tunnel into the frosty morning. A light snow had covered the ground, lending a soft and peaceful appearance to the ravaged earth that lay beneath. He looked behind him and saw the outer wall of Dullahan torn apart. From the northern side of the castle he could see directly through to the inner wall.

"For over a thousand years that wall has withstood every assault the four kingdoms have thrown against it. Now, in my absence of twenty years it is reduced to no more than a heap of bricks." He turned and pulled his cloak tight against the cold wind that stirred the snow. Looking ahead he saw the northern road was still adequately maintained as far as he could see. The braziers that lined it were gone and cobble stones were missing in places but it would still serve to carry an army with siege engines, let alone a solitary traveler.

"It's worth the risk," Draegan said and traced the *staminis* rune on his throat. He felt his body temperature begin to rise. "If I encounter any resistance I'll leave the road. Otherwise I need to make north as quickly as possible to catch the army of Stanrocc while they're still in the Iron Mountains."

With the sun rising on his shoulder, Draegan flew up the road, the leather and mail jerkin clinking softly beneath his cloak. In addition to the jerkin taken from the fallen brigand outside the Night Watch barracks, he wore on his arm the sigil of the Red Hand. He hoped this would be enough to gain him entrance into Erdrik's camp.

Draegan ran through the night and into late evening of the next day. He felt the air cool significantly as he watched small bumps on the horizon grow to become the foothills of the Iron Mountains. The road ahead became lost in the twisting foothills and

Draegan broke from the path and made his way to the top of a hillock. From this vantage point he saw the Iron Pass still standing, and made straight for it. The cold air helped cool him as he pushed himself up and over the hills, his aching legs devouring the frozen ground. The crunch of his boots and his labored breathing drowned out the sound of his mail as he ran. There were no other signs of life, save a few scattered crows cawing noisily as they took flight, disturbed by Draegan's passing.

As he neared the frozen peaks of the Iron Mountains the ground began to rise sharply. The rolling hills now rose more aggressively to meet the base of the mountain chain. From the top of one of the numerous hillocks he saw that the gate of the Iron Pass had been raised, though he saw no banners flying upon the two guard towers. There was a small wisp of smoke curling into the air over a hill near the guard towers, but he couldn't make out exactly where it originated.

"That's not enough smoke for a fire that heats or cooks food for more than five men," Draegan said, flying down the hill and making for the north road that approached the gate. "I think the odds are in my favor." A few hundred yards from the gate, Draegan broke the *staminis* spell and caught his breath, stretching his legs as he moved. He walked along the broken road and kept his cloak pulled tight about him.

"Ho, traveler," a voice said as Draegan rounded the corner and approached the Iron Pass. He looked up and saw four men gathered around a fire burning in the center of the road a hundred feet outside the two towers. A fat one stirred a small pot that hung over the coals while the other three rose to meet their guest.

"Make yourself known," the man in the front said. Draegan saw they were dressed the same as the three rogues in Dullahan's courtyard. They bore a great red hand on their chests, marking them as soldiers of Stanrocc.

"I see you are Erdrik's men," Draegan said as he walked toward them. He removed his hood and pulled his cloak back to show them his armband. "I too serve the Red Hand. I must make for Erdrik's camp to deliver pressing news."

The three eyed him cautiously and fanned out around him, blocking his path to the Iron Pass. "You come from Dullahan?" the one on his left asked while the soldier in front of him walked closer and squinted at Draegan's face. The fat man continued to stir the pot and stare into the fire.

"Indeed, with dire news for Erdrik. A force marches this way as we speak. I could not tell if they are Corvus or those of the Iron Mountains, but they are not our brothers."

The three men looked at each other. "Indeed? Dire? Our brothers?" the men repeated and laughed. "We have no brothers, my lord. Least of all a highborn like you." The three men pressed in on Draegan and moved their hands to their hilts.

"I don't know what Vek and his boys flushed out of that castle, but someone who uses such fine speech must have gold or something of value," the largest of the three soldiers said while the other two circled behind Draegan.

"You can keep his gold, I want his boots," the one to Draegan's right said.

"I want no trouble, men," Draegan said, raising his hands. "I make for Erdrik's camp and mean you no disrespect."

"You're gonna have a tough time catching up with them in your bare feet, old man. They must be past Brahne by now." The other two laughed and pushed in closer to Draegan.

In a flash Draegan pulled Carnis Fornax from his belt and swung at the larger soldier standing in front of him. The black flames blazed instantly from the hilt, causing the man to jump back and draw his sword. The other two backed off a few steps and drew their weapons. Draegan smiled and set his jaw.

"You could have let me pass," he said, anger tingeing his voice. He looked over his shoulder and marked in his mind where the other two soldiers stood. "And you would have lived. You may have even made it to Dullahan to see Vek and his friends' frozen corpses. But now you will share their fate."

He lunged forward at the large soldier who backpedaled and tried to parry the flaming blade. Before the other two could close in behind him, Draegan spun and leapt at the closest man, driving the blade clean through soldier's chest and out through his back. He felt a rush of energy as the sword drew in the man's soul. He withdrew the blade and the soldier collapsed in a heap. The remaining two had bunched up and stared in terror at the cloaked figure before them, brandishing his ferocious weapon of black fire.

Draegan coiled his muscles and in one violent gesture he sprung at the two and cut them down as his sword drank in their souls. He lowered his blade and walked to the fat man who stared at Draegan in horror.

"I'm not going to run, so just take what you want."

He looked at the stew, inhaled, and shook his head. "Where is Erdrik?"

"South of Brahne by now. We deserted a few days ago. They're moving slow so they couldn't have gone far."

He nodded and ran through the Iron Pass leaving the fat cook trembling in silence as he watched Draegan's cloaked form disappear through the towers.

With the aid of another *staminis* spell Draegan ran up and through the Iron Pass as it twisted through the mountains, burning through the rest of the day in a blur of snow covered rocks. He pushed onward as the light faded, continuing under the cover of darkness since his time was limited and the toll of the spell was heavy. The pass through the mountains slowed him even under the power of his incantation. It wasn't until the following night that he left the Iron Mountains behind and entered the frozen tundra of the north. He pushed through frost covered heath for hours and in the faint light of the waxing moon he saw the lights of Brahne flickering in the distance.

Draegan stopped the spell a few miles from the city and left the road. He slumped against a boulder and drained his water skin. He felt more tired than usual, his joints ached and the cold of the boulder bothered him enough that he leaned forward. "I am old, I am spent, and I may be a fool to think that my plan has any merit," he said and wove a sign with his fingers to check for seals around the northern capital of Brahne.

"Nothing." He smiled in relief, and then checked himself. "Is it wiser to circle Brahne to the south and look for Erdrik in the west or push east and see if he's camped before the Frozen Maw?" Draegan leaned back gingerly against the frozen rock and thought. "The eye," he exclaimed. He curled up in a ball and readied himself for the pain that was about to course through his body. He paused for a moment and relaxed. "I can't conjure an image of an Artifact I've never seen." He sighed and leaned against the boulder. "Do I risk going closer to Brahne and seek the World Render, or should I turn south and west to the Granite Hall of Stanrocc and await Erdrik's return?" He peered around the rock and looked toward Brahne. In the distance he watched the silent fires on the horizon wink like jewels in the black sky.

"Brahne has grown so much these past twenty years that now it lights the sky at night. Three miles out and it nearly matches the old splendor of Dullahan." He froze as an arctic breeze stirred something buried in his memory. He caught a faint trace of smoke and peered again at the lights. "Those aren't lights, the city is burning," he said and shouldered his pack as he stood. "The forces of Stanrocc must have been here recently if it still burns." Draegan rose and walked down the road keeping his eyes fixed on the flickering lights on the horizon.

Draegan was a mile outside the limits of Brahne and could now clearly see the city was engulfed in flames. He smelled the smoke as he approached and saw the horizon brighten from the sheer magnitude of the raging fire. When he was close enough and the fire bright enough that he could make out individual buildings, he began to hear voices rise over the sound of flames and the howling of the wind.

"They left days ago, and we'd be smart to do likewise."

"I say we see how far he goes this time and break if we need to. No sense leaving the party early."

Draegan stopped and flattened himself on the ground. The voices weren't far away and they clearly sounded drunk. He lay still behind a small lump of heath and continued to listen.

"It'll go bad for us when the War Chief and his main forces get word of what Erdrik did here. No mercy for us. I say we don't need to be here for the whipping."

"It's us'll do the whipping, coward. And if you do run off, where would you go? South through the Iron Pass to cursed

Dullahan? Or will you go home to be the laughing stock of Stanrocc?" The man speaking coughed. "Best to stay and see how this work out for us." There was a grunt and some indecipherable mutterings. "Stay in the rear if you like, then."

Draegan peered over the slight rise and saw a group of men crouched around a small fire ahead of him and to his left. With the light of Brahne in front of him he could see five men sitting around the flames. He crawled closer to the lump of heath and placed his hands on it to pull himself up for a better look. Draegan heard the shifting of iron armor and saw that what he had taken for a mound of vegetation was instead a still warm corpse.

"This is a recent kill," he said and lowered himself back down. "Then Erdrik's men must still be here, camped near Brahne." Draegan took a piece of parchment from his pack and drew a small symbol in the bottom corner. On his wrist he made the same mark. He pricked his finger and quickly fashioned a larger rune in blood, directly in the middle of the sheet. Tucking the piece of paper into his pack, he stood and limped over to the fire, grabbing his shoulder and breathing heavily. "Spare some water?" he asked as he neared them.

Two of the five men stood and put their hands on the swords in their belts. The others turned and looked as Draegan neared, their faces set in the flickering fire light. "Are you going to announce yourself or do we have to beat it out of ya?" one of the seated men asked.

"A messenger from Stanrocc, with news for Erdrik." Draegan limped forward. "Has he moved on or does the army camp here?"

One of the men who had stood walked toward Draegan and saw his arm band. The other man looked past Draegan into the darkness, checking for others. "Looks like one of us," he shouted over his shoulder. "What regiment you from and who do you serve under?" he asked Draegan.

Draegan smiled and hobbled past the soldier. He took a seat between two soldiers and held out his hands to the flame, wincing as he did so. "Doesn't matter now. I broke with some others a few days ago in the Iron Mountains. We went south."

"Dullahan?" a large bearded man opposite Draegan asked. "What good is it to flee if you're going to that cursed place? Better to die here on this frozen dirt then there."

"My sergeant Vek wanted to check the old place out. He didn't believe the stories." Draegan said and rubbed his shoulder. "He does now. I was the only one to make it out of that place alive, though my horse threw me and I made the rest of my way on foot."

"Why would a deserter come crawling home? You know the penalty, same as us all," said the bearded man. "The Red Hand knows no mercy."

The other two men had rejoined the group by the fire and sat to either side of the large bearded man who appeared to be their sergeant. The sergeant elbowed one and gestured toward Draegan. The soldier handed him his water skin and Draegan emptied it in short order.

"There's something evil in the bowels of Dullahan," Draegan said as he handed the skin back to the soldier with a nod of thanks. "I don't know who or what they are but we saw thousands of them. More than all three armies put together." He looked at the others' eyes as they all focused on him. "They're dark and move like shadows. Cut down Vek before he could draw his blade and spooked the horses. They wore a mark like this on their chests," Draegan said and produced a small paper from his pack. "Can you read?" he asked as he handed it to the sergeant who unrolled it in the firelight.

"Of course I can read," the sergeant said, "but I can't read this scratch. What kingdom speaks this nonsense?"

Draegan shook his head. "I've been thinking about it the whole time I been running here. It's not ours or old Docga's. Corvus looks different than that, I've seen enough to know. The Clan doesn't use marks like that either." He paused and looked around. "I think it's the mark of Iss," he whispered. "But whatever it is and whoever they are, they're marching this way. I have a few days lead on them, which is why I came back. Erdrik will forgive me if I bring him this news," Draegan said and held out his hand for the parchment.

The sergeant leaned back and looked curiously at Draegan as he tucked the piece of paper in his wide belt. He brushed aside Draegan's hand as he spoke. "Iss? That was a hoax. You look old enough to remember. The Usurper was behind it. I don't know you, old man, but I know enough that I think I'll be delivering this message myself. If he wants to see you, I'll come back for you." The bearded sergeant stood and looked at the four soldiers. "Keep him from running off again. I'm going to find the captain," he said and trudged off, his boots crunching the frost as he disappeared into the night.

Draegan looked at the other men who stared at him in silence. "So you managed to take Brahne? I didn't see any of the Clan of the Iron Mountains fleeing south on my way up here. I guess no one made it past you."

The four looked at each other and smiled. "Not many old men and women can outrun us," a lanky soldier said as he leaned in and handed Draegan another water skin. "It's good wine, drink it. Sharing the spoils."

Draegan took a pull and wiped his mouth. "So what happened?"

"Brahne was half empty. The Clan marched their whole army out a week ago, making west across the tundra to Corvus. Erdrik got word and knew we'd have an easy time of it coming here when their army was gone. Course, he didn't tell us the city was empty until we were at the outer walls." The lanky soldier took the wine skin back. "But Erdrik was right, we did have an easy time of it. Mostly women and children in there. A few of the home guard but they didn't do much."

Draegan grunted and looked over his shoulder at the burning city.

"Problem now is that Erdrik is gonna want to push us after the Clan's army and pick through the remains after they and Corvus go at it." He paused to take a drink. "But who's to say we don't run into them before? Who's to say it goes this easy for us again?" He shook his head. No, I'm done. We got lucky, we got our hides and a little loot. Time to head home." The others nodded in agreement. "Of course the old sergeant won't hear of it, but some more wine and it'll be easier to talk sense into his thick head."

"Aye, more wine is always the answer," Draegan said and looked at the small black symbol drawn on his wrist. It was beginning to fade. "Looks like the old sergeant is faster than I thought. Well gentlemen, I've got to run again," he said and smiled. Draegan's hand slipped to his waist and he curled his fingers around the hilt of his sword, feeling the carvings come to life in his palm. The blade flared to life as he pulled it from his belt and cleaved through the man sitting to his right. The others stood and shouted as Draegan leapt into the group, the black fire drinking the life from the soldiers as they scrambled to unsheathe their weapons.

In an instant it was over and Draegan tucked the hilt into his belt. He looked from the twisted corpses on the ground to the symbol on his wrist and saw it had vanished. He pulled his hood over his head as he crouched and removed his glove. He touched the palm of his hand to the frozen ground and saw the fire expand and contract as he tumbled and fell through the darkness.

***

"He's the one who gave it to me, your Highness," the Captain said as he bowed and ushered the bearded sergeant past the guards who stood near the entrance of Erdrik's tent. The sergeant entered through the heavy canvas flaps and shook off the cold of the night. Inside a fire burned in a brass bowl and candles ringed the edge of the tent, casting more than enough light to read by. Rich rugs and furs covered the ground, keeping the cold at bay, along with the heavy tapestries hung around the perimeter of the tent. Behind a richly detailed field desk, Erdrik leaned forward amidst a pile of papers and stared at a piece of parchment.

"What is this unreadable nonsense, and be quick. If it's a game, then you've had your laugh and now I'll have mine," Erdrik said as he leaned back and looked up at the sergeant. The captain took a step back toward the entrance to the tent and kept his eyes down.

"No game my lord," the sergeant said as he bowed stiffly. "Some deserter came from Dullahan with this paper," he said and pointed at it on Erdrik's desk. "He wanted to bring it here directly, but I knew it would be wiser to…"

"You take orders from deserters, fool?" Erdrik shouted. "Is this the class of men my officers train?" The captain winced and looked at the sergeant. "Leave us! Take the guards with you," Erdrik barked to the captain as he rose from his desk. The captain bowed and exited the tent, a rush of cold air swirling through the tent as the flap snapped shut. Erdrik still wore most of his blood red armor, though he had removed his breastplate and pauldrons. He stood a few inches taller than the sergeant, though he was leaner. His jet black hair was combed back save for a few loose strands that hung in his face. Black stubble lent a rough aspect to his angular features.

Erdrik thrust his jaw forward and narrowed his eyes. "I don't know what you're playing at sergeant but I have a feeling you'll tell me very quickly," he said as he ran his hand over the twisting figures carved on the black handle that hung from his belt. The sergeant's face paled as he shifted his gaze from Erdrik to the figure rising from a black cloud that suddenly billowed and spilled from the desk.

"You have something of mine, Erdrik."

Erdrik turned and saw the black mist rising from the parchment on his desk and pouring onto the furs that lined the floor. A figure in a black cloak rose from the vapor on his desk and hopped to the floor.

"It's him," the sergeant stammered as he pointed past Erdrik at Draegan. "It's the rider from Dulla..."

Before he could finish Draegan split the sergeant in two as Carnis Fornax came burning down through him in a vicious arc. Draegan turned and swung his blade an inch too high, missing Erdrik who dove out of the way. "I am getting old," Draegan muttered as he circled toward the tent's entrance.

"I don't know what dark magic you wield, but you won't stand long against the Burning Chains," Erdrik said as he snapped the black handle of his whip and great tongues of flame unfurled before him. Draegan watched six coils of crackling red flame writhe on the ground. He kept circling until he was directly in front of the tent's entrance and Erdrik stood in front of his desk.

Draegan held the blade in front of him for Erdrik to see. "This is Carnis Fornax, the Eater of Souls," he said and smiled as he feinted at Erdrik. Draegan stooped as the cords of flame cracked over his head, the intensity of the heat watering his eyes. As Erdrik pulled the whip back, readying for another strike, Draegan placed his palm to the ground and was swallowed in darkness. "It is more than a match for you." The tongues of flame parted the black vapor where Draegan had crouched, revealing nothing but the fur-lined floor.

"And the mark you couldn't read was the Shadow Walking rune," Draegan said from behind Erdrik as he sunk his blade of fire through Erdrik's back and watched it burst from his chest. Erdrik sputtered and dropped the whip moments before his body crumpled, lifeless on the thick furs.

The red coils of fire extinguished as the handle hit the ground. Draegan reached down and tucked the Burning Chains his belt alongside the hilt of Carnis Fornax. He looked through the loose papers on the desk and finding one, placed Erdrik's seal on it. He tucked it and his own parchment in his sleeve and crouched, placing his palm on the thick bearskin and closed his eyes as the ground heaved and pitched.

***

Draegan looked through the black mist and saw the corpses of the men by the camp fire, exactly as he had left them minutes ago. He shouldered his pack and began walking closer to the fires of Brahne where the main force camped. He passed many more camp and cook fires with soldiers gathered around them. Most didn't bother him, though a few asked him to stop and drink to their victory. Draegan declined and pressed on until he came to a group of men brushing down horses. Draegan approached the sergeant who was speaking with a smith and interrupted him.

"Word from Erdrik," he said and took a piece of paper from his sleeve and unrolled it. The sergeant squinted at it in the light of the smith's makeshift forge and cursed. "If we don't have enough horses to keep the officers mounted, then where does he think I'll get two more?" He looked up at the smith. "Should I have you make two for his Highness?" The smith ignored the sergeant and kept hammering, sending orange sparks into the cold, dark air.

"Erdrik needs me to take two horses west to scout the Clan's army. If you don't like the order, you can talk with him in his tent. And while you're there tell him I don't feel like going either," Draegan said and secured his pack to the nearest horse. Grabbing the reins of a second horse he spurred his mount on and rode toward the rising Tear of Helian in the west.

Chapter 18: The Spreading Darkness

Vangen stared at the black obelisk that floated gently before him, craning his head to watch the birds that wheeled lazily about it, their shrill calls piercing the stillness in the valley.

"You could have made this easier on yourself Dalken," Vangen said as he took his eyes from the gargantuan black iron spike before him and looked at the now quiet battlefield.

Vangen's forces were marching away, partially obscured in the distance by a cloud of dust. He could no longer hear their armor crunching in rhythm as they strode toward their next objective, but saw only the outline of their thousands of helmets, spears and banners etched against the red sky. In front of him lay thousands of fallen soldiers, their pikes and bodies broken and twisted into positions possible only in death. There was no blood soaking the ground, only rent armor and shattered weapons littering the dusty plain. A soft breeze stirred the dust that still hung in the air where the forces had clashed only moments ago.

"I will collect all of the half-spirits trapped in the Ashen Wastes," Vangen said to the fallen multitudes as he turned his back on the slaughter and watched his legions recede into the horizon. "And your forces will be reborn as my wiling servants, deathless and obedient to me. I will lead them into Athar where together we will raise a new banner over the green pastures of Fyrian and all that lies beyond."

The obelisk shuddered and wrenched violently. Vangen whipped around and snarled at the massive splinter of iron.

"I see you need to be chained, Shadow Walker, the same as your brother. If you fail to see my power and think it some stroke of luck that I have bound you and Pyr, then now I will instruct you in the finer points of my authority."

Vangen raised his hands over his head and brought them down to his sides in one swift motion. Great chains erupted from the ground and launched themselves at the obelisk, snaking their way around it and grinding it within their coils. The black metal shuddered as the lengths of iron bound the obelisk, freezing it in place as it turned translucent. Vangen saw within the glowing crystal shard the shadow of Dalken Tor thrashing against the faces of the obelisk, congealing into an almost human form, then dissipating and slamming into another side.

"I presented you with an opportunity to come without force, and you declined my offer, causing me to lose precious time. Now my army marches across the Ashen Wastes collecting the shades of your fallen warriors and joining them to my ranks. Soon Talus Sen will be presented a similar overture, and I hope you will stand as an object lesson for the remaining Blades of Darkness. You have no option other than to join me in my conquest of Iss and Athar, but as a generous Emperor I will extend all the remaining Blades the privilege of accepting peaceably before I exert my will upon them." Vangen narrowed his eyes at the obelisk. "You foolishly rejected my benevolence, and now you shall suffer."

Vangen snapped his fingers and the chains tightened and contracted, slamming the obelisk to the ground. The force of the strike shook the entire basin and lifted a cloud of dust high into the crimson sky that was large enough to obscure the wall of Dalken Tor's fortress. A crackling blue energy shot from the chains and enveloped the crystalline shard. The seething shadow within howled in torment, clawing with cruel, human-like hands at the facets of the obelisk.

"Louder Dalken Tor," Vangen said as he turned and walked across the basin, following the footsteps of his departed army. "I want your cries to carry across the wastes and echo in the ears of Talus Sen, that he may know my power and learn from your folly."

***

"Enter Vangen Atrox," came a sickening whisper from the yawning gate. "Enter and know your doom."

Vangen stood at the base of a great black tower that rose from blackened earth and soared into the sky, its summit lost in the clouds. It was constructed of great blocks of heavy black stone, fitted together so expertly it was difficult to discern the joints. There was no ornamentation on any of the four faces of the tower, save the great open portal Vangen stood before. In the plains behind him, Vangen's forces spread like a great red blanket over the gray ash that covered the ground. He now commanded ten thousand unliving soldiers, who stood motionless and rigid, waiting for his command. Again their banners, relics of their old masters, hung lifelessly in the still air. Again the quiet was broken intermittently by the ear-splitting cries of the dark birds that spun in wide circles above the legions of soldiers.

Steam issued from the ground in billowing clouds that rose and dissolved as they climbed into the ruddy sky. Several grated vents were dug into the ground around the base of the tower and two large channels radiated out from the tower, splitting the open plain in half. They carried a fetid green liquid outward from the tower that sputtered in the open channels.

Vangen threw his cloak over his shoulder and took a step forward. "I have brought my army to your door from across the Ashen Wastes. I would treat with you but you deny me. You have not learned well the lesson I taught your brothers, Talus Sen. If you will not greet me on the open plain but force me to come to you, then your fate will be the same as the other Blades who have rejected my offer." He waited a moment for a reply and heard nothing but steam escaping the vents. "So be it, Talus Sen, the Spreading Darkness. Your mastery of the Dark Ichor will not avail you in this realm. You too shall be bound."

Vangen stepped across the threshold into the dark tower and paused. A winding staircase rose up before him, twisting and curling into the blackness of the upper reaches of the tower. At the base of the staircase another flight of stairs descended several steps before being swallowed in darkness.

Vangen wheeled around as a mass of black rock slammed shut behind him, sealing the gate and closing him off from his legions. He heard a guttural grinding noise through the sealed entrance that shook the ground. The sounds of bolts retracting and locking into place were soon drowned out by the familiar echo of plate armor and heavy boots thudding in unison.

"So you would unleash your forces and press your advantage with me trapped in here, Talus Sen? You have erred most grievously. As your soldiers swarm onto the plains to meet mine, you are alone in here with me." Vangen closed his eyes and breathed deeply. His eyes snapped open and a cruel smile spread across his pale face. "And what is left of your wretched soul cowering in your dungeon, awaiting your end."

Vangen heard the sounds of war behind him. Cries and howls erupted over the shrill scream of iron and steel clashing in violent song. He smiled as he placed his palm against the cold rock that blocked the gate and felt his great army swelling and surging over the lesser numbers of Talus Sen's forces. He took his hand from the rock and descended the stairs.

Vangen walked down the stairs. They curved and twisted, carrying him ever deeper under the great tower. The perfectly hewn rocks that comprised the shell of the edifice had disappeared as he descended and now the walls were carved directly from the bedrock. There was no light, though Vangen had no need of it to see, his eyes turning an inky black as he swept down flight after flight of chiseled stairs. At regular intervals the stairs would spill onto a landing from which opened many corridors, but always Vangen descended, pushing further and further beneath the tower. The temperature began to drop slightly, though the air still held a dampness that came from the rock walls.

Finally the staircase ended and Vangen stood at the threshold of a massive empty chamber that spread before him. The ceiling climbed hundreds of feet into the air and was supported by two rows of great pillars, larger in circumference even than those that supported the dome of the Council Chamber in Dullahan. The rows of pillars in turn supported sweeping arches that leapt across the room, spanning the width of the huge chamber and holding aloft its expansive ceiling of stone.

Vangen looked around and saw a barred opening at the far end of the chamber, opposite the staircase he had just descended.

"Will you show yourself, or must I drag you like some petulant child from your hole?"

A cold air stirred in the hall, rustling Vangen's cloak before it died out. "When the Elder Gods of Light banished us to this realm thousands of years past, they made several oversights in their haste to punish us. You shall now see the folly of leaving me with my tools, and giving me resources to work with," Talus Sen said, his whisper reverberating through the empty chamber.

A heavy iron gate slammed shut behind Vangen, sealing off the stairs he had just descended and shaking the entire room. At the far end of the hall the thick iron bars retracted into the arch, and Vangen heard a heavy thumping, almost mechanical in its rhythm. It grew louder and more rapid and was accompanied by an anguished hiss. The pounding became deafening, shaking the very walls until it suddenly stopped, and an eerie silence fell over the chamber.

Vangen watched in disbelief as he saw issuing through the now open gate thick white coils of scale covered flesh, churning and seething over each other in their frenzy to enter the room. The scales and folds of heavy muscle poured over one another creating a grating, rasping noise. Vangen stood still and watched the sinews of armored flesh, as thick as any ancient oak, roil forth from the gate until at last he saw them begin to twine their way up and around the columns. He saw now that the muscular ropes of flesh were in fact all part of the same great beast.

Vangen smirked. "A snake no matter how large is still a snake, Talus."

Talus's laughed echoed through the hall as the immense wyrm began to uncoil itself. Vangen steadied himself as he saw what resembled plates of armor unfold from the creature and scrape against the flagstone floor. Down the entire length of the monster a profusion of thin, rib-like protrusions in the creature's body unhinged and lifted the beast from the ground.

"Hundreds of needle sharp legs," Vangen whispered under his breath. "Like some twisted form of a centipede."

Talus's laughter grew louder and from the coils of flesh Vangen saw the thin head of a dragon rise up on a thickly muscled and segmented neck. The creature sniffed the air, it's tiny, blind eyes useless in its bony skull. It unhinged its snakelike maw and Vangen saw several rows of knife-like teeth lining its pink gums. The beast exhaled and a noxious green vapor escaped its mouth, pouring over its fangs and settling to the ground in a thick fog. The creature continued to pump volumes of billowing green gas from its gaping jaws until the chamber was blanketed in a bilious haze.

"The Elder Gods tore a hole in the fabric of this realm in their haste to exile us here," Talus hissed. "And from the void I pulled this magnificent wyrm and fed it in the bowels of my fortress. It is still young, but its breath is toxic and its bite as deadly as the poison of the Dark Ichor itself. The very touch of its skin can dissolve flesh. In time, as it feeds upon the shades in the Wastes, it will surpass the Dark Ichor and become a living weapon that I will use to reclaim Athar for myself."

"You get ahead of yourself, Talus," Vangen said, never taking his eyes from the creature. "I will soon show you your place."

The beast shrieked at the sound of Vangen's voice, its head whipping in his direction as it pinpointed his location. Vangen saw streams of viscous liquid issue from its slavering jaws as the beast snapped its mouth shut, rising on its thousand legs and began to speed toward him. It shrieked again as it charged, its legs pushing its grotesque bulk fluidly across the flagstone floor. Rows of fins sprung up upon its head and continued down the creature's back, cruel barbs that jutted out from the flesh and leaked a green fluid down the beast's white scales, promising a painful death should Vangen come in contact with it.

Vangen stood perfectly still as the wyrm slithered toward him, howling in fury and bristling with blind rage. When the creature was twenty feet from him it rose in the air, its massive head soaring above Vangen. Pausing for a moment the creature dove at him, its dagger filled mouth rushing toward him as Vangen stood unmoving before the beast. An instant before the wyrm snapped its jaws shut around him Vangen smiled, shut his eyes and was gone.

The monster smashed into the flagstones, the power of its strike carrying its body forward as it tumbled over itself. Bits of stone flew into the air and the creature raised its head, searching for its prey. Shards of stone were embedded in its lower jaw from its failed attack, and green liquid oozed from its mouth, dripping onto the floor, hissing and bubbling as it etched the flagstones.

Vangen shook his head and walked toward the entrance the wyrm had spilled through. "A pity to take this magnificent creature from you Talus, but unless you leash your pet I will be forced to kill it," Vangen shouted into the chamber.

With incredible speed the wyrm righted itself, uncoiled and turned at Vangen's words. Lowering its head to the ground once again, it sped toward him, the insect-like legs carrying its hulking body over the flagstones at tremendous speed. Within seconds it was behind him. With mouth agape, it drew its thin, bony head back for a strike. Vangen did not turn to face the beast, but continued to walk toward the entrance as the creature lashed out and struck, swallowing him in one fluid motion.

The chamber echoed with the venomous laugh of Talus Sen as the wyrm lowered its body to the stones and gathered its legion of legs underneath itself. The beast began to slowly propel itself toward the entrance like some gargantuan snake. As it neared the arch it retracted its rows of barbed fins that ran down its serpent-like back. It paused before the threshold as Talus's laughter quieted. The white beast convulsed once and shuddered. From its thick throat the tip of a sword protruded and split an opening down its length. Green bile burst from the wound and when the flow subsided, Vangen crawled out onto the stones and rose, wiping the slime from his body. Behind him the wyrm contracted and convulsed in its death throes, the scale-covered rope of its body coiling around itself and thrashing uncontrollably. It smashed into the columns and fell, picked itself up and tried to employ its myriad legs, only to have them collapse again, sending the beast slamming to the ground, where it writhed in agony.

"What blade can pierce the hide of such a creature?" Talus Sen's cold voice, filled with frustrated disbelief, asked above the tortured screams of the wyrm.

"A special blade," Vangen answered, wiping the blood and various poisons from the sword before placing it back in the scabbard he wore down the length of his back. "A blade quenched in the blood of a priestess of Vatn. Their adherence to the old ways gives them certain properties that they carry with them even in death. It proves much stronger than a simple blessing and a dip in their sacred river."

Vangen passed under the arch and into the darkness of the corridor as Talus screamed with rage.

***

Outside on the plains beneath the black tower, Vangen's army stood at attention. Their legions spread across the great expanse to the horizon. The fallen of Talus's warriors littered the plains at their feet and were scattered over every inch of ground. Vangen's soldiers waited in silence as the great black birds wheeled in slow circles above their heads.

A low thumping grew louder and more insistent, shaking the floor of the plain. Cracks began to appear in the wall of the tower and massive stones fell from the crimson sky, crushing the dead that lay beneath the great tower. The blocks sunk into the ground with resounding thuds that shook the entire plain. Within minutes the tower that had stretched into the clouds was nothing more than a heap of rubble. A slight breeze gently lifted the banners of Vangen's army and carried away the dust that clung to the pile of rocks.

Smaller stones began to shift and loosen in the pile and Vangen emerged, picking his way confidently down the small mountain of black rock to stand before his legions. He raised his hand to the sky and the entirety of his forces turned and marched off toward the Ashen Wastes, their footfalls raising a cloud of dust that obscured them as they headed for the horizon.

Vangen set his jaw and brought his hand down to his side. From the pile of rubble an obelisk burst into the sky, hovering over the mountainous heap of rock.

"I will not give you any opportunities to defy me Talus," Vangen said over his shoulder. "You will be bound like your brothers."

As he spoke, great chains burst from the rubble, spraying shards of rock as they launched toward the obelisk and attached themselves. Behind him Vangen heard the pained screams of Talus as the metal became translucent. A greenish crystalline shard that held within it a seething cloud slammed furiously into the imprisoning walls in a futile attempt to escape.

Vangen began walking after his army. He reached behind his neck, feeling the hilt of his blade and smiled cruelly. "Oh Draegan I wish you would hurry back. I cannot wait to tell you the story of how I forged this blade."

Chapter 19: The Tundra

Draegan pushed his charger through the night and covered as much ground as his horse would give him, his spare mount following closely behind. By dawn of the next day his steed was lathered and nearly spent. He stopped by one of the hundreds of frozen lakes that dotted the landscape and chipped holes in the ice. His horses drank greedily as he unsaddled the first and watched the orange sun rising over eastern sweep of the Iron Mountains, its rays turning the sky a soft rose and causing the frost to shimmer.

"I don't need you wandering back to camp and leading anyone after me," Draegan said as he pulled his hunting knife from his belt. He paused and looked over the frozen landscape. "Although they should be in such a state of disarray from the loss of Erdrik that they would be unable to pursue me if they wanted." He put his knife back in his belt and scratched the horse's head. A few minutes later he was off again on the second horse, leaving the first still drinking from the small hole in the ice. The sky turned an icy blue as he rode through the day, with only a few streaks of clouds breaking the vastness of the scene. He stuck to dirt paths to keep his horse from faltering in the rocky tundra. The sun warmed his back as he rode and melted the hoar frost that clung to the heath.

After riding through the rest of the day and into evening he stopped his horse at the base of a hillock, dismounted and walked to the top. Looking out across the flat tundra he saw little that caught his eye in the waning light. He turned to descend the hill when he picked up the scent of smoke. Looking out again he saw a faint light on the horizon that he had initially taken for a flickering star. He pushed his horse toward the light and arrived at a clapboard shack shortly before midnight.

"I know this place," Draegan said as he rapped on the door. A small sign swung in the breeze, though it was too dark to read it.

"Come on in, we're always open," came a sleepy voice from behind the door. Draegan pushed the door open and stepped into the claustrophobic cabin. There was little room to maneuver in front of the counter as he inhaled and pushed the door shut behind him.

In front of him a young man smiled and stood to greet Draegan. He opened his arms and nearly hit the pipe that rose from the pot-bellied stove and poked through the roof. "Buy anything you like," he said, indicating the wares that surrounded them both. Draegan peered around him into the back room and saw the legs of an old man protruding from a rocking chair. Draegan scanned the tiny room and smiled slightly. Every open space and shelf was crammed with food and dry goods. Behind the counter that split the room in half there was a small path cleared between barrels of oil and sacks of flour that led to a back door. Lanterns and garlic and snowshoes hung from the rafters, and the shelves overflowed with rope, canvas, and various sundries.

"Go away, we're closed," came an old raspy voice from the back room.

"Oh, don't mind Grandpa Tun," the young man said, tilting his head to indicate the source of the voice. The young man lowered his voice and continued. "I mostly run the store these days. He doesn't do well with customers. Chased away four good ones about twenty years ago, and it's brought us bad luck since. Not another soul stopped by this place until a few days past." The boy nodded and leaned on the counter, knocking over a display of various dried beans. He bent to pick them up and continued. "Of course he didn't buy anything," he said and stopped gathering beans to gesture over his shoulder at the back room. "Grandpa, chased him off before he even had a chance to look around." He stood up and put the beans back in their display on the overcrowded counter. "I don't think Grandpa likes those folks from Vatn much. He's not as open-minded as me."

Draegan look quizzically at the boy. "A priest from Vatn this far north?"

"Yeah, big fella too. Looked like he could've eaten everything in the place," the boy said shaking his head. "Could have made a fortune on the jerky alone."

"Which way did he head?

"West, after the Clan's army, about two days out."

Draegan thanked him and began the tedious task of turning around to open the door without disturbing any of the stock.

"Sure you don't need anything? We've got everything you could want," the boy offered as Draegan shut the door behind him and felt the cold night air against his face.

"Did you tell him we're open, boy?" Draegan heard the old man's muffled shouting from the back room. "We need to move inventory lad, get him back in here to buy something." Draegan smiled and mounted his horse.

He pushed west through the night and by the first light of early morning he could make out a cloud of dust on the horizon. "Tor Valdin has mustered an impressive army if I can see them this many miles off," Draegan said as he dismounted. He took his pack from the saddle and sent the horse back along the path. "Back to the store with you, old girl. Maybe old Tun can make good use of you now. You'll only get me spotted that much faster riding out here in the tundra."

***

Draegan moved swiftly over the frozen plains, keeping the looming cloud of dust on the horizon directly ahead of him. As he covered ground, he could make out birds wheeling slowly in great circles above the dust cloud.

"Carrion birds. Tor and the Clan of the Iron Mountains march for war," Draegan said and picked his way easily down the hillock and found a footpath that matched his direction of travel. By late afternoon he began to see signs of the army's passing. Burnt out fires and half frozen latrine pits marked where they had recently camped. The heath was trampled and bare dirt covered an area a quarter mile wide.

"A host that could trample this much vegetation must number in the tens of thousands." Draegan moved swiftly through the old camp site and easily found their path west. "Where did Tor find this many soldiers? I didn't think the north had this many people, let alone this many fighting men."

As he continued to move west he saw the marks of horse hooves riding on either side of the foot soldiers, the horseshoes making distinct marks in the ground. But mixed in with the horses near the rear of the host he saw the prints of an animal he couldn't identify. He paused to try to make sense of the imprint. "Bears?" he wondered and held his hand over the indentation. "Not unless they're three times the size of any bear I've ever seen." He sat back on his heels and looked up at the cloud of dust on the horizon. He put his ear to the ground and listened. Draegan's eyes widened and he stood up, peering straight at the horizon.

"Tundra beasts," he whispered under his breath. He blinked at the dust cloud on the horizon and thought for a moment. "The histories say they were hunted to extinction, but these marks would argue otherwise. Where did Tor find such ancient animals and how did he tame them?"

Draegan continued west through the rest of the day and into the evening. As the sun began to set he thought of the Ashen Wastes of the shadow lands. He balled his hands into fists as he recalled Vangen and his army. "Though I fear I may be placing too much trust in these Dark Artifacts, I know of no other way to stop Vangen. His power is so great that only meeting him with equal force offers me any hope of victory, and even then I do not know if it will prove enough." He sighed. "I must focus on the present, for my strategy relies on accomplishing my tasks here on Athar first. I need that axe."

He looked at the sky reflected in the icy waters of an unfrozen tarn to his side and thought of the World Render. Suddenly, Draegan shouted in pain and dropped to his knee, clutching at his eye. His head swam with visions of a great man clothed in bear skins and in his grip the World Render flared to life. Around him was death and shadow as he held the axe aloft. Draegan took a deep breath and stood. He steadied himself and looked at the dust cloud in front of him. "So Tor wields the World Render. Then I must find Tor and relieve him of his burden."

Draegan placed one hand on the hilt of Carnis Fornax and the other on the handle of the Burning Chains. He drew in a quick breath of cold air before taking off and pushing off down the hill toward the dimming horizon.

Chapter 20: The Secret of the Blades

"Rise, Isarn and take these vestments," Isirah said, holding out a white robe, trimmed in crimson. "The raiment of the Clade is now yours to wear. Bear it with honor."

Isarn stood and draped the thick white robe over himself. Now twenty one, he stood as tall as Isirah, though he was leaner than his mentor. His close-cropped black hair framed his square jaw and his deep set black eyes flared with excitement when he saw the hood.

"Though we wear a robe similar to that worn by our brothers and sisters in Vatn our hood is crimson, to symbolize the blood guilt we suffer." Isirah held out his hands. "Take the cowl and remember the burden we brook for all people." Isarn placed the red cloth over his head and let it fall down over his wide shoulders. He bowed his head.

"Follow me to the vault," Isirah said as he exited the hall. Isarn moved silently behind him, feeling the heavy cloth conform to his body. "It moves better than I thought. It's quieter too."

"Follow its lead and silence yourself," Isirah said. "We approach the vault." The older man stopped before a pair of heavy iron doors and pressed his thick hands against them. He motioned for Isarn to do likewise. Isarn leaned forward and placed his palms against the iron doors. Immediately a red light pulsed in the seal carved in the center of the doors and began to trickle outward, following a series of channels carved in the iron. As the light flowed outward, the door was consumed in a scarlet flash that caused him to shut his eyes. Isarn heard locks clicking and bolts retracting. The doors gave way and swung silently inward.

Isirah stepped into the small chamber and motioned for Isarn to follow. The circular room contained a thin banner hung opposite the doors and embroidered with the seal of the Clade. In the center of the room a simple pedestal draped in crimson cloth held two daggers that gave off a faint blue and red light.

"The Vaghat awakened twenty years ago. It has yet to sleep, and I believe you know why."

"Bhel and Asai thirst for vengeance," Isarn said as he stared at the twin blades, pulsing in the dim room. Though he had read of them and pressed Isirah continually to see them, now that he stood within a few feet of them, Isarn stood in motionless awe. "Greydin Vir forged these?" Isarn asked in whisper.

"They were his blessing and his curse."

Isarn touched the red cloth on the pedestal, unable to contain his excitement any longer, yet fearing to grab the blades directly. Even in the stillness of the room, they looked deadly and promised great power. "I will atone for his sins. I will slake their thirst in the blood of the Usurper."

"They are yours to use by right, but be not rash, young man. Though these weapons are the better of any Artifact, they are only as capable as their master. You must prove a better man than Draegan, for your battle is with him. The Vaghat will fulfill its obligation against the dark sorcery of the Artifacts and prove superior. But between you and the Usurper it is a test of your mettle."

Isarn's eyes stayed focused on the soft glow of the daggers as he spoke. "I was forged in the crucible of the Clade, hammered and shaped upon the anvil of our teaching, and quenched in combat. My metal will prove more than a match for the Usurper's mettle."

Isarn took the daggers from the pedestal and held them firmly. "They feel lighter than they appear, but still they are beautifully balanced." He made a few feints toward the banner and looked at Isirah in astonishment. "They add a speed and power to my movements that I've not experienced before. What magic is this?"

Isirah nodded. "I felt it too when I trained with them. A great power is gifted to the bearer of the Vaghat, but its magic is beyond any understanding." He pointed at the blades. "Look at the edge. As keen as the day they were forged though they are over three thousand years old. Even blessed and holy blades, imbued with the enchantments of the priests of Vatn weaken over a period that long. But not the twins, Bhel the Flame and Asai the Frost." Isirah shook his massive head. "Their magic is a secret at the heart of the Clade. And although we do not understand it, we can wield it." Isarn looked confused. "Come to the training hall and I will show you," Isirah said and nodded over his shoulder.

The pair exited the vault and heard the doors lock shut behind them, the thud echoing through the hallway. Isirah walked briskly through the main hall to an antechamber as Isarn followed by habit, engrossed in the etchings that lined the metal of the blades. He looked up and saw Isirah waiting for him at the threshold of the training hall.

Isarn stepped through the doors and looked around the familiar hall that had been his home for the past ten years. The space was enormous, big enough to hold the remainder of the underground compound in its entirety. The ribbed vault soared hundreds of feet above him and was lit by rows of iron chandeliers that each held hundreds of candles. Constructed of large granite blocks, the chamber was roughly a quarter mile in length and width, making it a perfect square. As he entered the space he noticed how the candle light softened the gouges and scrapes in the floors and walls, signs of the violence of past training sessions.

Since he had been inducted on his name day, he had spent the majority of his waking hours in this room. If he wasn't training with Isirah or practicing on his own, he was cleaning the floors and repairing equipment. Lining the walls were racks of weapons, from basic short swords and simple clubs to masterfully wrought gisarmes and ancient war hammers larger than himself. He had learned how to use each one, and how to defend against them. Isirah had been a thorough educator and had at first taken great pleasure in showing Isarn how very different was their level of understanding and mastery of these weapons. But in time he had caught up to and eventually surpassed Isirah.

"Go to the middle of the circle," Isirah said and brushed past Isarn who looked at the gleaming weapons, so recently polished by his hand. He wondered how much of his own blood he had cleaned of each off those weapons during the past ten years. Isarn broke away from his thoughts and caught up with Isirah as they neared the center of the great hall, marked by a seal of the Clade thirty feet in diameter carved into the black granite floor.

"Stand opposite me, at the edge of the seal. I will awaken the flame and attack." Isirah waited until Isarn had reached the other end of the seal. "You need do nothing but stand there with the daggers.

"I would be a fool to stand still while you pummel me with those massive fiery fists."

"Do as I say," Isirah growled and began interlacing his fingers in a strange pattern. He mumbled under his breath and blew into his hands. As he breathed both his hands ignited in a burst of orange fire. He ran straight at Isarn, his fists leaving trails of flame as he closed the distance between them. Yet as the colossal man in his white and red robe with flaming fists neared the center of the seal the fire sputtered and went out.

Isirah stopped a few feet from Isarn and held out his hands. "You see? Nothing. Yet I did not break the spell."

"But how?"

"The answer is in your hands," Isirah said. "Hand me the twins and I will show you how it feels to be on the other side."

Isarn reluctantly gave the blades to his master. "I know how it feels to be on the receiving side," he said, casting a wary glance to the racks of weapons. "I've spent ten years on that side."

When Isirah was back at the far end of the seal and Isarn at the other Isirah shouted, "I'll stand perfectly still. Approach me with the shadow dance and see if you can get close enough to land a blow.

Isarn smiled. "I know you set me up to fail in some way, yet I can't overcome the urge to break your nose," he said as he sat down and crossed his legs. He closed his eyes and breathed slowly, feeling a heat build up inside him, growing hotter as he chanted the words of the spell. A moment later the heat had turned to ice and he felt a chill through his whole body. He stood slowly and took a deep breath. Holding it, he ran directly at Isirah and watched the world slow down.

Isirah saw Isarn stand and take a step toward him, and then the boy vanished from his sight. Though the older man knew the power of the enchantment, he was always surprised by how well Isarn had mastered it. Isirah focused his eyes on the ground and tried to find a shadow to track, but as he looked up he saw Isarn, faint and flickering as if a shimmering vapor. Isarn moved in and out of existence, first on Isirah's left, then right, then at the far end of the hall. Isirah knew it was an illusion, but so convincing was Isarn's spell that he had trouble keeping his eyes focused on the ground for the telltale sign of Isarn's shadow.

Isarn felt like he was moving through water. Though he was running, everything felt thick and heavy. The air slowed him and he had to push with all his might to keep each leg moving forward toward Isirah who stood frozen before him. He knew the shadow step was bouncing light off him, obscuring his true self while creating illusions that scattered all around him, distracting his target. He knew that he had mastered this spell, as he had hundreds of others, but now he felt inexplicably sluggish and weak. The closer he moved toward Isirah, the more he felt like he was losing control of the enchantment. His lungs bursting, Isarn exhaled.

Isirah smiled and grunted. "You see?" Ten feet before him at his feet, Isarn lay on the ground, breathing heavily.

"I couldn't hold it any longer," he said, picking himself off the floor. "I cast it perfectly at the beginning, but as I approached, I felt weak, and it slipped from me."

"You did better than most. Ten feet away from me is impressive. Most would have dropped at twenty."

"I still don't know what I did wrong."

"Nothing. You simply can't use magic near the blades," Isirah said, holding up the daggers and admiring them in the light of the hall. "Any spell that is cast near them is unraveled by the forces that live in the Vaghat." He held them out to Isarn, who took them. "The problem then becomes that he who bears them can't use magic either." He pulled up his hood and walked toward the weapons racks.

"A magic that counteracts all other magic?" Isarn said, dumbfounded. "These must be the most powerful weapons on Athar. What army could stand against the might of these..." Isarn felt a bolt of pain slam through his head and he pitched forward. He caught himself and looking down he saw a rock on the ground near his feet.

Isarn looked up to see Isirah holding a bag of stones and leaning on a rack of halberds.

"The Vaghat nullifies magic, not rocks. Or arrows for that matter." He set the bag of rocks down near a leather sling and sighed. "Bhel and Asai level the battlefield by stripping both combatants of their magical power. By the strength of their otherworldly art they can turn a Sage of Light or a Blade of Darkness into an ordinary human." Isirah wagged his finger in the air as he spoke. "That is when you must rise above your opponent and prove the better man by virtue of your training. This is why we make you into a hardened weapon. This is why your training goes deeper than any other soldier in Fyrian." Isirah pointed directly at Isarn. "You must stand against your foe on equal terms, and prove the victor."

Chapter 21: Encounter at Mirror's Gap

Draegan followed in the wake of Tor's army through the evening and night, keeping the firelights of their camps ahead of him as he worked his way through the frozen lowlands. This far west the tundra was riddled with hundreds of small lakes which were mostly frozen at this time of year and surrounded by heath and lichen covered boulders. The wind blew relentlessly, stirring bits of frost and stinging any exposed flesh.

Draegan used one of the boulders as a wind break while he checked for any barriers or seals. He knew the Clan of the Iron Mountains was not as skilled in sorcery as those of the House of Corvus, but he couldn't be too careful this close to their camp. He traced a sign in the thin layer of snow on the leeward side of the rock and waited. He sensed nothing.

"It seems odd they wouldn't have at least some basic protection spells, especially if they march against Corvus and their Ravens." He peered around the boulder and watched the faint lights of Tor's army shimmering on the horizon. "Their overconfidence will make it that much easier to sneak through their ranks until I am close enough to Tor to kill him and take the World Render." Draegan sat back and leaned against the frigid rock, feeling the cold push through his cloak and chill his spine. "But it was far easier to make my way through the warriors of Stanrocc, as I look like them and still hold some of their accent in my speech. I will stand out sorely among these barbarians. If only Gron were still here, he'd have no problem talking his way right to Tor's tent," he said and trailed off in thought, recalling with anger Gron's horrible end at the hands of Ceredyn. Draegan closed his eyes for a moment, tormenting himself with thoughts of the fight in the catacombs.

Draegan awoke with a start. He scrambled to his feet and slung his pack over his shoulder. Looking behind him, he saw the dark black sky softening in the east. "I was only out a few hours." He shook his head. "I need to expand the limits of my older body if I have any hope of matching Tor, let alone Vangen," He began moving west and saw that all but a handful of the fires of Tor's army had died during the night.

He walked through the early hours, watching the sky brighten as the sun crept over the horizon behind him. The air was cold, but the morning light warmed his shoulders as he approached the awakening camp. When he was a mile out from the stirring army, he began to make out distinct shapes in the gathering dust cloud. Tents were being taken down and a handful of riders strayed far enough away from the main group that he could make out their silhouette against the flat, white landscape. Draegan paused and looked up, watching the carrion birds take flight and begin their accent in an ever widening gyre.

When he looked back down at the main force he noticed that the horsemen he had seen earlier were gone from sight. He scanned the frozen tundra and spotted them riding toward him from the south. He cursed his luck and ran for cover behind a group of rocks that lay near an unfrozen tarn. "If they were dispatched from the main force to ride me down, then the army is aware of my presence. I can't kill them without arousing their wrath, nor can I allow myself to be taken prisoner, or they'll strip me of my Artifacts," he said and ran his hand over the hilt tucked in his belt.

Draegan climbed the rocks and stood, waving his hand over his head in an exaggerated gesture while the riders approached. They were six in number, and rode swiftly, splitting evenly when they encountered the small lake that stood between them and circled it, pinching Draegan from both sides of the shore.

"What business does Stanrocc have in our lands," the nearest rider shouted as he reigned in his mount forty feet from where Draegan stood on the rocks.

"Stanrocc? No. I am a traveler, sir, once of Skeldus, but now Fyrian is my home. I mean no harm, only gleaning what I can from the castoffs from your camp." The other riders had closed in behind him and surrounded the outcropping Draegan stood on.

"A thief? We've plenty of things missing from camp. Come down and be searched, or stay and be killed," the man said as a rider to his right took aim with a bow. "We take every precaution with crows around. Though most crows aren't stupid enough to wear black in the tundra. Now get off that rock."

Draegan looked at the men that surrounded him. The speaker was a tow head, young and without the typical braided beard worn by so many in the north. He wore a wolf pelt draped from his shoulders, while the other five were all red-headed and wore what looked like ragged bear hides, though the furs were so old it was impossible to tell. They all looked like hard men, and accustomed to riding as they shifted easily in their saddles. As he looked them over Draegan realized he had little in the way of options. They would have to die and he would have to find another way to hunt Tor.

"I have nothing of value," Draegan said, casting a quick glance toward the main force. He heard the faint blast of horns, signifying the army was preparing to move. The riders looked toward the camp and in the moment of their distraction Draegan pulled the hilt from his belt and ignited the blade. He sprung from the rock and onto the rider with the bow, cutting down man and beast in one fell swoop. An arrow whistled past him and struck the rocks as he turned and ran toward to blonde soldier.

"A Raven of Corvus," the leader of the riders shouted. "Send word to camp. Now!"

One of the riders broke from the group leaving the other four to deal with Draegan. They began to circle him, keeping him ringed in while he stood fast near the fallen rider and horse. Draegan's hand slipped to his belt and he grasped the handle of the whip.

"Nowhere to fly, crow," one of the riders said. "Put down your toy before it burns you."

"He killed Rung with that toy, so keep your distance," the blonde rider said. "The War Chief will send a battalion back here to deal with him and scout out any others." He looked over his shoulder. "Just keep your eyes on him and make sure none of his friends are around. Crows don't usually fly alone."

"You've got the wrong man," Draegan said, pulling the handle of the Burning Chains from his belt. "I'm no Raven." He snapped his wrist and six great thongs of living fire poured from the black handle. The riders tried to steady their terrified horses and widened the circle they rode around Draegan, giving him a wide berth. "And it will take more than a battalion of soldiers to stop me in my quest." He paused and tilted his head thoughtfully. "In truth, it would be best to just send the war chief. That will reduce the number of unwanted deaths." He raised the whip overhead and brought it down to his side, the six roiling tongues of flame cracking in response. A peal of thunder split the sky, startling the horses and nearly throwing one of the riders.

The blonde soldier regained control of his mount and broke off to camp at full speed. "He is no mere Raven. I must inform Tor," he shouted as he sped away. Draegan smiled at the other three riders.

"Your leader is a coward, but at least he is a coward who has the sense to flee." He watched the soldiers circling him, staring at each in turn. "You would be wise to follow his lead. I will not judge you ill should you choose to return to camp. But if you stay you will die." Draegan nodded toward the fallen rider.

Draegan waited for a moment and when none of the riders broke their canter, he lashed out with the Burning Chains and struck the rider closest to him. "I gave you more than fair warning. My time is at a premium and I will not waste any more with you." The flames burned through rider and horse alike. Draegan spun and rushed to his right, snapping the thongs of flame in front of him. The soldier turned his horse too late and was struck down, screaming in agony as the fire consumed his body.

The last rider broke off and drove back to camp. Draegan cracked the whip, splitting the sky once again with a terrible thunder that caused the horse to start, throwing its rider. In an instant Draegan was upon the downed man, splitting him in two with his black blade even as the disoriented rider stumbled to regain his footing. Draegan watched the horse speed back to camp and sheathed his weapons.

"They know I'm here now, and they know I'm a threat. Perhaps I've earned the attention of Tor."

As if in response Draegan heard the blast of a great horn followed by the steady pounding of war drums. He looked to the horizon and saw a force break from the main army and begin moving toward him. The carrion birds shrieked in protest, not knowing which group to follow.

"I might as well make them come to me," he said as he scrambled back atop the rocks to get a better view. "No sense running after them." He sat and peered into the distance. He could make out riders from foot soldiers, but they were too distant to count. "It'll be half an hour before they get here if they move together," he said and scrambled down from the rocks and picked his way through the fresh corpses. "I will prepare for their arrival."

To his left was the large unfrozen lake, and to his right the heath was littered with smaller, frozen ponds as far as he could see.

Between them was a space roughly two hundred yards wide. "A force that big will be bottled up here, unless they decide to circle the lake. The horses can do so in short order, but it will slow the foot soldiers down." He looked around and thought. "This is a fine place for them to pinch me in. Move the cavalry to the rear to block my escape and push me forward into the pikes of the foot soldiers. And in order to do so it means they'll be bunched together and not spread out. Exactly what I want."

Draegan set out from the pile of rocks and began drawing a massive circle in the snow. Every few feet he scratched runes on any rocks he could find with his hunting knife and tossed the marked rocks near the edge of the circle, after adding a drop of blood to each one. When he had made his way back to the boulders near the shore of the lake he climbed them and admired his work from a greater height. "That will dissuade them from turning tail and running."

He waited and watched the mass on the horizon grow larger. He listened to the steady pounding of the drum, keeping time while the sun rose higher in the sky. It was shortly after noon when the forces were close enough to make out individual figures.

"They moved slower than I expected. Now I see why. One hundred horsemen and four hundred foot soldiers. I don't know if I should be flattered or insulted." He stood and stretched, letting the rays of the sun warm his back again as the battalion approached. A cold wind began to blow, kicking up bits of frost and taking away what little warmth Draegan felt.

A few minutes later he saw the cavalry break from the battalion and circle around the lake at a slow trot. "Just as I thought. Hemming me in." He watched in silence from the rocks as the foot soldiers moved into the gap between the lake and ponds to the fixed rhythm of the war drums. As they drew nearer he could feel the earth shake from their heavy footfalls. He watched the cavalry finish their circumnavigation of the lake and reign in their horses a hundred yards behind him, blocking his escape. Ahead of him the foot soldiers halted at the blast of a horn. The drumming stopped and a breeze blew over the lake, rippling the water.

Draegan rose and let the wind snap his cloak in the sudden silence of the tundra. He heard the tamping of the horses behind him, champing at their bits as the iron in the bridles clinked softly from their nervous movements. Before him he listened to the sound of leather boots crunching and packing the frost as the soldiers settled into position, their hauberks jostling under their leather and fur cloaks. A shadow passed over his head and he looked up to see a group of carrion birds circling overhead.

"They will feast today, unless Tor Valdin brings me the World Render," Draegan shouted. The birds shrieked in response. A few of the foot soldiers laughed but were silenced by a deafening blast from a horn.

Draegan watched as the foot soldiers began to split their ranks, creating a passage down the center. In the distance he saw three men begin to move forward, each easily a head taller than the surrounding foot soldiers. Each of the three men wore a hammered iron helmet with great ram horns curling down to their thick shoulders. They pushed their way through the soldiers who were still jostling into position, trying to make way for these giants. The foot soldiers began to bang their axes and swords against their shields, raising a terrible din until the three massive men had pushed their way to the front. The soldiers once again fell silent. The sun glinted on their helms as they approached the base of the boulders Draegan stood upon.

"We're here to take you to Tor, crow," the giant in the center bellowed. "Come down off that rock." The three men were well over six feet in height and bore white bear furs over their wide shoulders.

The blonde man in the center carried a massive war hammer strapped to his back on a wide leather belt that covered most of his torso. The two men to his sides were red headed and wore great beards, the one to Draegan's right in three thick plaits that hung to his waist. He carried a huge battle axe, while the other man on Draegan's left bore two axes.

"Aye, we're taking you to Tor. In pieces," the beast of a man to Draegan's right said. He began unbuckling his axe from his back, while the other unhooked his bear pelt and laid it on the ground. The blonde giant in the center stared unmoving at Draegan.

"You killed their brothers, crow," the blonde giant said. "So I'm going to let them get their fair share of you before we take your entrails and that fancy whip back to Tor."

Draegan saw that each man wore a necklace of bear claws. "Berserkers," he whispered. "Like Gron." He looked over his shoulder and saw the cavalry had backed off a few hundred feet. "This is going to be a bit of a challenge."

"Quit your yapping and get off that rock you spindly vulture," the blonde giant shouted. All three men had removed their helmets and he saw that the blonde was missing an eye, while the other two were missing parts of ears and a few fingers. "Don't make me come up there and drag you down. You look thin enough that you wouldn't survive the trip.

Draegan noticed the other two men had each removed their necklaces and were beginning to breathe heavily. He saw beads of sweat running down their faces, though it was bitterly cold. The giant in the center of the group began taking off his necklace when Draegan made up his mind.

"I've seen what one berserker is capable of. I'd rather fight two than three," he muttered as he crouched then leapt from the rocks directly at the blonde giant, his hand moving to the hilt of Carnis Fornax tucked in his belt. He felt a crushing blow in his ribs and was slammed to the frozen earth, his head cracking off the ground.

"Caught him mid flight."

Draegan struggled to move. His vision blurred and his senses swam as he looked up and saw a read-bearded giant straddling his chest, his wide grin showing more than a few missing teeth. He pulled a hand axe from his belt and raised it over his head, his eyes glowing red and flecks of foam clinging to the beard near his mouth. Draegan pressed his palm to the ground and let the darkness swallow him.

Draegan rose from a cloud of black mist behind a group of foot soldiers, each craning his neck to see over the shoulders of those in front for a better view of the fight. Draegan pulled his sword from his belt, ignited the black flame with a thought, and cut through three men before him. The men screamed and fell, while those in front turned to look at the noise behind them.

"He's back here!" they shouted. "Don't let him escape!"

"Escape?" Draegan repeated. "I wouldn't dare," he said and cut down four more men in a flash of black fire before he dropped to his knee and put his palm to the ground again.

Draegan felt a rush of cold air as the wind gusted, carrying the black mist that surrounded him across the lake. He stood behind the boulders, looking out at the cavalry. He smiled as he took the handle from his belt and charged directly at the horses, covering a hundred yards in a few seconds. With a flick of his wrist the handle spat out six long streaks of blazing fire. The horses, though used to battle, shied away as Draegan ran at them, their riders struggling to keep them under control. When he was within striking distance he stopped short and cracked the whip over his head, a peal of thunder splitting the sky and momentarily deafening all those within a mile.

The horses scattered. Some threw their riders while others broke ranks. Draegan turned from the chaos of the cavalry and sprinted back to the gap where only the blonde giant now stood.

"He's back here," the massive man shouted over the heads of the foot soldiers. Draegan saw the two berserkers, head and shoulders above the rank and file turn and push their way back through the men to join their blonde comrade who stood alone near the rocks.

Draegan wasted no time and charged directly at the blonde giant, his sword lending a manic energy to Draegan's movements as it crackled in the icy air alongside the whip he dragged through the heath behind him.

The giant roared and charged to meet Draegan, his eyes glowing red as he closed the distance. He had unstrapped his war hammer and began to raise it as Draegan neared. At the last moment, the giant planted his foot, spun, and threw the hammer with all his strength directly at Draegan. He moved with such speed Draegan barely had time to dodge the hurtling missile of iron as it shot past his face, the leather strap on the handle cutting his ear as it sped toward the cavalry that was busy reforming its ranks.

The hammer plunged into the beasts, crushing horse and rider alike, while Draegan launched himself into the air and brought the whip down with all his might at the raging berserker. With astonishing speed for someone of such great size, the man lifted his arm as the thong of flame coiled around him, burning through his skin. He ground his teeth and shot his other hand out, catching Draegan by the throat as he descended from his attack.

Draegan pulled back on the handle of the whip, all six coils neatly severing the giant's forearm. He howled in protest and tightened his grip on Draegan's neck. Pain raced through Draegan's body as he fought to stay conscious. The giant roared and tightened his grip again, smashing the bloody stump of his arm into Draegan's face with terrible violence. Draegan plunged his sword into the man's mouth and watched it burst from the back of his skull. He took a deep breath of cold air and felt it freeze in his lungs as the giant fell to the ground, dead. The two red headed berserkers burst from the edge of foot soldiers, who were so densely packed together to watch the fight that several of them spilled to the ground.

"He killed the War Chief's brother," the men began to whisper loud enough for Draegan to hear.

Draegan kicked the amputated forearm at the soldiers and circled to his left, trying to keep the other two berserkers bunched together. He cracked the Burning Chains at the two giants, splitting the sky again. The men responded with roars and charged Draegan.

They rushed at Draegan single file and as the nearest charging hulk of bearded fury brought his massive war axe down in a ferocious swing, burying it in the frozen tundra, Draegan slid beyond its murderous stroke, passing through the legs of the first man and sprung up behind him. He drew back his arm, about to crack the whip at the second berserker who charged in after the first, when he felt his body seize. He craned his neck to see that the first giant had recovered from his failed swing and left the axe buried in the tundra. He wheeled quickly enough to grab Draegan's wrist before he could crack the whip. The second red bearded berserker charged in and grabbed Draegan's other arm, causing him to drop his sword to the ground. The throng of foot soldiers let out a triumphant roar as the two giants lifted the struggling captive over their heads, both of his arms held fast as if by irons.

"Balandar! Bandil!" the soldiers chanted as the red bearded giants held Draegan aloft, intending to rip his arms from their sockets. Their grip was like iron, and Draegan could feel the pressure building in his shoulder sockets as they began to pull. His head swam with pain and he cried out in a foreign tongue.

Instantly the ground erupted in flame. A jet of liquid fire burst several hundred feet in the air, consuming all within a forty foot radius of Draegan. As quickly as it appeared, the fire was gone. The cold arctic air whipped the black smoke across the lake revealing a giant ring of charred earth. In the center was a lone rock. It started to move and moments later, Draegan stood, brushing ashes from his cloak. At his feet lay the twisted and charred corpses of the two berserkers.

Chapter 22: The Battle at Mirror's Gap

Draegan turned his attention to his surroundings. He saw scores of charred bodies in front of a line of wide-eyed foot soldiers. The first three ranks of men had pushed so close to the fight they had stepped inside the circle and also been consumed by the conflagration spell. Turning, he saw the cavalry had escaped mostly unharmed and had reformed farther back after Draegan had charged them with the Burning Chains. He shook his head.

"I say again, if Tor Valdin brings me the World Render I will spare you all and these birds will go hungry another day," Draegan said gesturing to the birds that had begun wheeling above his head. He kicked one of the charred helmets of the three giants, its burnt ram's horns crumbling as it rolled across the blackened earth. A biting wind stirred the ashes as the foot soldiers and cavalry watched Draegan in stunned silence.

Suddenly, the pounding of the war drums began. Draegan turned to face the cavalry and discern the source of the steady thumping but he saw nothing. The chargers whinnied and shied as the drumming grew louder. With a blast from a horn the nervous horses parted as the foot soldiers had before, creating a path wide enough for three wagons to ride abreast.

Draegan peered down the channel and soon saw the source of the heavy war drums. "A tundra beast," he whispered, his eyes growing wide as he saw the lumbering shape smash out a rhythmic tattoo with its every footfall. Riders held their mounts in check as the horses snorted and champed their bits as the prehistoric creature lumbered by. "They were thought extinct after the Sundering of Athar."

The ground began to shake as the beast drew closer. It was only a few hands taller than the war chargers of the cavalry, but it was more than twice as wide with four thick, squat legs and shaggy wool that hung in matted clumps to the beast's knees. Its heavy, leather-skinned head swung from side to side as it labored up the path between the horses, gnawing on its bridle. It wore spiked iron plates over its considerable bulk, adding even more mass to its incredible size. Atop the beast, in a leather saddle, sat a shirtless man, his arms folded over his massive chest.

"Today I will make you famous," the voice boomed from atop the lumbering beast as it came to a halt a few feet from Draegan. The beast snorted a cloud of steam that passed over him, and began to gnaw its bit, white slather falling from its giant mouth. Draegan stood firm in its considerable shadow. He stared into the animal's beady black eyes behind the plates of iron covering its mammoth skull. After a long moment of consideration Draegan moved his gaze from the beast to the man who rode upon it.

"You will be known through the Iron Mountains as the crow that delivered the missing Artifacts to me," the shirtless man said as he jumped from the back of the behemoth and landed in the scorched earth, his legs planted wide. He was nearly seven feet tall and heavily muscled. He wore leather breeches and fur lined boots, but no shirt despite the biting winds. Only a thick leather belt slung over his shoulders offered any protection from the chill. His black beard hung in a single braid and reached the middle of his intricately tattooed chest. Over his powerful shoulders hung the World Render.

"I don't know how you came across them, but my scouts tell me you have the blade of the Usurper and Erdrik's whip." He smiled at Draegan. "Lay them at my feet, or I will lay your head at yours," he said, standing to his full height. Draegan saw the cords of muscle that wrapped around Tor's thick forearms tense, straining the leather wraps at his wrists.

"I am no crow, as I told your scouts." Draegan threw back his cloak and gripped his weapons tightly. "I am Draegan Ferus, Emperor of Fyrian, and you're wearing my axe."

Tor threw back his head and laughed. When he had collected himself he looked quizzically at the man before him. "For twenty years the four kingdoms have scoured all of Athar trying to find you, and at last in your old age you come seeking me. Tell us Usurper, where have you hidden all these years? It's a question all of Fyrian has been wondering, your people in Skeldus most of all." He pointed his giant finger at Draegan and continued. "They spat upon your name as your kingdom was torn apart by the squabbling generals and bickering bureaucrats who tried to seize the throne you left empty when you murdered your brother. Your name became a curse when your people were slaughtered by the four kingdoms which poured over your defenseless borders and turned Skeldus into a wasteland." He spat on the ground and glowered at Draegan. "So speak coward, and defend what little honor remains in your frail bones before I break you."

Draegan took a step back prepared to launch himself at Tor. Immediately Tor's hand flew to the leather strap that held the World Render and in one furious motion he unbuckled the axe and swung the great weapon at Draegan's chest. Draegan ducked, bending over backward at the waist and planted his hand behind him on the ground to keep himself from toppling over as the massive blade carved a murderous arc inches from his neck. Tor bellowed as Draegan muttered a word and felt the ground pitch up under him.

In another instant he stood atop the boulders near the lake, several feet above the scorched earth and let the cold wind dissipate the black mist of the Shadow Walking spell across the rippling lake. "You'll never catch me, barbarian," Draegan shouted. He glanced quickly around and saw that the soldiers had pressed back to the edge of the blackened earth and reformed their ranks. Behind Tor the cavalry had pushed in tighter and closed the gap they had formed to allow the Tundra Beast its passage. With his eyes locked on Tor, Draegan shouted above the winds. "Throw down the World Render and take your battalion back to the front lines. Let it be known that I will spare all your men if you do as I ask, but also know they will all die if you do not obey."

"My men would lay down their lives if I but asked, Usurper. It's the kind of loyalty and respect they pay to a true leader." Tor raised the huge axe over his head. "Not that a coward like you could understand." The foot soldiers cheered and began banging their axes on their shields drowning out all hope of a reply.

The War Chief began spinning the axe in a giant circle over his head until it began to hum. He shouted and, grabbing the handle, swung at Draegan's position atop the boulders, releasing a swath of fire that burned through the air. Draegan ducked as the arc of flame passed over him, only to find that Tor had followed his attack with another in rapid succession. The War Chief buried the World Render with vicious force into the ground, rupturing and splitting the earth in a zigzagging line that erupted from the bit of the axe and shot toward the boulders upon which Draegan stood. The force of the blow, though it originated nearly a hundred feet away, was enough to cause Draegan to lose his footing and tumble from the rocks. He caught himself on the burnt ground. He had just tucked the hilt of Carnis Fornax into his belt when he heard the thundering of the war drums once again.

Looking up he saw the massive bulk of the tundra beast charging toward him. The behemoth bellowed and closed the distance with surprising speed for a beast of its size carrying a payload of iron plate. Thick white strands of spit flapped from its mouth as its pounding hooves ate up the blackened dirt. Draegan dove out of its path at the last instant, sprang to his feet and watched as the beast smashed headfirst into the boulders. With a crack like thunder the boulder split. Unfazed, the tundra beast began the slow process of turning itself around when Draegan heard footsteps rushing up behind him.

Wheeling around he saw Tor had charged in behind the beast, using the diversion to make up the distance between them. As the axe carved through the air Draegan knew he had no time to dodge so instead he planted his feet and leapt into the swinging blade as it passed over his head by mere inches. Draegan landed inside the arc of the World Render and within the reach of Tor. The giant war chief released the axe and grabbed Draegan in a crushing bear hug. He felt his ribs beginning to crack as Tor lifted him easily from the ground. He lost his hold on the Burning Chains and the handle slipped to the ground as the tongues of flame extinguished themselves. Tor ground his teeth and bore down with his tremendous strength. Draegan writhed in agony as he felt the life being crushed from him. He heard the foot soldiers begin to cheer, though they sounded faint and distant. He looked down and saw the giant smiling as he was squeezing the life from him. The ground began to waver. As his vision blurred he noticed a piece of paper slip from his belt and float to the ground behind Tor. Draegan closed his eyes and felt the darkness swallow him.

Tor waved frantically at the black mist that clouded his eyes and dove for his axe, but it was too late. As he gripped the handle and turned he saw six great thongs of flame parting the black haze as if in slow motion. He raised the axe instinctually to defend himself and felt the burning chains curl around the handle and pull it from his grasp. He fell forward to his knees, clutching after the Artifact as Draegan dragged the axe to himself.

Draegan stood a few feet from where Tor lay on his knees, his giant head hung in defeat. The foot soldiers kept beating their shields and yelling his name, hoping to offer some support to their fallen leader. Draegan looked at the axe as it lay on the ground at his feet and sheathed the handle of the whip in his belt, opposite the hilt of Carnis Fornax. "You're mastery of this weapon is impressive. It obeys you as easily as mine bends to me," Draegan said, looking from the finely wrought carvings on the handle to the giant War Chief on his knees. He bent to pick up the weapon and wrapping his fingers tentatively around the grip looked past Tor to watch the last vestige of the black mist blow out past the boulders toward the lake. An instant later Draegan's eyes widened and he quickly curled into a ball when he saw the cloud part in a violent swirl.

Punching through the mist the great tundra beast came crashing directly at Draegan, its footfalls drowned out by the din raised by the chanting soldiers. The beast lowered its massive head and drove into Draegan's chest at full speed. He went flying, losing his grip on the World Render as he tumbled over the scorched earth and into the ranks of the cavalry. Draegan looked up and saw the hooves of a war steed crashing down. He rolled away just in time as the steel shod hooves trampled his cloak. Pulling the handle of the Burning Chains from his belt he lashed out at the rider, the crackling orange flames of the whip severing the man's body. The horse started and the halves of its charge fell with a heavy thud to the frozen earth.

Draegan stood and with the Burning Chains lashed out at the closest cavalry, forcing them to back their mounts away. The horses stamped and whinnied nervously at the sight of the hungry flames. He turned quickly to see Tor once again swinging the World Render at him from nearly fifty feet away, a great arc of flame cutting its way through the air toward Draegan. He dove to the side as the flame tore into the cavalry, consuming rider and mount alike, some four ranks deep before it dissipated.

"You would kill your own men so easily?" Draegan shouted. "And yet you make haughty claims of leadership," he said and crouched to the ground, placing his palm on the earth. In an instant he was gone as the glowing red blade cleaved through the black mist that rose from where Draegan had just knelt.

"Coward!" Draegan heard Tor bellow. Draegan rose near the pile of rubble, where earlier stood the boulder on which he had waited for the battalion to arrive. The sun was setting behind him and cast his shadow across the smoldering earth toward the growling tundra beast. He charged the behemoth from behind, cracking his flaming whip at its haunches, sending the terrified animal into a frenzy. It stampeded forward, eyes rolling in its sockets and bellowing madly, trapping Tor between itself and the cavalry. Tor planted his feet, and realizing he had no other option, hefted the mighty axe overhead and brought it down in a crushing blow directly into the beast's skull. He cleaved through the iron plate and thick skull of the beast with ease, but the momentum of the frenzied animal carried it forward, and it fell, tumbling over itself, trapping Tor beneath its lifeless bulk. The World Render protruded from its skull like a twisted black horn.

Draegan approached the beast cautiously and saw that Tor was firmly pinned to the ground. The legs of the beast still twitched convulsively as the life drained from its broken body. Tor's head and torso were free from the beast, as well as his left arm which he was using to frantically try and extricate himself from under the crushing weight of the tundra beast. Draegan circled around the carcass and approached the War Chief from the right. He pulled the hilt of Carnis Fornax from his belt and raised it over his head, the black flames bursting to life from the carven hole in the cross guard.

"Such an ignoble death for a War Chief," Draegan said. "However, I am a man of my word and I recall making a promise earlier." He turned and extinguished his blade, returning the hilt to his belt. "I told these men they would die because of your arrogance, and I am honor bound to oblige." He looked at Tor. "Though you can still save them if you gift me the World Render."

Tor spat at Draegan. "I'd rather have that sword and cape for myself," he said with a pained smile and drew a deep breath. "Archers! Cavalry! Soldiers! Kill him!" he shouted at the top of his lungs. Draegan heard the blast of a horn and quickly brought both his hands above his head and dropped them in one swift motion. Instantly the foot soldiers and cavalry froze in position. Archers held their bows drawn, but loosed no arrows. Foot soldiers drew their blades but made no effort to rush forward. Draegan stumbled with the exertion from his spell and caught himself on the warm carcass of the tundra beast. He drew a few deep breaths and righted himself.

"Now you see the extent of my power," Draegan said between gasps of air. "Your hundreds of men, held captive in one enormous binding spell." He looked around and saw the entire battalion in both directions frozen as if carved of stone. "I will slay each and every man while you watch. Know that their blood is on your hands and know that you could have prevented this had you simply listened to reason."

Draegan turned and pulled the Burning Chains from his belt and lashed out at the cavalry. A peal of thunder split the sky and Draegan walked slowly past the vanguard of the cavalry, staring at the frozen men and beasts. He stopped, sighed, and walked back to Tor who still struggled vainly against his captor, veins bulging on his face as he desperately fought to free himself.

"But there has been enough blood spilled over these Artifacts," Draegan said when he was near Tor. "I would ask again that you release me from my promise and spare your men." He held out his hand, the tongues of fire searing and hissing on the frozen ground as he dragged the whip behind him. "Give me the axe."

Tor continued to struggle against the fallen beast that trapped him. He clawed violently at the ground with his one free arm, trying to free himself. With a desperate cry and a monstrous push of his thick legs, Tor heaved the massive corpse off his body and rolled out of the way of the flaming chains that smashed into the hard-packed ground where he had lain.

"I was a fool," Draegan muttered and saw the bloody War Chief bending over the armored skull of the beast, desperately trying to remove the axe buried in its head. Tor's crushed right arm dangled at his side. The giant man began kicking desperately at the handle of the World Render as Draegan shouted in anger and sprinted toward him.

Draegan brought the black flame of his blade down with furious might as he rushed at Tor. At the last moment Tor spun and catching the handle of the freed axe, swung upward with his immense strength, catching the falling blade mid-stroke. They stood there, frozen for an instant, Draegan's blade crackling with hunger as it licked at Tor, while the World Render prevented it from biting into his flesh.

"Even with one arm, I'm more than a match for you," Tor shouted. The bit of the World Render began to glow red as Tor set his jaw and shifted his weight, preparing to throw off Draegan. Draegan pushed down on his sword with all his might, then when he felt the most resistance from Tor he immediately withdrew the sword and leaned back as the axe shot upward, releasing an arc of flame straight up into the sky. Tor stumbled forward but caught himself, bringing the axe back down in a sloppy strike intended to keep Draegan from taking advantage of his misstep. But he was too slow. Draegan pulled the Burning Chains from his belt and wrapped the tongues of flame around Tor's arm, dragging it and the World Render to the ground. Tor fell to his knees. Draegan rammed the black fire of his blade down through Tor's neck and deep into his chest. He felt a surge of power rush through is body as the sword drank the soul from its victim.

He sheathed the sword and whip and bent to pick up the axe, keeping his eyes focused on the Artifact while he purposely avoided looking at the statues of men and horses. Draegan took the sling from Tor and after some adjustments made it small enough to support the giant axe on his smaller frame. He began heading west, picking his way through the frozen soldiers as fast as he could and pushed into the setting sun. The carrion birds began to descend and work through the bloody remains of the battlefield.

"I will end your binding when I've put enough distance between myself and your blades," Draegan said and marched off toward the setting sun. Draegan pulled his cloak around him as a cold wind blew across the tundra. He wiped a sheen of sweat from his brow and shuddered, the spell and his effort in the fight catching up with him. The sun was now just an orange sliver above the horizon. As Draegan scanned the tundra for any sign of Tor's main forces he noticed a figure clothed in white outlined against the fiery sunset.

"Another challenger for the Artifacts?" Draegan wondered aloud as he pressed onward. "This grows tiresome, and I have yet to acquire the Black Horn." He took a deep breath of the frigid air and shook the exhaustion from his bones. After a few minutes Draegan paused and eyed the man more carefully. When they were within two hundred yards of each other they stopped.

"Hello, Draegan," the figure in white robes shouted over the howling wind. A smile spread over Draegan's tired face.

"I thought you were dead, Gron."

Chapter 23: The Initiation

Isarn sat against the trunk of an old oak tree and listened to the deafening racket of the crickets and cicadas. Beads of perspiration ran down his face and soaked into his already damp robes. He had been waiting in the forest since sunset, when he was blindfolded and left by Isirah for yet another training session. He felt the weight of the specially crafted harness looping over his shoulders and across the small of his back where the extra bulk of the device held the twin blades of the Vaghat.

He straightened his back and slowed his breathing, feeling the humid air of the forest move slightly as he focused himself and blocked out the din of the insects. All at once he heard a soft vibration and tensed.

Isarn sprung to his feet and wheeled around, pulling a dagger from the scabbard on his back as he sliced blindly through the air in front of his chest. He felt the steel connect with the shaft of an arrow, the shock of the bolt rippling up his arm to his shoulder. The arrow splintered, and Isarn was crouching behind a tree before it fell to the ground.

Though still blindfolded Isarn slipped easily from tree to tree, pushing closer to the hidden archer. The twang of the bow string and whistle of the arrows were muffled by the cacophony of the insects and few night birds that inhabited the island. But he felt the air part moments before the bolts struck and avoided every shot, moving like wind through the trees.

"You gave away your position when you fired the first shot, Isirah," Isarn shouted from behind the trunk of an ancient locust tree. Two arrows struck the opposite side, sending showers of bark into the undergrowth.

"How little you know," Isirah said, his voice echoing through the heavy, humid air of the forest.

Isarn spun, turning his blindfolded head in every direction trying to locate the source of Isirah's voice. It came from everywhere and all directions at once, impossible to pinpoint.

"He's using magic to disguise his location," Isarn whispered as he crouched into the tangled growth near the base of the tree. "I can play at that game." He slipped the dagger back into place beneath his robe and folded his hands, weaving his fingers together as he began chanting. After a moment he launched himself from the thicket and ran across a small clearing before diving behind a small bank, arrows speeding past him as he moved.

"Your enemy will not allow you the time you need to perform complex incantations. You must learn to summon them without signs or words," came the echoing voice of Isirah. "It must all be etched into your mind just as this forest is burned into your muscles."

Isarn pressed himself into the soft earth of the bank, slowing his breathing. He had trained in this forest for over ten years and knew every tree, every root, every rock and every rise and fall of the ground. For the past several years Isirah had resorted to blindfolding him during the training sessions to compensate for his acute awareness of his surroundings.

"I need to find him before I can tag him," Isarn said, racking his brain for a plan. The symphony of the wildlife in the forest rose in a tremendous crescendo, causing Isarn to lose his focus. "I need to silence these beasts so that I may find the old man and unweave his spells."

He crawled through the dry ditch, keeping himself pressed flat against the ground as arrows whistled over his head. He pushed toward the far end where a large sandstone boulder lay, the roots of an ancient oak coiling over it and into the ground. A heavy storm several years ago had washed out much of the earth from beneath the rock and Isarn squeezed himself under it, pressing his back against the underside of the boulder.

"You cannot spend your time hiding Isarn," Isirah said, his voice booming through the forest. "You have superior strength and speed and a weapon from the Elder Gods, yet you cower under a rock while I send arrows chasing after you."

Isarn curled his body further under the rock as more arrows came whistling by him, even closer than before and sank into the hard earth of the opposite bank. He drove his feet into the floor of the dry stream bed and braced his legs, pushing with all his strength against the boulder. It moved an inch, but would move no further despite Isarn's efforts. He pulled a dagger from the sheath and began sawing furiously at the great roots that wrapped over the boulder.

"I admit I have not tended this forest the way old Ieros did, but I should hardly think now is the time for pruning," Isirah said as he sped two arrows at the white robed arm he saw protruding from the side of the boulder. "You also do a great injustice to the Vaghat. It is no gardening tool," he said his voice rising with anger as he stepped into the clearing and fired two more shots at Isarn.

As the second arrow sunk into the bank Isarn stepped out from behind the boulder and threw the blade in the direction from which the arrow had come. As soon as the dagger left his hand he slipped back under the rock and driving his heels into the dirt, he wedged his back against the massive boulder and strained against it with all his might. Great veins twined up his neck as tendons stretched to their limit, his muscles nearly bursting with the effort.

Isirah dropped his bow as soon as he saw the flash of light leave Isarn's hands and clapped his palms together, catching the blade inches from his throat. "You are a fool to throw away your weapon," he began and stopped mid-thought as a mighty crack silenced all the noise in the forest. Looking ahead he saw the great oak shudder, its uppermost branches and leaves rustling though there was no breeze to stir them. A moment later another thunderous crack confirmed his suspicion and Isirah leapt to the side as the great tree came crashing down where he once stood, the trunk sinking a foot into the earth as the force of the blow shook the entire island.

Isirah scrambled to his feet, reaching for the blade he had dropped when he leapt to avoid the falling tree. He looked up and saw Isarn crouching over of him, the other blade of the Vaghat inches from his face.

Isarn lifted his blindfold and smiled. "I would like my blade back, please."

Chapter 24: The Man in White

Gron approached Draegan, who stood frozen in place. "Nothing to say? Just going to stand there with your teeth in your mouth?" Gron pulled his white hood back to reveal his great red beard and sun burnt face. He was just as large as before, though wider in the middle. His hair was mostly gone and what remained was shaved to the skin. Of the face that had been so familiar to Draegan only the fiery red beard and laughter around his blue eyes remained.

"How about a 'hello' or some sort of casual greeting for a man who cheated death?" Gron asked. Draegan smiled.

"Hello Gron," Draegan said, extending his hand which Gron took and nearly crushed in his exuberance. "Though I must admit I thought you to be some sort of apparition. I saw you in the catacombs…"

"Apparitions aren't usually so fat," Gron said, pulling Draegan into a hearty embrace before releasing him. Gron slapped his one remaining hand on his stomach and chuckled. "The catacombs? Don't remind me. Terrible story." Gron motioned to a stand of stunted, windblown pines. "Let's have a seat out of this wind and I'll tell you. Maybe get a fire going?" he said looking expectantly at Draegan's pack.

***

Gron settled back and leaned against the trunk of a pine once the fire was lit. He looked at Draegan's pack lying by the fire. "Any food in there? Been walking a long time trying to find you."

"I have little provisions, but they're yours if only you tell me how you survived."

Gron dug into Draegan's pack and emptied out several tomes, snorted in disappointment, and then dug out a piece of frozen hardtack that he placed gently on a rock near the fire. "While that warms up I guess I'll tell you. Terrible story, really. But here we go." He rubbed his back against the tree and looked at Draegan. "That's all the food you brought?" Gron began before he waved his single remaining hand and stopped his own line of questioning. "Sorry to complain. Haven't eaten in a few days and it's getting to me." He chuckled mostly to himself as he tugged at his beard.

"As you can see Ceredyn took my arm," Gron said gesturing to his shoulder where the cloth of his robe lay flat against his side. "You remember all those years ago when I grabbed that axe and got burned by the pyrrhic fire, well Ceredyn did something to my arm when he fixed me up. He stopped the pyrrhic fire from spreading alright. But he never extinguished it. It was trapped, burning in my arm and he controlled its intensity. But when he used his blood on me to stop it from spreading he must have done some sort of sorcery that allowed him to touch the World Render without being consumed, like I had been." Gron thought for a moment. "Glad he did though, because he used the axe to cut the flaming stump clean off at the shoulder, stopping the fire from burning me alive once and for all. Said something about dying a warrior's death, though I never could understand why he lit my arm on fire in the first place if he was only going to cut it off. Crows don't have much sense as it turns out."

Gron shrugged and continued. "Of course I don't have any either. After he cut my arm off, he fled down the access hatch with the Artifacts while I dragged my bleeding body over to the bear claws and ate a handful. I never felt so much pain in my life. Went berserk of course." Gron chuckled at his own joke but when he saw the subtlety had escaped Draegan he continued. "Usually one is enough to get the spell going, but I must have had four or five."

Draegan shuddered at the thought of the three berserkers he'd just faced and imagined the amount of power Gron could summon with a handful of imbued claws.

Gron shook his head and poked at the still frozen lump of hardtack on the rock. "So in a frenzy I took off down the shaft after him and through the cistern. I was bleeding everywhere, like a stuck pig. I had no idea where he went after that so I just went back the way we came. Hard to think when you're consumed with rage and have lost half your blood. Anyway, next thing I know some fisherman's hauling my carcass into his boat. He found me floating in Lake Sias, so I didn't get too far before I ran out of steam. Or blood."

Gron decided to have a try at the frozen hardtack and began gnawing bits off the side as he talked. "He patched me up and let me rest at his cabin for a few days. Or weeks, I forget. But soon enough he sent me packing. I couldn't do much to help him with only one working arm, and only three fingers on it at that. But I think the real issue was he may have figured out who I was. We're not too well like in Fyrian, you and me." He placed the hardtack back on the rock to continue thawing and wiped his hand on his robe. "So I left and went to Vatn. I always thought it was a nice place. A bit warm, but restful. They took me in of course, which explains the white robes," Gron said, gesturing at his white robes. "Always looked good in white too, so why not?"

"You're an acolyte of Vatn?"

Gron wagged a finger. "A priest. They made me take the vows after Ieros died a few years back. So I'm in the library now. Makes sense since I'm not much use in the gardens or the kitchen considering…" Gron held up his mangled right hand and pointed at his missing arm. "The library's nice enough, though it has too many scrolls for my taste. Old Ieros taught me a lot before he passed on.

Now I've got a pretty easy life compared to what I used to do. I don't want any part of this worldly nonsense anymore. But I do miss this breeze," Gron said as a bone-chilling wind whipped through the trees and nearly scattered the fire. He picked up the hardtack and continued to gnaw away at the frozen brick.

"Old Ieros was ancient even in my youth when I studied there with him…" Draegan said and trailed off before shaking his head and looking back at Gron. "Then why are you out here? And how did you find me?"

Crumbs flew as Gron spoke. "I was looking for Tor. I got word he was marching his whole army against Corvus, so I wanted to talk some sense into him. He's my uncle's wife's second cousin's oldest boy after all." Gron looked at Draegan, his expression turning serious. "I guess you got to him first. Artifacts don't change their owners peacefully," he said staring at the World Render strapped to Draegan's back. "When I saw the jet of fire shoot into the sky a few hours ago I wondered where I'd seen something like that before. Then I remembered what happened in the Vilkas when we fought our Night Watch brothers." Gron shook his head. "I remembered what you did in that clearing. I couldn't believe you were back so I came searching." Gron shoved the remaining hardtack in his mouth and licked his fingers. "But here you are. Now it's your turn. Where have you been these twenty years, Draegan?"

Draegan was silent for a moment as his mind drifted off. "Fighting Vangen." Draegan stared into the fire and thought back to the Red Keep and the endless army that poured from its gaping doors. "He lives in the shadow realm of Iss. I followed him there using blood magic and lost twenty years in that cursed place. When I came back everything was changed. I was changed. I didn't know. But soon I must go back and finish him before he opens a portal back to Athar."

Gron furrowed his brow. "I figured it was something I wouldn't understand. I'll just tell people you were hunting Vangen."

"When I left you in the catacombs I thought you were dead. I pursued Vangen back to his study where I killed him with Carnis Fornax." Draegan's hand slipped unconsciously to the clasp at his neck and was quiet for a moment as he listened to the wind howl and watched it stir the embers. The cold metal of the Great Aegis warmed quickly to his touch. "But I didn't know the depths of his power. When I watched his body burn I thought I had ended him, and saved us from his wickedness, but he still lives. He had planned his death by splitting his soul in two and sending half of it to the shadow land of Iss. The other was trapped in my blade. It wasn't until I read through the book he had written that I discovered this."

Gron exhaled and watched the wind carry his breath into the darkness beyond the firelight. "So when exactly did you leave us? And what became of the bow? Like you, it's been missing from Fyrian for a while."

"After Vangen fell, I went back to look for you, but found nothing. I slew the beast that we had fought and decided Vangen's study was the best place to find clues to his whereabouts. The eye told me of the bow," Draegan said, tapping his temple. "A week or so later I had returned from Docga with the Dark Ichor that cost Aran his life. As I recovered from the wound Tior inflicted on me I muddled my way through Vangen's hand written tome and learned of his ultimate plan. I immediately opened a portal to Iss not two weeks after I killed Vangen and pursued him there."

Gron nodded. "So you thought I was dead?"

"Sadly yes, along with Aran and everyone else Vangen had ultimately deceived. He had spread the Artifacts throughout the Kingdoms once again and war was coming to Dullahan." Draegan drew a deep breath and looked from the fire to Gron. "But I had a decision to make and I judged Vangen to be the greater threat and pursued him across the void into Iss. I encountered him there, but he proved more than a match for me. He sent me here but not before telling me that he plans to gather an army of shades and open a gate to Athar, unleashing his evil upon us. He is raising Iss from the shadows and returning here. I now seek to gather the Artifacts before I once more return to Iss in the hopes of using them against his furious might."

Gron grunted. "Ieros used to mumble something in his sleep about Iss returning. Never gave it much thought. So Vangen is still around." He paused and smoothed his robe. "But why were you gone so long?"

"I thought I was gone for days, weeks at the most. I learned when I came back that time does not exist in that realm as it does here. I found my kingdom fallen and my people dead or scattered. My name is a curse, all because I left Fyrian putting vengeance ahead of peace. But am I wrong to do so? If I don't stop Vangen soon, then it will not matter what kingdom holds power or wields what Artifact. All will fall before his deathless army."

Gron blinked and looked at Draegan who had picked up the leather straps he used to fasten the World Render to his back and began to rub them with oil. "So you are still hunting Vangen. I don't know if that's right or wrong to do. Who am I to judge?" He paused for a moment and his face brightened as he continued. "But there may be some hope, old friend. I told you I work in the library now, and while I'm not the best reader, the days are slow enough that I have plenty of spare time. And I found something that might interest you. A ray of hope you might say. I would have told you sooner, but nobody could find you."

"Hope is a word I've not heard or thought of in some time," Draegan mumbled as he wiped the straps clean and inspected his work in the firelight.

"You have a son."

Draegan's hands froze in their task. The straps slipped to the ground. He watched the embers dance and swirl above the fire as the wind whipped through their makeshift camp. After a long moment of silence a pine branch popped in the fire and Draegan looked back up at Gron. "A son? But how?"

"The usual way, I imagine," Gron chuckled. I discovered it one day as I looked through the old records down in the archives. I have keys to the place." Gron looked up at the stars. "Lots of odd stuff down there. Well I found a book of records that shows every birth and death on the island for the past four hundred years. I found your mother's entry. Issa's too."

"It feels as if it were yesterday that she was taken from me," Draegan whispered as the wind stirred the fire.

"Draegan, she gave birth to a boy a few months after you left. The only thing is, he disappears from the records soon after. There's no entry for when he entered school or took his oaths to become an acolyte or where he works on the island. Kind of a mystery."

"So he died. Like his mother. A false hope then," Draegan said. Any empty pit of grief spread inside him as he pulled his cloak tighter over his shoulders.

"Well, that's just it. He doesn't exist in the death records either." Gron shifted and rubbed his back against one of the pine trees before continuing. "He must have left the island as a young boy perhaps. It doesn't happen often but every so once in a great while a young one runs off with a trade ship headed back to the mainland.

From there it's anyone's guess." Gron ran his few fingers through his beard and tugged on it as he stared at the winking stars.

Gron and Draegan sat in silence for some time, listening to the wind blow and the fire pop and throw sparks into the night air. Finally the bear of a man broke the silence.

"You should come back with me and look through the archives. Maybe together we could find some clue as to his fate."

"Vangen!" Draegan shouted and smashed his fist into the frozen ground. "This is what he meant to tell me all those years ago in the study. Issa came to him with news for me, but he claimed to have forgotten her message. This must be the secret he kept," Draegan hissed through clenched teeth.

Gron leaned back and furrowed his brow at Draegan. "I tell you that you have a son, and your first thought is of Vangen? You haven't changed," he said as he tucked his arm under his robes.

"On the contrary, now I have more to lose than ever. But my son must wait. If none but you and I know of his existence then he will remain safely in the shadows until I complete my task. For if Vangen succeeds in opening a gate from Iss to Athar then it won't matter one whit if I had ten sons and Issa still lived. Vangen will devastate the whole of our kingdoms. He is still the greatest threat. He must be stopped and only I can do it."

He took his pack and looked at Gron as he stood to leave. "Thank you old friend. It brings me no small measure of joy to see that you're alive and have found peace. But I have not. I must return to Dullahan and stop Vangen as quickly as possible in order to keep it so. Only then can I return and find my son. If he still lives then some hope remains for the Empire, for I will teach him to be the ruler I have failed to be, and he will rebuild what I, what Vangen, has torn apart." Draegan placed his palm on the ground and a black cloud rose from the earth. Shrouded in dark mist, he didn't see Gron raise his mangled hand to stop him. An instant later the vapor blew away and Draegan was gone.

Gron curled up tighter against the wind and stared at the fire. "I wanted to warn you of another secret, long forgotten. Beware the Clade, Draegan, for they have a magic weapon that surpasses all others," he whispered to himself as he watched the shadows dance at the edge of the firelight.

Chapter 25: The Hunt Begins

"You are not ready," Isirah said as he closed the ornate cover of an old tome and sighed. He placed his fingertips on the rich leatherwork and whispered an incantation. Isarn watched the book shudder then settle back to the lectern. Isirah lifted it and carried it to the shelves that lined the library walls.

"What more is there to master?" Isarn asked as he followed Isirah up the curving stairs to the second story where he searched the walls for the book's home. "I am no novice with any of the weapons in the training room." He looked sideways at Isirah with a slight smile. "In fact I have proven your superior on many occasions."

"You are not ready," Isirah repeated as he slipped the book into an awaiting space in a shelf over his head. He turned to face Isarn. "Besting an old man who tires from climbing a flight of stairs is little to boast of."

Isarn raised his hands. "You are more than a match for any swordsman in Fyrian, and we both know it. But you seek to change the topic. I am more than proficient in all the weapons you have shown me. The sword and spear, the hammer and the axe, the stave and whip, they all obey me. I can pass the shield and know the weak point of every type of armor. I can pierce a swallow mid flight with my bow even as I run."

"You are not ready," Isirah said as he looked over the wall of books before him, searching for one in particular. "There is more to conquer than tactics, though I do not doubt your mastery of weapons."

"I have achieved a fluency in the empty handed fighting arts which outstrips that of Jagannath, a man who once bested one hundred warriors in a single day. I surpass all men in stamina. I do not hunger or tire or thirst. I can outrun a horse without aid of a *staminis* spell. You have seen me lift the breaking stone, a feat only you and Greydin Vir have ever accomplished. How then am I not ready?"

"You are not ready," Isirah repeated, brushing past Isarn as he made his way across a connecting bridge to the opposite side of the library, still preoccupied with finding the elusive book. "There is more to master than the physical, though you are indeed one of the greatest warriors Fyrian has ever known."

"Is it my training in the magical arts? Isirah, you yourself have seen my proficiency with magic. Your own words were that I had no equal. I can command enchantments without runes or signs, a feat possible only by the most accomplished mages. I can cast the Iron Hand and Stone Form with only a thought. If I will it, the elements bend to my wishes. You have watched me in the training room walk the Folded Path of Udros unscathed. Who else has done it without aid of protections and runic symbols but me?"

"You are not ready," Isirah muttered as he ran his hand across a row of tomes, pausing at one, only to curse softly when he saw it wasn't what he was looking for. "There is more to learn than spell weaving, though you are perhaps the greatest living mage in all of Athar."

"Then what more is there? You say I am a great fighter, a great warrior, a great mage, but still I'm not ready. When I am not in the training room, I live here in the library. I have read nearly every book this tower contains. I know the lore of the fallen Tribe of Docga, and can walk silently through the forest without disturbing a branch. I have studied the war histories of Skeldus and would be able to command battalions as easily as a battle-hardened general. I know the sea craft of the people of Stanrocc and can navigate without aid of instruments in open water. I have studied the dark past of all the five kingdoms and know the truth of our own. I have learned all these tomes have to teach," Isarn said opening his arms at the expanse of books that surrounded them.

"And still you are not ready," Isirah said, finally pulling a book from the shelf. He blew the dust off the cover and ran his fingers over the gold inlay of the title. "There is more in the world than books, though I do not dispute you are most learned for one so young."

"What then is my deficiency? Did I not master the seven precepts of Islak when I was only eleven? When I was fourteen you thought me ready for the Chamber of Hadith, yet even Ieros thought it unwise to enter before I turned sixteen. But I endured its tortures with your approval and emerged stronger than before, a feat that is unmatched by one so young in the history of the Clade. I unfolded the Shadow of Odoric and did not lose my sight. I drank from the Well of Sacra and my mind did not fall to its poison. I bathed in the Fire of Apah for three days and yet not one hair on my head was singed. I have passed all the tests. I have removed all desire from my heart. I am uncorrupted and incorruptible. My will is iron and my heart is as pure as the fires that forged me. I am ready."

Isirah turned from the books to face Isarn, his face clouded with anger. "Removed all desire? Tell me then why you persist in thinking you are ready to leave?"

"We have both seen the same images in the Scrying Pool, Isirah. Draegan has returned. He is gathering the Artifacts once again. You know as well as I do that he must be stopped."

"And that is precisely what you desire. You wish to be the man to stop him."

"Is that not what I've spent my life training for? You have beaten and shaped and taught me since I was but a child for one purpose, and now you would deny me this prize?"

"Only because you want it so desperately. You hunger for it, and your hunger makes you weak. You think it sharpens you, gives you a keen edge, but it opens you up to manipulation," Isirah said pointing his finger at Isarn. "This is why you are not ready."

Isarn threw up his hands. "What would you have me do? Spend my whole life training only to stay here and tend the hearth while the greatest evil since the Six Blades walks free? I thought you forged me to be the weapon that ends the suffering of the world."

"If you think that you or any weapon can end suffering then you are mistaken. You only serve to protect, to defend, and right now Fyrian is not under attack."

"So we wait until the rivers run red? Why, if we can prevent the blood from ever spilling? I can stop the Usurper now, before it's too late."

Isirah scoffed, then bowed his head and shrugged his shoulders. "If you were to go, what would be your plan, Isarn?"

Isarn stopped and looked from Isirah to the stories of books that soared a hundred feet over his head. He sighed. "We both know what Draegan is doing. The Scrying Pool has revealed that he now holds the Burning Chains and even as we speak he hunts the World Render. There is a good chance he already has it." Isarn looked back at Isirah. "I would go to Corvus and take the Black Horn before he claims it, forcing him to come after it and fight me here."

"So you would break through the seals of the most powerful mages in Fyrian, take the Black Horn and bring it here, defiling our sanctuary with its malignant bile? You would then lure the only man in Athar who is your equal if not your better to our home that he may not have to go through the trouble of taking it from the Council of Rune in Corvus?" Isirah rubbed his chin. "You are more warmhearted than I thought. And a fool."

Isarn balled his hands into fists, and then relaxed them. He watched Isirah descend the curving stairs to the center of the library where he placed the dusty tome on the lectern and began to read it, his hands touching the worn pages with care.

"What would you have me do then, master?"

Isirah looked up at Isarn standing on the balcony, and then returned to his book. He read in silence for a moment. "Go to Corvus and take the Black Horn. Bring it here and kill Draegan in the training hall. Or kill him in the dormitories. Kill him where you will and do what you will," he said, his voice rising in anger as he spoke. "For there is one thing the Clade, the histories, these books and the Trials have failed to impress upon you." He shut the book and looked up at Isarn. "It is all futile."

"I know you Isirah. For twenty years you have been my master and I know you. Though you say these words nearly every day, you do not mean it. You cannot mean it, for your actions stand witness against your words."

"I spent twenty years forging a man of iron and now I see it is folly to try and bend him," Isirah said and sighed as he looked at Isarn. "I truly have failed if you think there is anything to gain from your encounter with the Usurper. If you killed him, then what?" Isirah shook his head and grabbed the sides of the lectern. "The flaw of the Clade is that it tries to push back the inevitable, rather than accept it. We are trained, beaten, broken and forged into living weapons that have but one goal, to kill the man or men who wield the Artifacts," he said holding up his hands. "And then what? We cannot destroy the vile things, nor can we keep them from the greedy hands of men who seek power and dominion."

"But we must try," Isarn said as he began to descend the stairs.

"To what end? All will be swallowed in darkness, all life has its end in death. As long as the Dark Artifacts exist in this world, our fate is poisoned. It is only vanity that would have you think otherwise." Isirah folded his arms. "Go, kill Draegan, and kill Kelthus Artel sitting in his nest in Corvus. Keeping killing and what will you gain? A brief reprieve from the inescapable doom of Athar. A chance to bask in your self-importance as the hero who saved the peoples of Athar, though they still march blindly to their inevitable doom."

"And you would have me stay here, dusting books and mopping floors?"

"I would have you accept the truth. Whether it is this year or ten thousand years from now, the Artifacts will have their victory over man, because man is frail, greedy, vain, and prideful."

Isarn stopped at the bottom of the stairs and looked at his master. Though he was still powerful, he could see how old age was slowly creeping upon him, bending Isirah's back, softening him and making him weaker.

"Is this why you didn't stand against Draegan twenty one years ago when you had the chance? Or are you simply bitter at your cowardice and use this untenable rhetoric to support your lack of heart?"

Isirah chuckled softly, though there was no humor in his voice. "I truly have failed you. Do what you will. Go then."

"I go with hope in my heart. I go with the conviction that I can make this a better world. I go with the belief that even if I can only stay the doom of Athar for a short time, than this time is the most precious gift that I can give to the people of Fyrian and to my brothers and sisters in Vatn," he said as he walked toward Isirah. "And I would go with your blessing."

Isirah looked at Isarn and sighed. A slight smile spread across his sun burnt face, the wrinkles in his leathery skin making him appear much older. "I wish you well."

Isarn bowed and left the library in a hurry, his robes snapping behind him as he ran down the hall to the armory to prepare for his journey.

Chapter 26: The House of Corvus

It had been four days since Isarn left the sanctuary. He'd left the island he'd spent nearly his entire life on shortly after nightfall in a small boat and worked his way northeast as he rowed against the winter winds and through the white capped peaks of the frigid ocean. It had stormed during the second night, sending him off course from his destination of the western shore of Corvus. He had spent most of his third day bailing his small craft and correcting his course such that he found himself near landfall that night.

By dawn of the fourth day he had sunk his waterlogged boat a few miles off shore and swam with his light pack to the gray cliffs that rose from the sea. Dripping and freezing he found a small sandbar that sheltered him from the wind as he dried out his clothes and pack.

"I can't risk a fire," he said as he sat with his back straight against the frigid cliff wall, staring out over the churning sea. He sat perfectly still and regulated his breathing, closing his eyes and chanting softly under his breath. Slowly, his body relaxed and he stopped shaking from the freezing wind as his core temperature rose.

Throughout the day he meditated as his belongings dried out. In the evening, as the light began to dim behind the leaden clouds that obscured the once blue sky, Isarn rose and collected his possessions. He wore gray leather pants tucked into black boots that rose to his knee. Under his gray woolen tunic he wore a small hauberk of finely wrought chains he had forged himself under the guidance of Isirah years ago. Under cover of darkness they had taken it to the River of Falling Light that flowed from the White Temple in the center of Vatn and Isirah had blessed the mail in the crystal waters, though he had chided Isarn to not place too much faith in his empty words.

Isarn smiled and felt the mail slide softly over his silken shirt. His costume as a disciple of the Rookery with his short black cloak and gray clothes was deceptively simple. In his boots he carried two dirks and slung over his shoulder was a short bow and quiver of black fletched arrows. His leather belt held a special scabbard that Isirah had given him before he left. Cradled in the small of his back were Bhel and Asai. Isirah had told him how the scabbard was imbued with the same otherworldly metal as the blades, masking their magic when carried securely in the sheath. This would allow him to weave signs and cast enchantments without interference from the peculiar properties of the twin blades of the Vaghat.

He packed little for his journey, carrying only medicinal herbs and poultices as well as a few vials of powder that could not be found in the fens of Corvus. Isarn carried no sleeping mat or blanket, no food, nor means to prepare any in his small rucksack. This lack of extraneous gear allowed him to easily scale the sheer wall of sandstone behind him without undue weight. Through the evening and into the night he climbed unaided until a few hours before dawn when he pulled himself over the precipice.

Isarn felt the salty air that had been buffeting him all night mix with the cold air blowing across the marsh. A light rain began to fall as he searched for cover. He headed for a strand of stunted swamp oaks a few hundred yards inland from the cliff, where he could still hear the waves crashing against the sandstone wall. He took off his pack and sat against the trunk of a nearby tree, flexing his bloody hands in the darkness. Taking a small tin of paste from his pack he applied it liberally and settled in against the rain that had begun to come down harder. He awoke three hours later at first light. His hands had begun to mend while he slept. Pleased with the salve's progress, he broke camp, removing all traces of his presence and headed due east at a steady jog.

The Rookery lay outside the capital city of Rhyke, in the swamps at the base of the Spire of Heaven Mountains. He would need to make his way across the fens of Corvus unseen, and then enter the Rookery where the Black Horn was kept. The disciples and masters of the Rookery were the most feared mages in all of Fyrian, yet Isarn smiled to himself and felt reassured when he placed his hand under his cloak and felt the handles of the Vaghat.

"Soon I will test you, Bhel and Asai. The Ravens of Corvus will make fine sport."

Traveling through the marshes, it was a trivial matter to collect and purify water. He took one rabbit at dusk and after cleaning it in a small stream lined with sparse pines, he ate it raw, loathe to risk drawing attention with a fire. Isarn moved through the night, finding solid ground to carry him through the swamps until a few hours after midnight, when he crested a small hillock and decided to move out of the driving rain. He made his way into a valley and found an outcropping of boulders that sheltered him from the worst of the downpour while he slept.

The following morning as he broke through a stand of pines shortly after sunrise, he saw two figures walking along a footpath that followed a slight ridge rising from the marsh. They were silhouetted in the morning light, both carrying large packs and baskets as they trudged slowly up the slight incline. Isarn moved closer, careful to keep out of their sight.

"What's wrong with the marsh down by Telkyn's farm? If we'd have just gone there, then we wouldn't have to slog so far in the rain," the man in the rear complained. He was roughly Isarn's age, though shorter and thinner. He carried a shovel and a pick axe in addition to a large rattan basket strapped to his back, the size of which caused him to stoop almost as much as the old man in the front.

"The bank's been worked out completely is what's wrong with it. The Rookery needs peat for fuel, not mud with some moss in it," the older man replied. "We're heading up to the mire by Telkyn's brother's farm."

"Fyn," the younger man replied. "Fyn's farm."

"Aye, and we're paying that buzzard too much to dig if you ask me. Telkyn must have told him how much he charged and now he's squeezing us hard."

Isarn followed the two for another quarter mile in silence, moving unseen through the sedge on the side of the footpath. He had met them as the path turned south then east and found following much easier than forging through the fens directly. After following the older man for some time in silence, the younger one spoke.

"There's no living in this," he said and stopped to adjust the straps on his back. "Those men at the tavern we heard the other night, that's how to make money."

The old man stopped and waited while the other reslung his basket and tightened the buckle. "You think working the drainage pipes of the Rookery is better than this?" The old man said and waved his hands emphatically in front of him. "Out here at least you're free. Once you go into the Rookery you're not your own master anymore. They let you out once a month. That's a bad sign. There's dark magic in that place."

"You're superstitious. It's a fair wage for the work they do. You heard them talking the same as I did. The Rookery is built in a fen and they use conduits or channels or something to keep the water from building up and seeping into the place. When something breaks or gets clogged those men get paid to go out and take care of it." He tested the straps and started walking again. "At least you'd be out of this rain."

"Conduits? They can call it what they want, but it's still a sewage tunnel, young fool. They have to put all that mess somewhere, and you want to be the one to deal with it?" The old man grunted and turned back up the path. "I'd rather dig in this dirt than dig in the filth they wash out of that cursed place." He spat and kept walking. "And what are we doing with all these Ravens anyway? We don't hire them out to the other Kingdoms anymore, so what good do they do us? You ask me," he said gesturing toward his chest, "that place is going to be shut down by the Council of Rune."

Isarn paused in the rushes and let the two men continue walking out of earshot. "I remember reading about that in the histories," he said. While the two men bickered about the future of the Kingdom, and the quickest way to get rich, Isarn thought back to the lessons Isirah had taught him and the books he had read. The Rookery was constructed shortly after the founding of the House of Corvus. Given this kingdom's unfortunate climate and limited natural resources, people from the House of Corvus became adept at magic, having little else to offer as a means of defending themselves. The great kingdom of Skeldus to the east had vast fertile farmland, as well as the largest standing army of the five kingdoms, while the Clan of the Iron Mountains to the North, though lacking the rich earth of Skeldus, had much more land and many more people which kept Corvus always under threat of attack or invasion.

So the Council of Rune, the ruling body of Corvus, quickly saw its unenviable position as the smallest and weakest of the five kingdoms and founded the Rookery to train its people in the magical arts, which was their sole means of protection. But it was not long before those in power found another use for the disciples of the Rookery. It was no secret that the Ravens produced by the harsh training of the Rookery made the best spies, and they quickly became a coveted commodity by all the kingdoms in Fyrian. For centuries Corvus profited by selling their Ravens to the other kingdoms. However, for the past twenty years, the House of Corvus had closed its borders and kept its disciples close to home rather than sell them to the highest bidder. Thus they accumulated a powerful army, well versed in the magical arts and now the Kingdom of Corvus was no longer the easy prey it once was. Once the favored battleground for newly risen War Chiefs to assert their power and the puppet of those ruling in Dullahan, Corvus was now mostly spared the border skirmishes that had plagued them until the rise of the Usurper.

"The Rookery itself is thousands of years old," Isarn thought. "Sage Corvus carved it from the granite cliffs of the Spire of Heaven Mountains three thousand years ago. As someone who dwelt underground I know that living in solid rock requires ventilation and a means to pass waste. There must be forgotten ways to enter and exit that have long since passed from memory," Isarn paused and smiled. "And the drainage system those men spoke of promises to be one."

Isarn moved through the fens through the afternoon, never pausing and heading always west. The sporadic rain kept travelers off the roads and the few people Isarn saw never noticed him as he slipped easily through the cattails and sedge that lined the hundreds of pools. By evening he had passed into another forest of swamp oaks and stunted pines that brought him to the edge of the Dosan River. The Dosan had its headwaters in the Spire of Heaven Mountains and ran northwest where it emptied into Lantern Bay. It acted as a natural border between the House of Corvus and the Clan of the Iron Mountains and it was the source of many disputes, skirmishes and even wars between the two kingdoms.

"The Rookery must empty its sewage through the marsh and into the Dosan," Isarn said as he peered into the greenish-gray waters that flowed lazily by him in the dimming light of the setting sun. The rain which had stopped during the afternoon began again as the temperature dropped.

Isarn followed the river, staying back from the bank and under the cover offered by the reeds and scrub trees that grew along its edge. He continued through the night, encountering no opposition in the form of patrols, magical seals or barriers. By dawn he had covered many miles and saw the outline of the mountains ahead of him as the sky lightened to the foreboding iron gray that was so familiar in Corvus. He stayed tucked in a stand of pines as the sun rose, further etching the mountains against the sky and giving him enough light to make out the Rookery across the river.

"So there it is, the training ground for Fyrian's most powerful mages," Isarn said as he looked across the Dosan at the gray granite wall that soared hundreds of feet into the air, its top lost in the low hanging clouds that blanketed the land. "And my proving ground." He reached behind him and felt calmed as he touched the handles of his twin daggers.

He rested and watched the Rookery from his vantage point under the pines and across the river. On the far side of the river there was a small patch of marshland that ran up to the base of the escarpment. In it he saw carven channels lined with stone that emptied into the Dosan. The channels were open at the top, though where they penetrated the cliff wall they were barred and gated. Higher up on the wall he saw barred openings that served as ventilation chambers. After an hour of waiting, Isarn saw several of the vents open, the metal doors making a grinding noise as they retracted into the wall. He heard a great sucking sound as the air rushed in and watched as the gates closed after a few minutes.

"There isn't enough time to scale the wall and make it into the vents," he said as he looked around him. "It looks like my only way in is the drainage system."

Isarn continued to scan the sheer wall of granite for any weakness. There were few windows carved in the cliff face, and those were hundreds of feet up, nearly covered by the clouds. At the base of the mountain, between the channels and sunk deep into the granite wall, a large gate was shut tight with heavy iron doors. At no time did anyone enter or exit by the gate. As the day wore on, he began to doubt his plan when he heard a metallic groaning and saw the bars of the channel lifting into the walls. A surge of waste came pouring from the opening and slid down the channels where it spilled into the Dosan and muddied the waters before it was swept downstream. Birds that had been roosting in the trees above him began to dive into the water and return to their perches with small fish that had come to the surface to feed.

He smiled. "So I'm going to have to get dirty."

Isarn sat and watched the Rookery all afternoon and timed the opening of the air vents and the release of waste. The vents opened every hour whereas the drainage gates only rose every fourth hour.

"They should open shortly after midnight," Isarn said, looking behind him to try and gage the time from the position of the obscured sun. It hadn't stopped raining all day and he was soaked to the bone. "I'll head in before they open and be ready to swim in when they do." He looked at his soaked clothing and shook his head. "I guess I'm not going to dry out until I get back to the enclave."

It was four hours before midnight when Isarn took off his boots and hid them under some pine boughs along with his pack and cloak. A few hundred yards upstream of the drainage channels he found a large rotting log along the bank and pushed it into the frigid waters of the Dosan, slipping in silently behind it as the cold of the water shocked his senses. He swam underneath it, holding his breath as he guided the log across the river. When he reached the other side of the river he came up a few feet above the channel outlet and clung to the bank, taking deep breaths, and keeping the log from slipping downstream. He came to the mouth of the upper drainage channel and wedged it in at an angle. When he heard the iron bars begin to protest as they were raised into the cliff wall he took a deep breath and plunged to the bottom of the river.

Lifting a great stone from the river bed, Isarn brought it to the surface as quickly as he could and placed it on his shoulder. As he broke the surface he used all his strength to roll the boulder into the mouth of the channel and rammed it against the log. He heard the bars lock into place and the thumping of an unseen machine that always preceded the rush of sludge down the channel. He dove again and brought up another rock, wedging it beside the first. He heard the onrushing waters and dove again, surfacing with another rock just as the sludge impacted the other two boulders. The force of the collision pushed the boulders slightly out of the channel, but they caught on the log and jammed themselves tighter together, forming a dam.

The sewage hit the obstruction and began to spray Isarn with considerable force. He grabbed onto the log and swung himself and the rock he carried on his shoulder into the channel. He placed the rock against the others, and was about to dive back in and cross when he heard something slam into his hastily built dam. He looked past the log and saw a pale shape in the darkness.

"A hand," he whispered. His eyes followed it back to see the bent and mangled body to which it was attached. "So the rumors are true. They flush more than sewage." He shook his head and slipped back into the water, diving to the bottom and crossing the Dosan once again.

On the opposite shore he slipped back into the scrub wood and waited, trying to find a spot out of the rain. "This is a miserable country," he said as he lay down in the fallen pine needles and watched the cliff wall.

He awoke a few hours later to a sound he couldn't place. He looked at the Rookery and saw the great iron doors in the cliff wall begin to part. A bluish light poured from the opening and he saw several figures emerge into the marshlands ringed in by the Dosan. He heard voices but couldn't make out words.

"Now's my chance," he said, and taking his pack, he ran upstream and slipped into the freezing water as the figures crossed the fen to the edge of the river. Isarn came up a few yards below the bottom channel and hugged the bank. As he did so he heard voices drift toward him. He controlled his breathing while he listened to the conversation taking place above him.

"This one's clear. Must be the other."

He heard groaning and cursing as the voices faded along with their footfalls. In a few minutes he heard them again and saw the bluish light casting a reflection out onto the water.

"Here's the blockage," came the same voice as before. "Storm must have washed this debris downstream."

Isarn pushed off the bank and looked out past the overhang. He saw a slim figure standing near the mouth of the drainage channel casting an illumination spell. The man stood directly under it and was well lit enough for Isarn to see he was dressed as a disciple of the Rookery. The four men standing near him were common laborers carrying axes, staves and shovels.

"Let's make this quick before they open the grate," the disciple said.

"Tonight's our lucky night," came a rougher voice as Isarn saw the four men descend into the channel. "We got a body."

"You know him, Raven?" one shouted up at the disciple.

The disciple leaned over the edge of the rock lined ditch and spat. "No, one of their failed experiments I'd say. Now hurry up and let's get out of this rain.

"A little water ruining your feathers?" came the same gruff voice. Isarn heard the others laugh.

"When that grate opens in three minutes we'll see who's laughing," the disciple shot back.

Isarn moved back to the bank and peered into the empty channel upstream. "They may not break any protective seals and barriers on these channels when they flush their waste, but they certainly must have taken down their enchantments for the work detail." He heard the grate begin to retract and he pulled himself up into the rock lined channel. Downstream he heard the workers yelling and scrambling to get out of the way of the oncoming sewage. Ducking low, Isarn sped up the opposite, empty channel as far as he could until he heard the mechanical thumping. He dropped and flattened himself on the ground. He placed his hands on one side and anchored his feet on the other, pushing as hard as he could to make his body as rigid as possible. He heard the rushing waste coming down the channel and held his breath.

It poured over him, knocking him loose and tumbling him several yards down the channel until he managed to catch hold of a rock that protruded slightly from the wall. As the sludge passed, the pressure relented and he took a breath. He swam upstream against the lessening current.

At the base of the cliff where the channel met the grate, the water level had lowered enough that he could stand and trudge the remaining few yards on foot. He strode ahead just as the gate began to lower, rolling under the bars as they slipped into sockets drilled into the ground. He was inside a tunnel not much over four feet in diameter. He moved forward in total darkness, hunched over and feeling along the walls for any variation that might aid him in finding his way out. Several times he felt panels that were locked in place. "There must be other tunnels or pipes that connect to this one," he said as he kept running, wasting no time trying to open them.

After a few minutes of running through the filth that had failed to drain from the tunnel, he heard voices echoing ahead.

"Hurry it up, the basin's going to refill soon."

"I can't see anything."

Isarn saw a light ahead and ran straight for it, his boots sloshing in the waste.

"Wait. I hear something."

"That's just the other waste chambers echoing through the main pipe. We're all connected together. Now do you see a cloak or not?"

As Isarn approached the light he felt his boot tramp on something uneven. In the faint light from the opening ahead, he saw a filthy and torn woolen cloak, much like his own, caught on a small projection from the rock wall. "Must be from the dead student," he said quietly. He quickly picked it up, ran the last hundred feet to the opening and poked his head up and into the light.

The man looking down the tunnel screamed and fell backward, kicking and clawing as he tried to put distance between himself and Isarn, who had sprung from the opening.

"The dead've come back," he yelled his eyes white with terror as Isarn pulled himself from the tunnel opening and stood in the bottom of a twenty foot diameter basin that was roughly seven feet deep.

Isarn heard laughter and looked up to see another man standing at the far lip of the basin.

"That's not the dead, you fool. We flush the dead out of here naked, not dressed as disciples." The man at Isarn's feet stopped scrambling backward and began to rise cautiously. "Probably some poor soul who fell in the basin of another emptying chamber."

"I found this," Isarn said, holding out the filth covered cloak.

The terrified man reached forward tentatively and then snatched the garment from his grasp. He looked it over and nodded. "It'll be fine once I clean it up." He looked up at Isarn. "How'd you end up here?"

"You two quit chatting and get out of there fast before they start filling this basin back up," the man on the far wall shouted.

A moment later Isarn was standing at the edge of the basin, dripping with filth and introducing himself. "Telkyn," Isarn said, holding out his dripping hand, which neither of the other two men took.

"So they must have sent you down to one of the emptying chambers on punishment detail. I see you decided to take a dip." The larger of the two men chuckled and looked Isarn over. "I'm Raff and this is Tab," he said gesturing to the man beside him. "Never seen you before. This your first time in trouble?"

Isarn nodded and looked around the room. "Yes, I'm in trouble indeed," he said as he looked for exits from the dimly lit hall in which he stood dripping. The room was narrow with only a few feet of space around the basin carved in the floor. Pipes twisted down from the ceiling and ended several feet above the bowl of the basin. At the bottom of the bowl Isarn saw the opening he had crawled through along with several other valves which were shut. At the rear of the room he noticed a wooden door and several levers on the floor next to it.

"Down the hall on the right is the gray water collection tank," Raff said while he looked at the tattered cloak Tab was holding. "You better get back before you're missed." Raff turned back to see the door at the end of the hall closing.

"He sure didn't waste any time," Tab said. "Nearly scared me to death, him popping out of the drain valve like that."

"Why'd you go down there after that old Raven's cloak anyway?

"They weave magic into the cloth. Even a scrap like this is bound to have some enchantment."

"I hope it has an enchantment to keep it from smelling so foul," Raff said as he pushed away from Tab and his new treasure.

Chapter 27: An Encounter in the Rookery

In the dimly lit hall Isarn noticed a group of workers engaged in muted conversation as they headed toward him. He bowed his head and walked by in silence as he passed. They paid him no heed and Isarn soon reached the end of the corridor. He pushed open the door to the gray water collection room and entered. He exited moments later, having cleaned himself in the tank and dried his clothes with a simple enchantment.

The hall was empty. Isarn heard the mechanical thumping he'd listened to many times as he waited in the tree line across the Dosan River. He made his way to the stairwell at the end of the hall, and in the darkened corner of the landing he used a *topos* spell to make out his surroundings. He froze in place. Three times the size of the Clade's sanctuary and far more complex in its layout, Isarn felt overwhelmed. The Rookery wasn't built around a central hall but rather was a disorienting series of chambers stacked on top of each other. The byzantine layout had more than several corridors that doubled back on themselves and many others that ended in solid rock. But even through the dizzying layout he felt the presence of the Black Horn many stories above him and deep within the granite walls of the cliff, kept toward the interior of the mountain. There was a massive staircase close to what he guessed to be the center of the Rookery, but it ended a few stories below the upper levels. Deep within the cliff face was a smaller stairwell that appeared to climb further toward the top.

"The small stairwell is my only option," he said as he climbed the flight of stairs up from the landing, leaving the humming of the sewage machinery behind. In a flash he slipped down a corridor that emptied into a grand hall. It was one of the largest rooms in the Rookery and had six massive fireplaces along its flanks and one at the far end. The ceiling rose sixty feet and was supported by two rows of columns that carried the stone ribs of the sweeping arches. The hall was dim, and only one fire burned at the far end of the dim space. Three figures were framed by the orange flickering light, talking softly though their voices carried far enough that Isarn could hear them. The floor of the hall was filled with long wooden tables and benches, ordered in tight rows.

"This must be where they eat. They could easily fill this space with one thousand disciples. It's big enough to hold the great hall of the sanctuary with room to spare."

He moved quickly across the width of the grand hall, unseen by the talking men, to a similar staircase which he took down into another dimly lit corridor. This hall was a mirror of the one that he had recently left but rather than doors leading to drainage rooms and cisterns this hall was lined with barred portals. Isarn peered through the grate of the nearest room and saw it was simply an empty cell. He continued on, every cell the same, empty.

"Perhaps an old prison, unneeded for these past twenty years, as no kingdom has attacked Corvus and given them cause to fill their cells."

He pushed to the end of the corridor and encountered a heavy wooden door braced with thick bands of iron. It was locked, but sealed with no magic. He took a small ampoule from his belt and crushed it against the rusty keyhole in the center of the door. He placed his thumb over the opening and spoke a word. He felt the liquid begin to get hot and removed his thumb to see a puff of smoke escape from the locking mechanism. A moment later he heard a bubbling sound and knew the liquid had melted away the delicate metalwork inside the lock. He grabbed the rusty lever and lifted it slowly. It made only the slightest noise as the gears inside the door began to move, retracting the bolts that held the door in place.

In an instant he was through the door and passed into another corridor that turned right at the end of the hall and then right again, where he descended curving stairs into a deeper part of the Rookery. The air grew damp and cold as he came to the bottom of the stairs. "I hate to go lower in this place when the Black Horn lies so far above me, but this feels to be the only way to get to the hidden staircase." In front of him a large portcullis blocked his path. Beyond it another corridor stretched into darkness. He checked for barriers and found an old spell still active in the bars of the portcullis.

Isarn smiled as he slid his hands into the small of his back and pulled Bhel and Asai from their sheaths. The moment he felt the blades glide from their scabbard the barrier began to unravel. By the time he held the blades in front of him, glowing faintly in the dark corridor, the enchantment on the bars had vanished. He slid the daggers back into their sheath and gripped the bottom of the gate. Planting his legs he locked his arms and set his back, lifting the gate slightly to test its weight. The old iron protested at first, groaning loudly, but it began to move as he heaved upward. When there was an opening large enough he slipped under the bars. Once through, he spun and caught the weight of the portcullis as it dropped, lowering it softly into the holes chiseled into the flagstone floor. He turned down the hall and pulled the daggers from his back. They gave a faint light, enough to see in the consuming darkness. He saw cells on either side of the vaulted corridor. Walking silently past them he saw the cells were empty, but ahead in the darkness he heard a faint rustling.

"A rat," he said as he slowed to pinpoint the location of the sound. He approached the cell ahead cautiously, but as he neared, the faint rustling turned to banging. Isarn stopped and waited. The banging noise intensified and soon it was joined by a pained moaning. He took a step forward and saw a red hand shoot into the corridor from behind the iron bars ahead of him. Isarn's eyes widened as he saw hand after hand reach through the grate, some clawing frantically at the air while others grabbed the bars and tried desperately to shake them loose. "Obviously I was mistaken, but even so how many can be trapped in such a small cell?"

He waited a moment longer, watching the clawing hands before curiosity overtook him and he stepped forward to get a better look. As he approached the chamber he saw the source of the tortured cries. Chained to the wall behind the bars was a creature composed of the flayed corpses of several men haphazardly fused together with bands of iron and coarse stitches of leather. Torsos and limbs were joined at impossible angles. The monstrosity's entrails dragged through the straw lining its prison, as it struggled to pull itself up on its various legs using the bars of its prison as support. Its many mouths hissed and spat at Isarn as he stared in awe at the monster. The creature howled and gnashed its teeth as it was alternately attracted to and repulsed by the light from his blades.

"I sense many tortured souls within that living host of decaying flesh," Isarn said as he stepped closer to the cell. Twisted hands lashed out, missing Isarn's throat by inches. He stood still and watched as the beast began to lower itself to the floor and moan. It made an almost human utterance as it exhaled plaintively through its many mouths.

Isarn recoiled in horror. "It speaks," he said. "This must be one of the failed experiments I've heard about. Isirah told me how the Rookery had begun to practice blood magic in the last forty years, but I didn't believe him." The beast lay its broken, bloody body down on the straw covered flagstones and tore at its own flesh with its myriad arms.

"Whatever dark magic binds you to life I will sever and speed you on your way to what little peace I can give you," Isarn said as he approached the cell with Bhel and Asai pulsing in the dark before him. The creature thrashed on the floor, trying to pull itself closer to Isarn. He plunged the blades between the bars and sunk them deep into the tortured creature. The beast made no attempt to defend itself. It shuddered before it exhaled in relief one final time and slumped to the floor, dead.

Isarn wiped the blades on his boots and rose to continue down the hall when he started at a sudden noise ahead of him. A wailing moan was joined by shrieks from the cells in front of him.

Isarn froze as the clamor grew to a din. Creatures began to stir and awaken, adding to the riot of noise that echoed in the dank, fetid corridor. "I must escape this dungeon. I have not the time to tarry here and give peace to all of the Rookery's abominations," he said and moved quickly through the darkness, his blades casting a pale glow to guide him. From the corner of his eyes he saw shapes and shadows torn from nightmares. Claws and tentacles grasped at him as he sped past. He raised his blade to send the light further ahead and saw a creature from the corner of his eye, vaguely human but with lidless eyes covering its pallid body. It opened its gaping mouth and shrieked as the light from the blades of the Vaghat passed over its twisted form.

He pushed on, stumbling through the corridor of horrors until he came to a heavy iron door that blocked his progress. He held Bhel and Asai near the door, but felt no trace of magic. "Another mechanical lock," he said. He sheathed his daggers and took another ampoule from his belt, crushing it into the keyhole in the door. Repeating the same incantation from before with his thumb over the hole he felt the liquid become warm and begin to corrode the inner mechanisms of the lock. After a minute of waiting he unsheathed the blades of the Vaghat and pushed gently on the door, testing for any hidden locks that would spring shut if a key wasn't used to open the portal. The wailing from the creatures in the dungeon had lessened while the light from the blades was extinguished, but resumed once the Vaghat began to glow in the darkness.

Isarn shouldered the door open, its rusty hinges giving way as he strained against them. He quickly shut the door behind him, muting the din behind him. He looked ahead and saw a faint light bathing a set of stairs in green as they curved up and out of sight.

"The stairwell at last," Isarn said, recalling what he had learned from the *topos* spell. "This should carry me to the top of the Rookery." He moved to the end of the hall and ascended the curving stairs for several stories until he came to a landing on which stood a door beneath a large arch. The door was carved from stone and had several runes etched in its surface. Isarn peered at them, and as the light of his blades fell across the stone, he saw another set of runes appear beneath the first.

"This is the old tongue of Corvus, from the days when the Sages themselves walked in Athar. I cannot read it, though I doubt anything but doom awaits beyond that door."

He continued up the stairs, bypassing several other landings with similar doors whose inscriptions spoke of ancient times. At last the stairs curved around a final time and emptied into a hall lit with a green light that pulsed gently from shallow grooves carved into the walls. Before him was a simple barrel-vaulted corridor with two pairs of wooden doors on opposite sides of the arch. At the end of the hall a small alcove housed a life-sized statue of Sage Corvus holding aloft a lantern.

"Sage Corvus the All Seeing," Isarn said moving from the landing to the shadows nearer the wall. He felt the Black Horn was close but was unable to pinpoint its exact location. "It feels near, as if it's on this floor, but behind which door?"

Looking again at the doors and the alcove, he noticed a shadowy mass lying on the ground near the base of the statue. He approached and saw the figures of two dead disciples lying motionless on the flagstones. They wore the same cloak and shirt as he did and were indistinguishable except for a red epaulet on their shoulders, denoting a special assignment.

"They've been killed recently though there is no blood," he said as he examined their corpses. He placed his hand against one of the bodies and recoiled in horror. "There is no soul." He looked around him and stared into the shadows. "There is only one weapon in all of Athar that could have killed these men in this manner. But where is the Usurper?"

Isarn drew a breath and shut his eyes, quieting his mind and slowing his heart. "There, behind the statue. I feel a slight current of air moving," he said and snapped open his eyes. "What secret do you hide Sage Corvus?" he said as he checked the statue for hidden switches. He found one and wove a sign to read for enchantments. Smiling, he slipped the blades from their sheath and felt the spell dissolve before him. Isarn reached up and grabbed the lantern that Corvus held outstretched before him, twisting it slightly. He felt the stone grinding as it moved slightly in the statue's hand. There was a small click and Isarn stood aside as the statue of Sage Corvus began to swing outward into the corridor, revealing a small chamber.

He entered the small room cautiously, looking around the dim space as he placed each foot gently before the other. The room was a perfectly hollowed cube of smooth black marble, devoid of ornamentation and windows. A single red orb was suspended a few inches from the ceiling, bathing the chamber in a ruddy light. In the center of the room a small pedestal rose from the black marble floor and on it rested the Black Horn of Malthier the Hideous.

"You're too late, disciple. The Artifact is mine," Draegan said as he stepped from the shadows and into the center of the room, his cloak trailing behind him as the black flames of his sword crackled in the still air of the chamber. Draegan rushed at Isarn aiming for his head, but as he swung Isarn twisted out of the way, dodging the hungry flames and jumping to the far corner of the room. Draegan circled him and stood in front of the exit, blocking Isarn's escape.

"You're quick, Raven, but now you're trapped."

Isarn ground his teeth and reached behind him, drawing the Vaghat in a single fluid motion. Bhel and Asai flared to life, lighting the room and blinding Draegan. Isarn threw himself at Draegan, his daggers slashing and plunging in a vicious series of strikes that drove Draegan back and out of the chamber, stumbling and struggling into the hall, desperately dodging each blow. Draegan leapt back putting some distance between himself and Isarn. Isarn paused and glowered at Draegan, his daggers casting an eerie light over his hardened features.

"I know not what cheap enchantment you've placed on your blades, disciple, but I assure you they will not stand against the fury of Carnis Fornax."

"The Vaghat will be your doom Usurper," Isarn said through clenched teeth. "I had thought to gain the Black Horn to lure you to me, but now I see there is no need. I shall simply kill you here."

Again Isarn plunged at Draegan, raining murderous blows which Draegan struggled to parry. The flame of his sword guttered in the dim hall, extinguishing completely for a moment which allowed Isarn's blade to pass through his defense and strike a glancing blow with the flat of the blade. Draegan retreated further and collected himself as he stared aghast at his sword, which flared back to life.

"You are no crow," Draegan said, moving forward cautiously and keeping his eyes locked on Isarn.

"I am Isarn, the Holy Iron, forged in the crucible of the Clade and I am your end, old man."

"I do not know how you found me or why you hunt me, but the Artifact is mine. Stand aside or die."

Draegan rushed at Isarn and brought his sword down in a wide arc, forcing Isarn to back toward the statue of Corvus. He swung madly, charging forward and forcing Isarn to retreat past the statue and into the chamber holding the Horn. Isarn caught the flaming blade in his crossed daggers. As the flames touched the Vaghat they sputtered and extinguished.

Draegan had placed his weight behind the blow, and now that the blade had vanished, he tumbled forward into Isarn and they both sprawled onto the flagstones. Isarn kicked Draegan off and each scrambled to his feet, Isarn slashing at Draegan as he rose. Draegan sprinted past the statue of Corvus and into the chamber. Isarn quickly followed, entering the red tinged room moments after Draegan had grasped the Black Horn from the pedestal and spun around to meet him. Isarn leapt into the air and brought both blades down at Draegan's throat with all his force. Draegan ducked to the ground and placed his palm on the floor as the glowing blades carved a murderous streak through the air, directly at his head. A swirling black cloud rose around him, blanketing his vision and slowing time as he felt the room contract. Through the haze he watched as the two curving blades cut a swath through the mist. He turned to avoid them but couldn't move as he felt his body pulled and stretched.

Isarn sunk his blades up to the guard into the black marble of the floor. He pulled them out and slashed at the black vapor, watching it dissipate as he felt it chill his bones. "I missed him." He looked over the room and turned to peer down the hall. "I still feel the Artifact, but where is he?"

He turned and ran down the corridor away from the chamber and kicked a wooden door. It splintered as it fell from its hinges and smashed to the floor. Isarn looked up and saw Draegan standing on a mahogany desk, smiling as he finished strapping the horn to his back. He winced as the cord from the horn dug into his wounded shoulder. Draegan clapped his hand to his arm and placed the other on the top of the desk.

"I don't know what magic you wield, stranger, but wounding me is quite an accomplishment. Yet for all your luck, still you reek of inexperience, and now the Artifact is lost to you." A cloud of black mist swallowed Draegan and he was gone.

Isarn shouted and threw the daggers into the black vapor, sprinting after them even as they left his grasp. Both blades of the Vaghat plunged into the roiling cloud of darkness and were lost for a moment before they shot out and stuck into the wall behind the desk, pinning an emerald colored tapestry to the rock wall. Isarn slammed his fists onto the desk in frustration. Drawing a deep breath, he circled the desk and pulled the Vaghat from the wall and slid them silently into the sheath in the small of his back.

Isarn looked down and saw a body crumpled on the floor behind the desk, his throat slit and eyes rolled back into his head.

"Dead for only a few minutes," he said as he placed a hand on the still warm corpse. He rose and saw a crumpled paper near the side of the desk. Isarn picked it up, and smoothing it on the desk, saw it was penned in a script largely unknown to him. He read what parts he could in the faint light pouring in from the corridor but the letter ended with a large rune whose meaning escaped him.

"It must be the tongue of Iss," he said and thought for a moment as he looked around the study. "Draegan sent this missive to Kelthus Artel and then used the sheave of paper to Shadow Walk into his study and kill him moments before he made his way to the Black Horn. Then he used this parchment to run from me, no doubt back to Dullahan." Isarn picked up the paper and crushed it in his hand, and with a whispered word it burst into flames. He let the ashes fall from his hand. "Then I shall hunt him in the cursed land of Skeldus, and this time he shall not escape me."

He exited the room and slipped down the hall toward the stairs, disappearing into the darkness of the stairwell.

Chapter 28: The Gate Opens

Draegan collapsed in his chair and clutched at his shoulder. He slipped the Black Horn onto the desk and winced as he pulled back his shirt to examine his wound.

"Perhaps Vangen was misinformed, and this trinket I wear is no Talisman of Light," he said touching the Great Aegis he wore at his neck. "I took the full brunt of a tundra beast charging into my chest with little more than a bruise, yet here nothing more than a carving knife has cut me as neatly as roast ham." He looked at his shoulder and saw the wound went deeper than he had thought. "The child was fast and had some skill with those blades, though his ability to stop my sword and confuse my Shadow Walking is most disturbing. I have seen nothing like it before, even from Vangen and the horrors that dwell in the shadow lands."

He placed his hand over his shoulder and began chanting as he stared out the small window in the study, the morning light casting a warm glow through the soot covered glass. After a few moments he looked down at his shoulder and saw the wound had barely healed.

"There is some strange magic in those blades indeed, if I cannot even begin to heal a wound of this size," he said as he pulled open the drawers of the desk, searching for thread. Finding none he turned to the curio behind him and pushed aside several containers holding vials of brackish liquids and tins of foul smelling pastes. Toward the back, lying upon a velvet cushion, he found a needle next to some glimmering thread.

"This will have to suffice until I understand more about this strange man and his sorcery," he said, grinding his teeth as he pushed the needle through the skin of his shoulder and sutured it shut.

When he had finished his work he applied a salve to the wound and slipped out of the study and down the hall to his abandoned bedroom. There he rifled through the mountains of books that littered the floor searching for a particular tome that Vangen had given him soon after promoting him to the Graywalkers. He looked for hours, distracted by bitter memories of the past and the volumes of books and piles of scrolls he had collected during his service to Vangen, until shortly after noon when he found the book he was searching for.

He took it, along with several others, back to the study and locked himself in, reading incessantly over the next three days. He took notes on every empty scrap of paper he could find, often writing in the margins of books, or flipping over scrolls to write on the reverse. He did not sleep and cast several spells to keep feelings of hunger and fatigue at bay.

By morning of the fourth day he had read nearly all of Vangen's books, becoming fluent in the language of Iss. His head swam with all the information he consumed, the exegesis and marginalia comprising nearly as much if not more than the original texts themselves. Draegan had taken such copious notes that they spilled from the loose, random papers he had scrounged and begun to climb his own arms as he had resorted to using his flesh as paper.

"I'm no better than Ceredyn or any Raven at this point," he said, running his fingers over the spells written in the tongue of Iss snaking up his forearms and disappearing beneath his sleeves. "In truth I now read and write the tongue of Iss so fluently I begin to question how I compare to Vangen." He thought for a moment, and then whispered, "Vangen. I will always stand against him as long as he attempts to force his twisted vision of order upon the innocent people of Fyrian." He looked at the Black Horn lying on the desk, half buried in scrolls and sheaves of parchment. Draegan stared at the figures twisting down its length, partially obscured by pages torn from books and thought back to the shades that assailed him in the Ashen Wastes.

"I have found no evidence to show me that what Vangen told me in Iss holds any kernel of truth. I dare not guess as to whether or not the realm of Iss will break its seal and return to Athar for I could not possibly stop such devastation. But I know I must at least attempt to stop Vangen. I have failed my family, my friends and Fyrian already, but I will not fail in ending him. From his writings it is apparent that he can open a portal between our worlds, so his threat of invasion is real. His army must be growing, even as I tarry here." He pushed aside a pile of books from the desk, knocking them to the floor in order to clear a space on desk's surface. "Knowing now how he bound me when last we fought in this study, and seeing how effective it was on larger numbers when I tested it on the battalion in the Iron Mountains, I hope to expand its power and shackle his entire forces before they can march on Athar."

Draegan stood and circled the desk as he walked to the window, looking out upon the ruins of Dullahan. The morning sun lit the piles of rubble and half-crumbled towers, casting strange shadows over the inner courtyard. Snow covered the parts of the roof that still stood on the Night Watch's dormitory, and near the entrance he saw the snow dusted corpses of the three looters he had killed days earlier. He shook his head and sighed.

"But with all the dark Artifacts under my control, I hope to stop Vangen long before he floods my lands with his unliving army." Draegan turned from the window and looked around the study. "I must waste no more time. Vangen prepares for war and every moment here is a wasted opportunity to end his madness." He gathered a handful of loose papers and a few books, which he threw into a small pack. He waved his hand above his head, opening the hidden gate to the stairs that led to the catacombs and descended into the bowels of Dullahan.

***

Draegan let the dank air of the catacombs fill his lungs as he walked purposefully across the damp flagstones to the center of the great chamber. Before the great pile of rubble and the rotten corpse of the hideous beast he had slain twenty years ago he turned and headed down one of the numerous side passages. He lit no light, for his eyes had grown accustomed to the darkness. At the end of the tunnel he reached beneath a pile of moldering shrouds and retrieved several objects which he carried with him back to the center of the massive chamber. There in a pile he laid the four Dark Artifacts and stepped back.

"I do not know if my actions will ultimately profit Athar, but I know if I do nothing to stand against Vangen, then all hope of peace is lost. He truly seeks to conquer Fyrian by raising the armies of Iss from the shadows and sending them here to wreak havoc, defying the Elder Gods. He is mad but he is also powerful beyond reckoning. I have little hope that these Artifacts can stop him, but for Fyrian, for peace, and for my people I must try."

Draegan marked a circle on the ground with the heel of his boot, and with his finger traced several runes around the perimeter. He tucked the handle of the Burning chains into his belt, opposite the hilt of Carnis Fornax. He slung the Dark Ichor over one shoulder and the World Render over the other, making sure it was balanced over his cloak. He sat in the circle and placed the Black Horn in his lap. He ran his fingers over the figures carved on its surface.

"I question whether the Black Horn will even be of use against soldiers who are unliving and know no fear." He tucked the horn into his pack and pulled on the string of the bow that ran across his chest. "And this hateful weapon that spreads death and disease cannot be used against Vangen's forces, for disease and sickness cannot kill what does not live."

He took his hunting knife from his boot and carefully cutting around a line of text written on his forearm, he dripped blood onto each of the symbols that lined the circle. He stood and took the hilt of his sword from his belt and lit the blade as he stared at the black flames leaping greedily before his face. The damp air of the catacombs became colder and Draegan saw his breath as he exhaled. He uttered dark words and the circle inscribed around him burst to life, flames reaching up toward Draegan as the blade shuddered in his hand, trying to escape the pull of the circle.

Draegan drove the blade deep into the center of the circle and felt the Artifact push against him as the flames of the spell drew the souls of those he had killed from within the hilt and consumed them. He watched the flames at his feet grow higher as the fire of the sword became weaker. Taking his dirk, he carefully traced a symbol already written in ink on his forearm. He watched the blood rise to the surface of his skin, pool, then run in a rivulet over the side of his arm and drip into the circle. The flames guttered for an instant, than flared back to life. "Once again into the land of shadows, this time to end Vangen."

"A noble sentiment, Usurper, but as you said before, you are too late."

Draegan turned and saw a figure clad in white robes with a scarlet hood approaching slowly from the staircase at the rear of the chamber.

"Isarn, I believe you called yourself. A strange name indeed, as it has the perfume of Vatn about it, but I see the cut and color of your cloth is different," Draegan said as he began to pull his sword slowly from the ground, readying himself for another battle. "Tell me Isarn, who are you and how did you find me?" His other hand began to slip toward his belt and the handle of the Burning Chains.

"Enough, Usurper," Isarn said as he raised his right hand over his head. Draegan instantly froze, unable to move as if he was bound by irons. "The last time we met you slipped from my grasp. This time I have taken precautions. A binding spell will be enough to prevent your Shadow Walking." Isarn walked toward Draegan, keeping a careful eye on him as he watched him twist frantically against the spell. He stood outside the circle, keeping clear of the flames that burned around Draegan's feet, and studied his prey.

Draegan tried to shift his weight as he struggled against the invisible bonds that held him. The spell was cast at a great distance and though powerful enough to hold him tight, he could still breathe. "You have changed your colors young Raven, but you still misunderstand. These Artifacts will never be yours. They belong to me, and now I'm afraid I must leave you once again."

He shouted a word in the foul tongue of Iss and instantly the red flames rose higher, licking at his body as the circle tightened around him. In a panic Isarn drew the blades from their sheath and raised them to strike down Draegan before he could complete the spell. Stepping into the circle he brought the weapons down toward Draegan's neck even as the flames sputtered.

"Again you are too late Isarn. I know not what deceit you use to unweave my spells, but this one has been written in my blood and can only be undone by my blood," Draegan said as he wheeled out of the way of the descending daggers. The use of the Vaghat had begun to unweave the binding spell as well as the opening of the portal to Iss. The moment Draegan felt the chains of the spell begin to loosen he twisted and raised his hands, catching Isarn's wrists in his vice-like grip.

"The spell is complete," Draegan whispered as he felt his body pulled and stretched. The fire turned black and the flames rose and swallowed Draegan, tearing him away from Isarn who stood dumbfounded in the cold black flames.

A moment later they flared again and consumed Isarn.

Chapter 29: The Shadow Lands

Draegan and Isarn tumbled through a great black void, falling and flying at incredible speed. Their bodies were bent and stretched in the utter darkness, though Isarn fought with all his strength to twist his body closer to Draegan as they careened through the abyss.

Isarn kept his hands locked around his blades, inching ever closer to Draegan as they were ripped across the void. Draegan lifted his hands and caught Isarn's wrist as one of the blades came slicing past his face. Isarn used Draegan as a fulcrum and wrenched his body around, plunging the other blade at Draegan's chest. Isarn's hand slowed mid-strike and the two were blown apart from each other, repulsed by some unseen force.

***

Draegan opened his eyes and lifted himself from the ground. He vomited into the dry dirt and stood, wiping his mouth. He saw he was in a basin, similar to the one surrounding the Red Keep, though this one was of a grayish hue, with no channels of magma carved through the earth.

Ahead he saw a great black fortress of iron split in half as if cleaved by the axe of some monstrous giant. Part of the structure was sunk in the ground and rested on the other half. Above both halves a large black obelisk floated gently, bound by massive chains. In the middle distance before him, strewn about the basin floor lay thousands of motionless soldiers, victims of some battle fought not long ago, for the dust had yet to settle. Pikes and spears jutted up from the slaughter at angles, many broken and splintered. A few banners hung limp in the still air, as lifeless as the soldiers they draped.

Draegan began moving forward, unsure of which direction to head in order to find Vangen, but hoping some gain might be had by inspecting the battlefield. As he strode across the ground, the Artifacts shifted uneasily on his person, digging into his flesh as he moved. He adjusted the axe and bow and pushed on, looking at the crimson sky with its seething leaden clouds as he scanned the wastes for any sign of life or movement. He vomited once more and thought back to the spell he'd cast in the catacombs.

"That spell was sealed with my blood. How is it possible that he could begin to unweave it, and then to follow me through to Iss?" Draegan turned and looked around him, checking for any sign of Isarn. Finding none he turned his gaze once again to the sky. "The weapon he carries is truly powerful. I suspect it is the weapon itself that unweaves my magic rather than through any skill of the child."

When again he shifted his gaze back to the ground he saw the sea of dead begin to vaporize before his eyes. They hissed softly as they dissipated into a great black cloud that rose over the valley and drifted off behind him over the mountains, carried on some unfelt wind.

Draegan began walking toward the obelisk, moving swiftly over the terrain. The ground shook violently, a great fissure appearing as masses of earth shifted and tilted. Vapors curled from the cracked ground and rose around Draegan as he steadied himself, the shock of the tremor rippling through the empty basin. After gathering himself and waiting a few moments for any aftershocks he pressed on, covering the ground and nearing the ruins of the great fortress.

"Perhaps Vangen was right after all," he said as he saw the massive fracture that rent the ground where the soldiers had laid only moments ago. "This realm is tearing itself apart. I must find Vangen and end him as quickly as possible." A great roar of thunder split the valley, deafening Draegan as he fell to his knees clutching at his ears.

"Vangen!" came a thunderous voice following closely after the hideous bellow. Draegan looked ahead at the devastated fortress and stared unbelieving at the great obelisk that was suspended over it. The once metal structure had become a glowing crystal and even at this distance, outside the broken walls of the fortress he could see within the obelisk a roiling mass of dark clouds that moved furiously through the floating shard.

"Who dares speak that cursed name in my presence?"

Draegan looked at the obelisk in surprise. The shadows that swirled within the giant crystal had taken a near-human form. He saw a sinister shape rise through the clouds and claw at the inside of the obelisk. Stepping forward he said, "I am Draegan Ferus, Emperor of the Fyrian Empire. I come to this realm seeking Vangen."

Again the basin shook with a terrible thunder. "The spell that binds this timeless void has loosed its bonds if two living souls walk again in the shadow lands of Iss." The ground shook with another quake. "Now two sons of Skeldus have walked the void, and both claim to be emperors. Surely you can have no love of each other."

Draegan paused and stared at the billowing clouds in the floating obelisk. "It is true. I came here to kill my brother and save Fyrian from his foul machinations." He paused again as another quake tore through the valley. "But who are you that you hate Vangen as much as I?"

A peal of thunder boomed through the sky. "I am Fet Reth, the Eater of Souls and mightiest of the six Blades of Darkness. By guile and deceit your brother trapped me in this prison and bound my army to his own. Even now he marches through the Ashen Wastes, collecting the shades of my fallen warriors. He seeks to open a portal to Athar and march his forces through to conquer and crown himself king."

"Then you know why I must stop him."

"And I would aid you, Draegan of Skeldus, for my hate of Vangen is strong. He has bound my brothers in prisons such as you see before you and endeavors to use our souls to augment his own. With some uncanny art he wishes to join our souls to him and use our powers to allow his wretched form to cross the gate into Athar unscathed."

Draegan stood stunned in the rubble beneath the ruined keep. "Always he stays beyond my grasp. I had thought him trapped here, unable to cross back from the shadows, but now I learn he has crafted a way to circumvent the very limits placed by the Elder Gods." Draegan looked at the crimson sky for a moment then brought his gaze back to the swirling mist in the crystal. "How then would you aide me in stopping him?"

"Release me from this obelisk, Draegan Ferus. I know not by what cunning Vangen fettered me to this crystal prison, but were I free of it I could easily sweep through his ranks and take the souls of his army for my own. With them I could free my brothers and together we would crush him beneath us and grind his bones to dust!" Fet Reth's voice boomed through the basin. "Release me!"

"Even if I knew how I would not," Draegan said. "I would no sooner have rid the lands of Vangen then set free the six Blades of Darkness, the greatest enemy Athar has ever known. No, this I will not do."

Fet Reth smashed into the obelisk, causing the chains to buckle and tense, a resounding boom echoing across the basin. "Seek vengeance, child. You must strike now. Release me that I may be his death."

A great tremor tore across the valley, splintering more of the ground and shifting masses of strata that jutted out from the basin floor. Great clouds of vapors issued from the cracks and floated into the scarlet sky. Draegan was knocked to the ground, smashing his shoulder against a large rock.

He picked himself off the rock and rolled his shoulder to relieve the pain. "The shadow lands of Iss are tearing apart. Soon they will free themselves from this void and crash back to Athar, sundering my world and devastating all those who dwell there." He sighed. "Only Vangen promises to stop this inescapable cataclysm, therefore I cannot kill him."

"Vangen's words cannot be trusted," Fet Reth hissed. "By placing himself in such a lofty position as the only salvation for Athar, he buys himself time. Free me from this obelisk and end him swiftly. In the hands of my brothers we can peel the truth from his soul layer by layer."

The great crystal shard hung suspended in the red sky, moving almost peacefully on its massive tethers of iron. Draegan watched it for some time, looking at the tormented shadow that thrashed within. He walked through the pile of rubble that lay scattered at the base of the fortress, picking his way carefully past massive boulders and over piles of loose scree until he was within the outer wall of the fallen fortress. He pushed forward until after some time he stood before the obelisk. He saw the size of the great chains that bound the pulsing splinter of black crystal, each link the size of a hay wagon, and shuddered at the thought of how powerful Vangen must be to bind such a creature.

Fet Reth's thunderous voice boomed forth from the obelisk. "I sense something I have not felt in many ages. A feeling I cannot quite place." The shadows swirled then paused, settling to the base of the crystal. "Come closer Draegan Ferus, son of Skeldus."

Draegan strode forward and was within twenty feet of the base of the obelisk, though it levitated three times as high above him. He placed his hand on the hilt of Carnis Fornax, and looked up at the black light emanating from the crystal.

An ear-splitting roar of thunder burst from the obelisk, knocking Draegan to his knees as he clapped his hands over his head in pain. The thunder of Fet Reth's bellow shot across the basin and echoed off the distant mountains.

"You carry with you Carnis Fornax," Fet Reth rumbled, his voice seething with rage. "For three thousand years I have hungered to hold my blade again, and now it is within inches of my grasp. How cruel to be trapped within this prison," he said, his voice lowering to a venomous whisper.

Draegan smiled. "I see your true intentions now, Blade of Darkness. You are the same great evil that once terrorized the hosts of Fyrian, and you wish to do the same again." He pulled the hilt from his belt and the sword erupted to life, the black flame spewing in a dark jet from the carven maw. "I will free you from your cell, but you will like the irony of your new prison even less."

He swung himself up onto the thick iron chain and ran up its length toward the obelisk, Carnis Fornax held behind him, its flame snapping greedily as he moved. Fet Reth screamed in horror, recoiling within the crystal as Draegan rushed toward him. He plunged the blade deep into the obelisk. The crystal offered no resistance as the black flame passed easily through the surface. Draegan felt an icy bolt course through his body and braced his feet as he held the hilt tight against the obelisk, fighting with all his strength as the shadow within tried to repulse him. Inside the crystal, the churning vapor slammed and recoiled from every facet until at last it was drawn into the blade and Draegan collapsed.

Taking a moment to catch his breath, Draegan stood and pulled the sword slowly from the crystal and stared into its dancing flames as he walked back down the chain. He had covered less than thirty feet when the forged links went slack, sending Draegan plummeting to the ground. He hit the pavers of the inner courtyard and rolled. Around him the chains had gone limp and lay on the ground while above the black crystal had once again become metallic. It hovered for an instant, trembled slightly, then crashed to the ground with a shock that splintered stone and sent Draegan reeling back with the force of its fall.

He picked himself up and saw the metal obelisk buried several feet in the ground, jutting from the earth at a skewed angle. He picked up the burning blade that he had dropped in his fall and extinguished it, placing the hilt back in his belt.

"I must delay no further. Vangen prepares his army in the Ashen Wastes and there is little to gain by tarrying here."

Draegan wended his way carefully through the ruined keep and returned to the empty basin where he moved across the fissured plain, slipping past jets of steam and vapor that shot through the newly formed cracks. A flash of light blinded him and he raised his hands to cover his eyes when he was stunned by a bolt of pain that racked his body. The eye of Islak flared to life, filling his vision with smoke and clouds. Amidst the chaos he saw a host of soldiers standing at attention on a barren field. The vast legions spread around a great gray metal disk, several hundred yards in diameter. It was etched with runes and symbols, hardly a space was left unfilled. He could make out little, other than it was written in the tongue of Iss. Behind the multitudes of soldiers and far beyond the perimeter of the iron circle stood six great obelisks, marking an even larger circle that contained the first. In the center of the metal disk stood a lone figure.

"Vangen," Draegan said. He took a scrap of paper from his sleeve and tucked it under a rock before sprinting across the basin and making his way toward the mountains on the horizon.

Chapter 30: The Wastes

Isarn slammed into a boulder and rolled, using his momentum to spring to his feet, blades drawn and legs braced wide as his eyes darted about, searching for Draegan. After a moment of looking he relaxed.

"So this is the shadow land of Iss," he said as he took in his surroundings. Isarn stood atop a large escarpment that stretched to the horizon on either side of him. Above he saw the ruddy sky with its roiling clouds. Directly beneath the cliff face the ground sloped for miles, covered in what he thought to be the burnt remains of a once massive forest. Beyond the limits of the forest he could see little other than gray ground that ran flat for miles until it met the crimson sky.

"Not a sound of life is to be heard," he said. "No whisper of birds in the sky, nor chatter of insects on the ground. The whole of this land feels dead." He sheathed his blades and studied the sky once more. Perplexed, he drew a symbol in the air with his hand and watched a rune flash to life then slowly fade away as its green glow died. "I cannot find any direction here by craft or magic. I sense no water or vegetation, save what appear to be the remnants of a dead forest. Even beneath the ground nothing stirs in the soil." He walked to the edge of the cliff and peered down.

"I must have been caught in Draegan's spell and cast aside at the moment of its completion. If he is here in this land with me, I must find him and quickly, before I too fall in this lifeless land." He drew a symbol in the dirt and sat before it, folding his hands together as he drew his breath in practiced measures while he closed his eyes. He was perfectly still for only a moment when his eyes snapped open. "There," he said and stood, taking the twin blades of the Vaghat from their sheath. He pointed them at the horizon and watched as they glowed more strongly. When he pointed them in the opposite direction their glow faded substantially.

"You are here, Usurper and I am coming for you," he said as he slipped the blades back into their sheath under his robes.

Isarn began climbing down the face of the cliff, finding his way carefully among the many fissures that ran through the rock. It took him more time than he thought but after what felt like hours he had descended nearly to the base of the escarpment when a quake shook the cliff and caused him to lose his grip. He plummeted a hundred feet and landed with a sickening thud in a heap of scree. His robes were torn and he had lacerations in several places but he felt no broken bones as he stood and checked for his blades.

"Some small luck that I broke no bones in that fall," he said as he pointed Bhel and Asai toward the horizon. "Perhaps even here the Servants of Light watch over us," he said watching for the blades to glow more prominently as he scanned the horizon. When again he picked up the direction of Draegan he began scrambling down through the loose stone, making sure to keep his footing.

After some time the ground lost a bit of its precipitous slope and he neared the edge of the charred forest. This close he could see the twisting black trunks of the trees, scorched to utter charcoal and frozen in place. The forest was massive and even without the covering of leaves the branches and trunks were intertwined in such a way that they began to blot out much of the crimson sky as he walked closer to the dead woods.

"I have been traveling for what seems hours and have yet to see any change in this foreboding sky. If it is day then by now the light should be waning and some sign of night should be apparent," he said as he peered over the tops of the trees. He drew his gaze down to the thick trunks of the ancient dead trees and looked deep into the burnt forest. "I know not what awaits me in there, but I must pass through and on to Draegan."

He took his blades and drew a series of symbols on the ground near the base of a massive tree. "Stand guard over this, old sentinel, for I may have need of it later," he said and sheathed his weapons once more. He wove a sign with his fingers and spoke several words before plunging past the burnt trunk and into the shadowy darkness of the forest. Behind him the runes glowed softly before fading slowly into the ground, leaving no trace in the dirt.

Isarn ran through the forest, ducking twisting branches and curling roots. He continued for hours, never tiring or thirsting. He would pause every few miles and use the daggers of the Vaghat to scan the horizon for Draegan, always correcting his course as he was unable to find landmarks to guide him in the dense twining trees of the blackened forest. When he looked to the sky it was always a deep red, never giving sign of sun or moon or stars. After some time he stopped checking and worried little about it. He focused instead on finding Draegan and keeping the seared branches of the forest from taking off his head as he slipped by them at full speed.

"I sense a malignant evil off in the distance, though it is a different aura from the man I hunt," Isarn said as he looked to his left. "I must stay focused on my quarry, though the abomination that lies beyond this forest must be some great terror indeed if I can feel its presence without the aid of my magic."

He pushed on, fixing his direction as necessary and staying alert for snaking roots and low branches. At last he noticed the forest beginning to thin. The once dense canopy of interwoven black branches that only offered brief glimpses of the sky now thinned as the trees became less clustered. His progress quickened as he was able to move much more rapidly through the thinning forest. The trees became sparse and stunted as the ground leveled. In another hour he was past the trees and standing on a gray plain that stretched before him to the red horizon.

Behind him he saw the forest grow thicker as it receded into the distance. The ground rose and carried the giant trees even higher until at the very limit of his vision he could see the escarpment he had descended, jutting slightly above the horizon.

"I have run for hours if not days, and yet I do not tire or hunger or thirst, though I have cast no spell to prevent such." He looked back through the forest for any signs of life. "Still it feels wrong to see no birds or hear no noise. No wind blows and yet the bloody sky seethes with the promise of a terrible storm. This is a land of the dead."

As if in answer the ground shook violently, nearly knocking Isarn to the ground. After regaining his footing, he stood still for a moment, scanning the forest before turning back to the gray plain that stretched before him. Once more he found the position of Draegan with the blades and after sheathing them, sprinted out into the desert.

"What is this," he exclaimed after taking his first few steps toward the horizon. A swirl of fine gray ash rose around his boots and settled gently back to the ground. Isarn bent and touched the powdery surface, disturbing more ash. "The ground too has been burnt to ash. It is no surprise then that no life finds purchase in these wastes," he said and began running once more in the direction the blades had shown him.

Ear-splitting shrieks filled the sky as Isarn sprinted across the ashen ground. He stopped and craned his head in every direction, eyes darting about as he scanned the sky trying to find the source of the horrible cries. Directly above him, plummeting from the crimson sky he saw a mass of swirling shadows, vaguely human and with gaping maws and outstretched arms, talons curling cruelly and promising a quick, though painful death should they reach him.

Isarn leapt back and rolled as the shades poured into the ground where moments before he had stood. They struck hard into the soft ash and then rose again in a black vapor. Isarn stood horrified as the creatures congealed a hundred feet above him and shrieked once more and began to circle slowly. Their cries were answered and Isarn saw more apparitions screaming toward him from the distance, joining the other group that swirled in a widening gyre in the crimson sky.

There were now nearly a hundred shades swirling and shrieking in the air above Isarn. He set his feet and pulled the Vaghat from its sheath. The wraiths howled and flew up, joining together in a chaotic cloud that paused for an instant before diving again at Isarn. He lashed out as the nearest creature dove at him, its claws raking at his throat as he stepped back. His blade passed through the shade as if it was mist, but it did not reform. The other shades pulled back and hung in the sky above him wailing and hissing.

"So you are nothing more than departed souls," he said and smiled as he looked at his blades. "Come again and Bhel and Asai will give you rest." The churning mass of shades split the air with their screams and dove at him, a wedge of black vapor and hooked claws streaming down like thunder. Isarn crossed his blades before him and stood with his legs wide as he braced himself. He shouted a word as the chaotic throng fell upon him and Bhel and Asai flared to life, their glow creating a shield of light that curved in a shimmering arc in front of Isarn.

The wraiths slammed into the wall of light, driving Isarn's legs deep into the soft ash that covered the ground. He held himself upright, keeping the daggers crossed above his head as he strained to push back against their onslaught. The shades howled in pain as they touched the shield of light, dissolving with a burning hiss and clouds of dark vapor. The others flew off and circled back into the sky, screaming at Isarn as they gyred up and reformed their ranks.

"Worry me not, shades of the wastes. I have bigger game to hunt this day than you," Isarn said as he sprinted off toward the horizon. The wraiths followed behind him wailing as they went. A few would often break from the churning mass and dive at him, but he was always ready and caught them with his daggers, scattering their vaporous form into the void.

He ran for some time, losing track of time, heading always for a point on the horizon indicated by the blades. He had evanesced all but a handful of the shades, but those few still followed him across the ashen plains, though they had all but given up their attempts to attack him and instead shrieked from safety several hundred feet above Isarn.

"Your cries do naught but drive me faster to my quarry, piteous souls," Isarn said as he sprinted across the ground, stirring small eddies of powdered ash that quickly settled in the windless plain. He pressed on for what seemed days, neither tiring nor hungering from his exertion. The crimson sky frothed like a bloody sea, the light and tone always the same whenever he looked at it. Time had lost all meaning to him. If not for the blades guiding him he would have become hopelessly lost.

Isarn ran and ran until he noticed the sound of his boots crunching as they compacted the fine ash. "Silence," he said, a confused look on his face. He slowed and looked behind him as he ran. Gone were the tormented cries that had drowned out his thoughts and he saw the shades that hounded him for so long were departing. As he trained his gaze back to the horizon he saw a slight deviation in the endlessly flat ground. "Mountains? There is where I will hunt you," he said and pushed himself harder toward the horizon.

Before him he watched the imperfection on the horizon grow slowly into the faint outline of a range of mountains. As he covered ground he began to sense the enormity of the space he traveled across as he watched the range grow slowly in the distance. "This land is a nightmare, he said as he continued onward. "I run and yet the mountains appear no closer than when I first spotted them." A tremor shook the plains, causing Isarn to pause and collect himself before moving onward.

As he pressed on he stared at the range on the horizon, trying to see if he could pick up more details. He ran for what felt like another hour and stopped. He knelt in the layer of soft ash that blanketed the ground and drew his blades. Pointing them at the faint outline of the mountains he saw that Draegan was actually off to the left of the range. He returned them to their scabbard and placed the tips of his fingers on his temple. He drew a breath and held it as his vision blurred. Isarn's eyes rolled back in their sockets and he closed his lids. Deep in his mind he saw the range more clearly, only there were no mountains. What he had thought to be peaks jutting above the horizon were instead six massive obelisks that rose hundreds of feet from the ground, each of their tips crowned by a tapering pyramid. Around them hung a cloud of dust that obscured the rest of his vision. Isarn gasped and opened his eyes. "That structure looks man-made and a cloud of dust that low to the ground must be due to some sort of activity. Whatever it is, Draegan approaches it, and I must be there to meet him," he said before gathering himself and once more racing off toward the pillars.

He watched the obelisks rise before him as he made his way across the ash covered plains. As he neared them he saw they were fanned out along the perimeter of a great circle, though at this distance they seemed miles apart. Black clouds began to form in the crimson sky above the obelisks. He sprinted toward the nearest pillar and stayed directly behind it as he approached the structure. The ground rose slightly as he neared the obelisk. Within a few hundred yards of the massive obelisk he began to hear an ominous humming, as if the pillar was alive. He stayed in its shadow and scrambled up the small lip, keeping low to the ground. Lying on his stomach he crawled the last hundred feet and pulled himself through the ash and up over the edge of the slight rise. He gasped at what he saw.

Below him the ground sloped down into a gentle bowl, the angle so slight it seemed almost level, save for the fact that Isarn, lying on his stomach was several feet above the hundreds of thousands of soldiers that stood at attention in the basin. Around the edge of the basin he saw the other five obelisks, standing like giant sentinels over the host gathered in the depression below. The soldiers were split into six factions, and stood in orderly battalions that encompassed a great metal disk lying at the center of the basin. Above the disk, black clouds rolled and thundered as flashes of lightning danced from one cloud to the next. Beneath the gathering storm stood a single figure, his arms raised to the blackening sky.

The whole valley was silent save for the low humming of the obelisk closest to Isarn, and the distant rumble of thunder. His eye was drawn past the figure and the storm to the far rim of the bowl where he saw a person in black walking uncontested down a lane created between two factions of the huge host of soldiers. He drew a sharp breath.

"Draegan!"

Chapter 31: An Encounter in the Wastes

Draegan scaled the mountains leading out of the basin with little difficulty, finding crevices in the crumbling rock that held him easily as he navigated his way over the range and down the more gently slope of the opposite side. He ran through the loose stones and picked his way past boulders until again he returned to the Ashen Wastes. He scanned the mute sky for any sign of the shades that had plagued him during his initial visit.

"I suppose Vangen has called them all to service," he said and pushed forward, churning through the fine black powder as he moved toward the horizon. "Then he must be preparing to open the Grand Gate. I will waste no time," he said and sprinted ahead as fast as he could, eddies of ash swirling behind him.

After hours of running through the wastes he saw ahead of him a strange formation in the distance. Several times during his approach small tremors shook the plains, but he kept on, always moving toward the structure on the horizon. Another tremor rocked the plain, this one stronger than the rest and accompanied by a metallic sound.

"It must be some trick of the light at this distance," he said as he ran, "for it appears as if the range has changed shape. There is now a thin tower rising on the horizon."

Draegan was knocked to the ground by five additional massive quakes, each of which were followed by metallic thuds.

"There is no mistake, I see it clearly now. Six great spires have risen from the ground even as I speed toward Vangen. He readies himself for the final spell. I fear I may be too late," he said and pushed himself harder, trying to cover the ground as quickly as possible.

Draegan felt the land begin to rise gradually as he neared one of the massive obelisks. "I had thought these to be the obelisks from the keeps, but now I see they are larger even than those, and while those of the keeps are of smooth iron, these are riddled with symbols and runes, many of which I've no knowledge of. His skill has grown indeed to create such intricate glyphs on his own."

He climbed the last few feet of the rise and saw he was on the lip of a great basin that sloped gently before him. He peered out from behind the great obelisk. "It is as the eye showed me." Before him thousands upon thousands of soldiers stood at attention in regiments and battalions, gathered in tight formation around a metal disk lying atop the ash in the center of the shallow bowl. Around the perimeter of the basin he saw five other obelisks and noticed a low thrumming noise in the still air. Above the metal circle he saw the sky begin to darken as black clouds formed in the crimson sky. Beneath the lowering clouds he saw a figure, alone in the center of the disk, arms outstretched to the sky.

"Vangen," he hissed through his teeth. "How will I get to him through this massive host? My binding spell is powerful enough to hold thousands, but his legion nears one hundred times that. I fear that I am outmatched."

"Indeed you are. You have always been, brother." Vangen's voice came booming from the crimson sky and echoed across the empty plain. "You have arrived at the moment of my final triumph and I should like to have you watch. I recall being forced to watch you at many tournaments in our youth. Despite being bored to tears by your antics while father swelled with pride at your hollow victories, I was always afforded a great view of the spectacle. I would wish the same for you now." Vangen lowered his arms.

"Come down dear brother and join me here. I should like you to witness the birth of a new god."

Draegan stood still at the edge of the basin, watching the soldiers that surrounded Vangen. "You have every assurance they will not harm you. They obey me implicitly. Come, Draegan, I offer you a chance to witness the beginning of a new era."

"Being close to him is the best opportunity I have," Draegan thought as he rose and dusted himself off. He stepped over the lip of the basin, past the humming obelisk and descended into the throngs of armored soldiers, hands near his belt as his eyes darted about, looking through the mass of iron-clad warriors. He passed them uncontested, staring at their vacant white eyes. They all faced Vangen, completely motionless and with no expressions on their faces. Mouths slack, though they stood with an uncanny rigidity. As he descended the gentle slope he saw that the circular metal slab rose a foot above the ash, acting as a sort of dais. He paused several feet before it and looked up at Vangen. Behind him the soldiers stood frozen.

"It is not too late, Vangen. Leave the gate closed and Athar to its own fate. Leave me to my kingdoms to repair the damage you have caused and I will leave you here to rule this realm."

Vangen laughed. "You have seen the extent of my power and know you cannot stop me, so you attempt to appeal to my humanity in the hope that I will stop myself. How clever. But you insult me in your ill conceived request." He held his hands out and gestured around him. "You are so conceited and so blind to your own actions that you do not realize that all of this is due to you, brother. Was it not you who ripped the Artifacts from their temples and loosened the seal that bound this world? Was it not you who opened a portal here, pursuing me in your lust for vengeance, which served only to further weaken the ties that hold this realm in the void?"

"You lie. You deceived and manipulated me, Vangen," Draegan said gnashing his teeth. "You used me and played me for a fool. Do not dare to think that any of this was caused by me. I was involved only through you. You are to blame for the removal of the Artifacts, you are to blame for the war in Athar, and you are to blame for the thousands that have died by your deceit."

Vangen walked toward the edge of the disk. "You look much older this close. The years have not paid you any kindness. I would rather think you enjoyed your time in Athar, running about and collecting your Artifacts and lording over your empire. But now I see the task has worn you thin." He looked past Draegan and scanned the legions of soldiers before him. He turned his attention to the gathering clouds above him. "But I have little time to parlay with you," he said, moving back to the center of the circle. "The spell you are about to witness requires of me the utmost focus and precise timing. But be assured you will observe an event that outstrips any in history. I will surpass the Elder Gods and cast a spell as mighty as the one that created the world when I join together the two halves of Athar and restore balance to the world."

Vangen stood in the center of the disk and raised his arms to the storm that raged above him. Thunder rolled as flashes of lightning burst from the ever growing maelstrom. "I have gathered the shades from the wastes and now they swirl in the storm that rages above. Soon I will open the gate and march my unliving legions into Fyrian. The sun sets on the Athar, Draegan. The time of the living is near an end. My hosts will pour over the land like a creeping shadow, devouring all life and sending their souls here to me where I will press them into service, growing my ranks with every fallen soldier. Look around you. The pillars you see at the edge of the basin are matched to the obelisks of the Blades of Darkness that I have imprisoned. Once the land is prepared for my arrival I will subsume the souls of the six Blades of Darkness and walk through the gate, reborn as a god. In my wake I will pull this shadow realm back into Athar and rejoin the halves once again."

He looked down at Draegan standing outside the metal circle. "A pity you will die in the process, but as some small assurance I will let you live long enough to see the fall of your Empire."

Draegan pulled the hilt of Carnis Fornax from his belt and glowered at Vangen. "I shall have your soul long before that, brother."

Vangen looked up past Draegan, startled. "You brought company and neglected to tell me. How unlike you to be so rude, Draegan." He dropped his hand and balled it into a fist, locking Draegan in a binding spell. He walked toward the edge of the disk, keeping his gaze trained on an obelisk to his left. "Another of your Graywalkers to join the fray?" he asked Draegan. "Is it that beast of a man from the Iron Mountains? Grom or something?"

Draegan tried to twist his body to see where Vangen looked, but was bound too tight. He felt a great weight on his chest making it difficult to breathe. His hands were locked to his sides and his weight was taken from his feet as he was suspended several inches above the ground. A faint green light coiled over his body keeping him frozen in place.

"Come and join your friend." Vangen's voice boomed through the basin and echoed as the thunder rumbled softly behind him. "I promise you safe passage, though when you are by Draegan's side I will weigh your words and judge you then."

"I am Draegan's bane, though in truth I take no orders from you either, Vangen," Isarn said as he rose by the side of the great obelisk, stepping from its shadow and over the lip of the basin. His white and scarlet cloak seemed to glow next to the dark metal of the humming pillar. "And by your words I have already judged you." He walked down a path between two ranks of frozen soldiers, the blades of the Vaghat pulsing in his hands. "And I think you will find my sentence quite merciful considering your transgressions."

"A priest of Vatn?" Vangen asked, shooting a curious look at Draegan, as he saw Isarn approaching through the ranks of his soldiers. He turned his attention to Draegan bound before him. "I never would have thought you capable of carrying two souls across the abyss brother. Never would I think your skill in magic sufficient enough, and yet here I stand, being insulted by a white robed child in need of a lashing." He looked up at Isarn. "Announce yourself in my presence."

Isarn smiled and bowed mockingly, never taking his eyes off Vangen. "I am Isarn, the Holy Iron, forged in the crucible of the Clade. I am the heir of Greydin Vir's curse and the end of this madness. The Vaghat will drink the blood of both of you this day."

"You catch me off guard, Isarn. I have no idea who you are and had I more time, I would wish to question you further. But as I told your friend, time grows short. I am afraid I must attend to greater things than a child with daggers and an inflated sense of self-worth."

Vangen raised his hand in a swift motion, summoning a green light from the ground that coiled around Isarn's leg. The young man slashed at it with the blades and the light parted like mist. Freed from the binding spell, Isarn charged forward toward Draegan and the disk. "First you, Usurper," he said, blades poised above his head, "then I will tend to this mania."

As Isarn sprinted forward and neared Draegan the spell that held him loosened and Draegan was able to wrench himself free and twist backward as Bhel and Asia carved two deadly arcs through the air. Draegan crouched and sprung back out of the way of another vicious lash of the blades.

"Enough," shouted Vangen from the platform. "I shall blast you both into the abyss," he said, pulling his hands back as a sickly green energy began to crackle around them. Draegan looked from Vangen back to Isarn and saw the twin blades driving at him again. He raised the hilt of his sword and lit the blade, catching the daggers as they swooped toward his chest. Carnis Fornax sputtered and flared, a jet of black flame erupting from the guard and flying out as a fiery bolt into the forward most ranks of soldiers, felling a handful before it died and disappeared. At that same instant Vangen thrust his hands forward and released the green lightning that had been crackling around his hands. It was coursing toward Draegan and Isarn when one of the great obelisks that ringed the basin shuddered and exploded near the base, toppling over as if felled by the axe of a giant.

Draegan felt as if his hand was struck by a hammer. The hilt of his sword burst, sending fragments in every direction, several lacerating his face as they flew by. His ears rang and he felt a chill run through his body as if his blood had been turned to ice. He stared dumbfounded at his hand as he saw a green light begin to surround him.

Draegan and Isarn were struck by the green lightning as the obelisk collapsed, shattering mid-fall into a thousand shards of splintered iron that tore through Vangen's ranks. Draegan and Isarn were frozen for moment, loosed from time as they watched the soldiers near the obelisk crumple to the ground. Then all was black.

Chapter 32: The End of the World

Draegan and Isarn were swimming through blackness, cut off from their senses as they struggled against a dark heavy liquid that pressed in on them from all sides.

Isarn burst through the surface of the inky liquid and gasped for air. Moments later Draegan surfaced several feet away in the viscid fluid, gulping for breath and clawing desperately to keep from sinking. Small eddies of a bilious fluid swirled in the black mire, adding a sickly green tint to the black swamp.

Isarn swam through the tarry liquid, straining with every stroke, trying to make the shore several yards away. He struggled to land, pulled himself from the mire and collapsed. Draegan fought the glutinous fluid in the opposite direction, aiming for a small island of rock that rose above the surface. He made the island of rocks at the same time, and straining with every muscle, climbed atop them and laid prostrate.

"You have to come to shore some time, Draegan," Isarn said between labored breaths. "And when you do I will be here to greet you."

"Vangen must be stopped first." Draegan caught his breath while laying on the rock and tried to wipe the viscous globs of tar from his boots and cloak. "He means to open a portal and march his unliving army through it, killing all those who dwell in Athar," he said between labored gasps. "He has little time to complete his spell. We must hurry."

"You will not throw me from my hunt, Usurper. I will have your head first, and then deal with Vangen on my own."

Draegan sighed and stood himself up upon the rock. He looked at his hand and flexed it, some feeling returning to it as he moved. He checked for the remaining Artifacts and found them all still in place. "Is your head as thick as the tar that fouls the water in this swamp, boy? Killing me will do nothing to stop Vangen. Every moment we waste here brings all of Athar closer to its doom at his hands. He is the greatest threat Athar has never known. His evil surpasses that of the Blades of Darkness. What will you have gained when you sever my head, only to return to a land that has been wiped clean of all life? He means to make Athar a mirror of Iss, a dead land. Surely you see he is a greater threat."

Isarn walked back and forth on the shore watching Draegan, his blades at the ready.

"While you pace like a caged animal, Isarn, you are buying Vangen the time he needs to sweep through the Fyrian Empire and consume all life." Draegan said. "I do not know why I have inspired such hate in you, but surely you can look past it, if only momentarily, to see that Vangen must be stopped now."

"You loosed the shackles that bound Iss when you gathered the Artifacts twenty years ago. You unwove the spells of Greydin Vir and set Athar on a path that ensures its destruction. You abandoned your kingdom of Skeldus and left it undefended and leaderless while the armies of the other kingdoms swept in and gutted your land." Isarn raised a dagger and pointed it at Draegan. "Even now you carry the six Artifacts, weapons of such evil they should never have been touched by mortal hands. For these crimes and more you have been sentenced to death at the hand of the Clade."

"What is the Clade? Who is Greydin Vir? I recall fighting no such man."

"The details are inconsequential. Know only that the Clade spells your doom. I will return the Artifacts to their rightful place and restore peace to the lands."

"Was Greydin Vir your father? You couldn't have been more than a child when I first fought Vangen and gathered the Artifacts, but I suppose I could have killed him in my quest. I was party to many acts that I am shameful of, when I served as head of Vangen's Graywalkers. If this is the case, I am truly sorry and would wish his death undone."

"You have little time for a history lesson, Usurper. I will throw you a rope that you may come to shore. I promise I will not attack you until you are ready, but then I will grant you no quarter."

Draegan sat on the rock. "Still you persist in this irrational line of thought. I will waste little time with you Isarn. Vangen must be stopped before he ends all life on Athar. I hope to use these Artifacts to stop him, though I do not yet know how, for his power is unimaginable." Draegan looked across the swamp to Isarn, his white robes mired in black sludge and pacing on the shore where the hard packed gray earth met the thick waters. "But there is something to you and your blades that escapes me. Every time you near me my magic weakens. I felt it in the Rookery and in the catacombs. You unwove my blood spell and crossed the abyss to join me here in Iss, something that should be impossible. I felt it again when you attacked me near Vangen's metal disk. You unwove his binding spell, allowing me to elude your blades."

"You know little, Draegan, and now is not the time for your education."

"But if you can unweave a blood spell, let alone a binding spell of Vangen's then I think it possible that with your help we could stop him from devouring Athar."

"Again you delay. I will not bargain with the man who wields the six Artifacts. You are my kill, and I shall have you."

Draegan looked at his right hand. "Five Artifacts. Carnis Fornax is lost to me. It shattered as the obelisk did when we were struck by Vangen's spell. I suppose it gave its life to save us from Vangen's magic. He meant to send us to the abyss, blasting our souls out of time and beyond creation, beyond even the dead that dwell in this cursed place." He looked back up at Isarn. "But here we are, alive and bickering at each other across a foul swamp, presumably in some lost corner of this shadow realm."

Isarn paced in silence, his daggers held tight in his grip.

Draegan stood and held out his hands. "For the sake of our homeland, kill me later. If you seek to restore balance to Athar you can do so after you have saved Athar from the cataclysm that Vangen conjures as we speak. You heard his words and know his intentions. You have seen his forces and have tasted the smallest portion of his power. He has bound the six Blades of Darkness already and now intends to merge their souls with his, giving him more power than the Elder Gods. Can you not see the need for urgency in this matter? He must be stopped, and now, before the gate opens."

He paused and stared at Isarn, who had stopped his frenetic pacing and stared back at him, unblinking. "We both seek to stop him. Let us join forces to end his madness, and then you can have whatever revenge you seek from me. I promise you no deception is harbored in my words. I wish only to end Vangen. He manipulated me and played upon my sense of justice to twist and bend me into his service. He took from me those that I loved dearly and I would repay him tenfold. I admit that my actions were wrong but my intentions were always true. I sought the Artifacts to stop Vangen from acquiring them. Little did I know of the repercussions. He escaped me in our first encounter and came here where he built this army for the sole purpose of returning to Athar. And I have come here for the sole purpose of stopping him."

"How do plan to stop him?"

"With your help. You have a power I have never encountered in life or in any text. I have poured through the archives of Vatn and read texts penned by the servants of darkness themselves and still I have not heard a whisper of a magic that unweaves all magic simply by its presence. Now that I have seen and felt it work I believe it may afford us the opportunity we need to end Vangen."

"So you would use me and my powers to stop Vangen. But what then? What would stop you from assuming his crown and ruling over these corpses as you march back to Athar?"

Draegan shook his head. "I have never sought power, only to keep it from Vangen. I do not desire these Artifacts, but had only a small hope that they could prove of some use in my fight against him. I sought only to take them from Athar and keep their poison from my people. Here I hoped they would aid me in my task, but already I have lost my most precious Artifact, Carnis Fornax. I had hoped to take Vangen's soul and trap it within, now it is lost." He looked back at Isarn. "But with your blades perhaps we can get close enough to take his head instead."

Isarn looked at Draegan for a long while, then sheathed his blades and folded his arms across his chest. "I will aid you, and promise you safe keeping until Vangen is dead. I will not ask the same from you, for I would be foolish indeed to believe the oath of one such as yourself. But know that if you deceive me your death will be swift." He motioned to Draegan. "You have seen my blades before and know a small part of their power. If you make the slightest move to harm me while I aid you, I will have your head and heart."

"Yes I know those blades. What magic is in them that allow you to unravel even a blood spell?"

"Worry less about my daggers and focus instead on getting to shore. As you said, time grows short. Now come across and let us put this charge of stopping Vangen behind us. I would like to have both your heads this day."

Draegan took a length of rope from the small pack he wore beneath his cloak. Using the World Render he chipped off a bit of the boulder he stood upon and tied it to the rope to add weight. He threw it across the swamp and it carried to shore, where Isarn took it. Draegan looped the rope around a solid projection and tied it tightly, testing it with a few harsh tugs.

"There is no tree or rock on the shore, as you can see Draegan. What is your plan?"

"Hold it yourself," Draegan said as he clambered down the rock and entered the mire once more, sinking up to his neck as he stepped into the thick fluid. Isarn wound the coils around his waist and secured them. Draegan took the rope and held it overhead, moving hand over hand, pulling himself along at a torturously slow pace. "You have every opportunity to walk away and let me sink, Isarn," Draegan shouted tilting his head back to keep his mouth out of the ooze.

"You would test my word so soon? You are brave indeed to place your life so willingly in the hands of your enemy," Isarn said as he braced his feet and pulled hard against the rope to keep it taught. "That or a fool." He leaned back and lifted the rope from the tar and pulled Draegan the last few feet toward shore until he found the ground beneath his feet and walked himself in.

Draegan lay panting on the hard earth, covered in the viscous muck of the swamp. "You are stronger than you appear to pull me through that mire."

"You will see just how powerful I am when we face Vangen," Isarn said, untying the rope tossed it at Draegan's feet.

"Yes, Vangen," Draegan said as he rose and wiped the sludge from his body, flinging it to the dry earth. "We must not tarry here if we are to stop him, though I know not how to find him in this cursed realm of shadow and ash."

Isarn pulled the twin blades of the Vaghat from their scabbard on his back and held them out toward Draegan. Draegan crouched and put his hand to his belt, searching for the hilt of his broken sword.

"Do not fear the Vaghat just yet, Draegan. Your time will come, but for now they hunt Vangen." He swept the blades across the horizon at arm's length. "There," he said, nodding to a spot in the distance where the blades pulsed more excitedly. "He and his army wait beyond that range. I hope some climbing will not slow you down," he said and sprinted off toward the mountains in the distance.

Draegan finished wiping himself down the best he could and checked the fasteners of all his weapons. Finding them secure he took off after Isarn.

Chapter 33: Talus Sen

Draegan caught up to Isarn and pushed ahead of him as Isarn slowed.

"I'll keep you in front of me," Isarn said, measuring his breath as he ran. "I would have my eyes on you rather than the other way around."

They followed the shore of the swamp for some time until they came to a channel hewn in the hard packed earth and lined with carefully mortared bricks of black. Both men stopped and looked at the bottom of the groove where they saw a small trickle of thick green liquid empty slowly into the swamp, mixing with the inky black waters. Looking ahead they saw the channel run straight toward the mountains in the distance. Isarn hopped across the eight foot wide channel with ease and motioned toward the range.

"Let us follow this channel and have it take us to the wastes," he said

They ran for hours covering mile after mile as they crossed the barren landscape, watching the mountain range grow ever larger and keeping the channel between them. The ground was hard, unlike the ash covered plain, yet it was just as flat. Other than the swamp which they had left behind them there were no other landmarks. Ahead they watched the range loom larger until at last Draegan spoke.

"It's no range," he said between breaths. "It's the fortress of a Blade of Darkness. I don't know which one, only that it is not Fet Reth or the Red Keep of Pyr, both of which I have seen before."

"How do you mean?" Isarn asked as he slowed slightly, letting Draegan pull several steps ahead. His hand unconsciously moved toward the small of his back where the Vaghat lay sheathed.

"When first I came here I traveled across the Ashen Wastes and over a mountain range to a large basin wherein I saw the fortress of Pyr the Red Scourge, the Blade of Darkness that wielded the Burning Chains during the War for Athar. Within that great keep of iron and stone I encountered Vangen, sitting beneath an obelisk of red iron." Draegan slowed to a stop and turned to face Isarn.

"When this shadow land was rent form Athar three thousand years ago the Elder Gods of Light banished the armies of Iss as well as the souls of the Blades themselves into this void. They dwelt here in this deathless land, cut off from Athar until Vangen arrived. In that time they built great keeps and fortresses to house their unliving armies. When Vangen came here he used arcane magic to trap the soul of Pyr within a great obelisk similar to that which you saw standing around his army, though smaller and devoid of runes."

Isarn narrowed his eyes and stared at Draegan as they moved. "And what of the obelisk that shattered?"

"I know little, save that we were torn apart as we crossed the abyss. I was cast into a part of this realm beyond the Ashen Wastes which I believe to lay in the center of this realm. Around the Ashen Wastes must be the Keeps of the Blades of Darkness, for I exited the portal spell near to the fortress of Fet Reth.

"The Eater of Souls and wielder of Carnis Fornax during the ten thousand year war," Isarn whispered.

"No longer," Draegan said. "When I arrived here I found his Keep of iron split in two and his army lying decimated before his gates. But within his splintered fortress there floated an obelisk of metal similar to that which I had seen in the Red Keep. It called to me and beckoned me closer. Indeed it was the soul of Fet Reth, trapped within the pillar." Draegan lifted his eyes to the crimson sky. "He sought to have me free his soul so that he could end Vangen, but I did not wish to inflict greater evil upon the world and instead took him from that prison with his own sword, now shattered."

"Perhaps his soul died with the blade," Isarn offered.

"Perhaps, though I admit little understanding of these matters. For before I took him, he told me from his prison that Vangen had trapped the other Blades in similar circumstances and wished to join them to himself before he crossed into Athar." He thought for a moment before continuing, Isarn keeping his distance and watching him carefully. "If he truly needs the souls of the six Blades to cross between realms, then it is conceivable that Vangen could be weakened or kept from entering Athar altogether by taking the souls of the remaining Blades. Before us lays a fortress of some great terror, and beyond it Vangen. If we must pass by it or through it, it may aid our cause to attempt to shatter this obelisk as well."

"My blades can vanquish a soul as simply as they can unweave a spell. They are the greatest weapon in all of Athar and beyond," Isarn said, reaching behind him and touching the handles of his daggers. "But if time is short dare we waste it on some quest of dubious effect?"

"I cannot be sure. Vangen spoke of the obelisks that surrounded his army at the edge of the basin being matched to a trapped soul in the six Keeps. When I ignited my blade perhaps Fet Reth's soul escaped or was sent to the abyss and that is what shattered the pillar we saw falling before we were cast into that infernal swamp. If we can get to the other five souls in their Keeps before Vangen opens the gate we stand a chance of stopping his evil from passing through to Athar at the least."

"This is a gamble Draegan, and again I impress upon you the limited time with which we have to work."

"I agree, but let us at least try on our way back to the Ashen Wastes when we pass through this fortress. If it proves to be of some gain we will be able to reassess our options."

Isarn nodded and they both sped off across the dry plain heading for the walled keep they saw looming on the horizon. Within a few hours they had covered the distance and stood before a massive pile of rubble. Above it, held by two large chains, floated a metal obelisk of greenish metal. Clouds of steam issued through the pile of black rocks and curled into the bloody sky.

"There, the obelisk," Draegan said, climbing over the loose stones of the heap. Isarn followed a few steps behind, trying to avoid the stones that Draegan loosed as he climbed.

A sickening whisper filled the air. "The Dark Ichor."

Isarn looked up to see the iron obelisk flare to life, transforming in a flash of light to a crystal of green fire. Within it a dark shadow swirled and howled.

"Return my bow and I promise to end you painlessly," the icy whisper threatened.

Draegan stood and dusted himself off. "You forget that you are bound Talus Sen the Spreading Darkness. And the Dark Ichor is mine now, to be put to better use by piercing the heart of Vangen."

The ground shook, nearly knocking Draegan and Isarn to their knees. "Vangen!" came the shout from the chaotic mass of black clouds that frothed in the crystal. "Free me and I will spare you the trouble and rend him limb from limb myself."

Isarn climbed the rubble and stood behind Draegan in the shadow of the great hovering pillar. "We have a better use for you, Blade of Darkness," Isarn said and clapped his hands together as he sat in the dust beneath the obelisk. He closed his eyes and drew a deep breath. Draegan backed away and kept his gaze trained on Isarn. After a moment he snapped his eyes open and shouted. The obelisk slammed into the heap of rock with a tremendous crash that sent clouds of dust pouring into the air. Fragments of rocks flew in all directions as the ground shook from the impact. The great chains slackened and fell to the ground, sliding down the pile of rubble and coiling on the earth. Isarn stood and walked calmly toward the pillar.

"You will aid us in our quest to end Vangen, but you must be satisfied in knowing alone, for you will not live to see it." Isarn approached the roiling mass of vapor that churned within the obelisk. He slipped his hands behind his back and slowly drew his daggers. They shone a dull red in the crimson light of the sky, and then flared to life as he approached the pillar. Talus Sen screamed and clawed at the crystal's walls.

Isarn drove the blades into the obelisk and leaned on the handles as he watched the seething black clouds within curl and fly to the farthest reaches of the prison. "Your fate is sealed. Accept your absolution and go peacefully into the abyss, shade of darkness."

Talus Sen screamed as the blades pulsed within the crystal. The obelisk began to vibrate, growing louder until at last it exploded, sending shards of crystal spraying across the courtyard. Draegan ducked and pulled his cloak over him as bits of crystal rained down. Isarn stood firm, still leaning on his blades though the pillar was no more. Then he stood up, slipped the daggers beneath his cloak and walked through the rubble toward Draegan.

"On to the wastes and Vangen," he said.

A great quake rocked the ground sending both men tumbling. They sprang to their feet quickly as the pile of rubble began to shift and great stones rolled to the basin floor. After a few moments they began to move again, sure that the worst had passed. A clap of thunder tore through the sky and Draegan doubled over, falling down the pile of rocks and slamming his shoulder into a link of iron in the great chain that had bound the obelisk. Isarn raced down to him and saw him clutching his chest.

"The bow is gone, shattered," Draegan said gasping for air and trying to raise himself. Isarn grabbed his hand and pulled him up. Draegan massaged his shoulder and steadied himself on the chain. For a while he said nothing. "It exploded when the quake struck, knocking me down." He took another breath. "I do not know if stopping these Blades of Darkness has any effect on Vangen and his plan, but it surely is the solution we seek in ending the Artifacts," he said with a weak smile as he rubbed his shoulder.

"It proves even more successful than my Vaghat," Isarn said.

"I must know more of this weapon you carry," Draegan said, eyeing Isarn with caution as he dusted himself off. "Only Carnis Fornax when I held it was capable of such a feat."

Isarn shook his head. "His soul is not held within my blades as it was in your sword. Talus Sen simply ceases to exist. As I unravel spells so too do I unweave souls. He exists no more as shade or soul or being of any kind. He simply is not," he said and walked past Draegan down into the rubble of the courtyard. "Come, we must lose no time."

"A weapon that unweaves spells?" Draegan asked in disbelief. "Then surely they can undo the work of Vangen and take apart the great seal he is constructing in the wastes. How close must you be in order for them to have effect?"

"Come Draegan, we are short on time," Isarn said, turning back to look up at him. "And yet you prattle on more than old Ieros."

Draegan's eyes widened as a slow smile spread across his face. "Your frustration betrays you Isarn, priest of Vatn, for Ieros is known to me as well. I knew him from the library in the White Temple when I trained there in my youth, forever bent over those dusty tomes."

"I have few ties with Vatn. Do not let this white robe mislead you. Save for my mother who was murdered shortly after I was born I know only of Ieros for he, like me was a member of the Clade. We are separate from Vatn. While we both seek peace and stability, we use means they would not find agreeable with their beliefs."

Draegan froze for an instant, but gathered himself quickly and picked his way down toward him through the pile of rubble. "I too was once connected with Vatn. I was born of a priestess and wed one as well. But both are lost to me as are many other things now that I walk the path of revenge," Draegan said searching Isarn's face and seeing him as if for the first time. "But tell me of the Clade, for though I have poured through many ancient tomes and raided the archives of Vatn little mention has been made of your kingdom."

Isarn smirked. "We are no kingdom, for now we number only two," Isarn said as he turned. "But I will tell you the rest as we push for the Ashen Wastes."

The two wended their way back through the wall and ran across the hard packed earth at top speed. Isarn kept Draegan ahead of him while he related a few brief details of the Clade.

"How is it that those who read the Chronicle of Fire never once question the disappearance of the Sages? These are men and women so powerful that they battled the Blades of Darkness for ten thousand years, and then like that," Isarn said as he snapped his fingers, "they are gone from the text. Does this not raise any questions in your mind?"

Draegan kept pushing for the horizon, noticing the ground changing slowly from hard earth to a fine layer of powder. "We are taught the Sages left with the rending of Athar. When the Elder Gods sunk Iss and banished its armies to this shadow land the Elder Gods of Light and Darkness left. We thought they took their champions with them."

"It is a much darker story than it would appear then, for in fact the Sages were killed by one man, one man who bore the Vaghat that I now carry."

"Impossible," Draegan said, looking over his shoulder at Isarn.

"Greydin Vir, the founder of the Clade used these same otherworldly blades to end the Sages when they came to the Isle of Vatn shortly after the Failed Council. The Sages turned on Vatn and kidnapped her children, keeping them as ransom for the Dark Ichor. Greydin Vir, her consort, killed the children, taking away any chance of a future attempt to use them as leverage. In her grief Sage Vatn took her life and cursed Greydin who did not know until then that the children were his. That was the night the heavens crashed to the earth and Athar was rent. That was the sundering the Chronicle of Fire speaks of, but it is not the end of the tale, for in his wrath and consuming guilt Greydin forged these blades from a piece of the fallen sky and used them to kill the Sages when they returned months later with their armies. In single combat the Sages proved no match for a weapon that robbed them of their magic. It was then that Greydin proved the superior fighter, felling the five remaining Sages in brutal combat."

"But how is it that this tale is unknown to those in Fyrian?"

"Because Greydin made it so," Isarn replied as he pushed harder through the terrain, forcing Draegan to keep up. "The Sage's armies returned to Fyrian leaderless. Those who survived vied with one another for power but would not speak of the tragedy that befell them on Vatn, let alone record their shame for posterity. On Vatn, after the Fall of the Sages, the Clade was used to keep the Artifacts of Darkness from the hands of men. The mission and the members were shrouded in secrecy given the nature of their work. But over time, as the five kingdoms waged war with each other, few sought these relics of a lost age assuming they had disappeared with the Sages and Iss. As time wore on, the Clade dwindled in number, but not in power."

Draegan ran in silence for a few moments. "It is a grand legend and were it not for those blades you carry I would think you mad." He paused before continuing. "So there exists a secret society unknown to those in Fyrian charged with the keeping of the Artifacts. This is something that perhaps even Vangen is unaware of."

"And we should near him soon," Isarn said. "To our left hills begin to rise from the plain. They must serve as the break that separates us from the Wastes. In a few more hours we should be able to at least see Vangen and his pillars for there in the sky I can already see the storm growing."

Draegan looked up and saw a mass of black clouds above the horizon swirling slowly in the crimson sky. Flashes of light illuminated them, though at this distance they could not hear the thunder that echoed across the basin. In a few hours they had begun to climb the rolling hills Isarn had spotted. Soon they began to make out the great obelisks on the horizon, beneath the ever growing storm.

"Four," Draegan shouted over his shoulder. "I count only four pillars."

Isarn ran next to Draegan and squinted at the horizon. "So when Talus Sen was wiped from existence, then so too was the obelisk that Vangen had here."

"It would appear," Draegan said and mused. "Perhaps it is time to change tactics." He lay down behind a small rise on the ridgeline and peered across the plains to the structure on the horizon, motioning for Isarn to do likewise. "There remain four other obelisks. I have a Shadow Walking rune placed near the Red Keep of Pyr. This may be the time where we part ways, for the two of us working separately can cover more ground and complete our task that much faster."

Isarn sat several feet away from Draegan with his back against a rock. "I would not let you out of my sight to slip away so easily Usurper. Even if I were to let you go how could you possibly hope to take the soul of Pyr without Carnis Fornax?"

Draegan thought for a moment, folding his hands while staring at the black clouds in the ruddy sky. "Take my cloak and Shadow Walk to the Red Keep. There you will find Pyr trapped in an obelisk as Talus Sen was. I will press into Vangen's throng and buy us time. When you have finished with Pyr, return here."

"I wish to keep you in my sight and now you would have me lose you," Isarn said as he looked at Draegan. He held up his hand. "And I will not don the cloak of Dalken Tor and use its dark magic no matter the cause. There must be another way."

"If you can craft a better plan then I am not averse to hearing it," Draegan said, still staring at the clouds. After a moment of silence he continued. "I am protected by the Great Aegis that I wear on my neck. I do not fear death from Vangen's forces. I will charge into his legions with the World Render and make use of its awesome power as I lay low his soldiers. They cannot harm me, though I hope to turn them back to shades. It takes Vangen some time to place the shades of his fallen warriors back into hosts. This will distract him long enough for you to make off to the Red Keep with my cloak and end Pyr in his prison before you return here." Draegan turned to look at Isarn. "But from that point I am at a loss. I do not know where the other three Blades are or if we have the time to face them, nor even if what we are doing is of any use in stopping Vangen. I know only that it destroys the Artifacts, something that even the Sages failed to do three thousand years ago."

Isarn turned from Draegan and looked across the ashen plain to the great ring that held Vangen's forces. He looked at them for some time in silence. "I count fewer soldiers," he said, motioning to Draegan who moved beside him and peered out across the plain from behind the rock.

"The soldiers of Talus Sen and Fet Reth are no more," Draegan whispered. "This is some small hope indeed. Look how the ground is empty where the obelisks used to stand. Before each of the other four grand pillars gathered the legions of that Blade of Darkness, but in the empty space where Talus Sen's and Fet Reth's obelisk once stood, there are no warriors." Draegan turned to Isarn and began unfastening the pin at his throat in order to remove the cloak. "You see now we are having some effect upon him. His forces dwindle with each Blade you kill and so too do we profit from the loss of an Artifact." He removed the cloak and held it out to Isarn. "You must take it and go to the Red Keep and Pyr."

Isarn looked at the black cloth before him and set his jaw. "It goes against every fiber of my being to accept such a gift. I shudder to think of the evil that lies with its weave, but I cannot argue with the fact that Vangen's forces are diminished through our efforts." He reached out and drew the cloak around him. "It reeks of death and chills my blood at its very touch. Teach me the sign and quickly, for I would soon end this loathsome task and be rid of this foul burden."

Draegan drew the sigil in the dirt behind the boulder and told him the words to speak. "I carry with me parchment with that same mark should you need to shadow walk to me," he said. Isarn nodded and folded his hands, closed his eyes and uttered the dark words of Iss. Draegan watched the black mist swallow him and felt a chill in the air as he stood and stepped through the vapor and out onto the ridge looking down into the valley.

"I wish him good hunting," he said as he fastened the pin of the Great Aegis through the leather of his belt and pulled the carven handle of the Burning Chains from its loop. He gripped the handle firmly in his hand. "And I wish the same for me," he said as he stared down into the plain and at the throngs gathered at Vangen's feet. He looked up at the lightning flashing through the sky and taking a breath, plunged down the hill and across the basin floor as fast as he could, churning through the gray ash as he sped directly for Vangen.

Chapter 34: The Battle on the Wastes

Draegan crossed the plain and charged up the slight incline near a thrumming obelisk. He paused for a moment on the lip of the basin and saw before him the multitudes of Vangen's unliving army spread out beneath him. Pikes and spears rose sharply above the masses of iron plated and helmed soldiers below. Banners of the Blades of Darkness, whom these souls served previously, flapped in the air stirred by Vangen's storm. At the center of the depression, atop the great metal disk, Vangen stood with his arms held out to the sky and his head tossed back as he chanted into the raging storm above him. Lightning struck around him, scorching the metal circle on which he stood and a green mist began to swirl about him at his feet.

"Still his forces are thousands more than all the armies of Fyrian combined, and together Isarn and I have cut his numbers by one third. I have little choice but to throw myself into the fray and hope for Isarn's success."

He took a breath and plunged down into the bowl moving straight toward the flank of a large regiment of soldiers clad in reddish armor. They stood frozen as he approached, not even turning to look at him when he was but several feet away. Draegan yelled and lashed out with his right hand, the Burning Chains issuing forth from the black handle. Six great tongues of flame snapped through the air, hissing as they tore into the soldiers that stood at attention. The flames ripped through them as easily as a scythe fells ripe wheat and Draegan watched as they crumpled to the ground, armor piling in heaps upon the gray ash.

Draegan swung relentlessly, the coils of flame decimating throngs of soldiers as he cut a swath of fiery death through the frozen ranks of soldiers. Draegan heard a tremendous crack of thunder over the hiss of the searing flames of his whip and looked to the sky. The lightning had stopped and stillness quieted the air.

"You test my patience, brother," Vangen said, his voice echoing across the basin. "I am intrigued as to how you avoided my divine wrath, and felled two of my obelisks, for truly your soul should be shrieking across the abyss and I should count six pillars about me. I would dearly love to question you, but I am rather occupied with an onerous portion of my enchantment and cannot spare the time." Vangen turned his gaze skyward once more and raised his hands. "I shall have my legions gut you and bring me your head upon a pike, and then we shall talk of your cunning."

"I will turn your soldiers to ash," Draegan shouted over the howling wind that had begun as Vangen started to chant once more.

"And I will give them life again," Vangen sighed. "You cannot triumph."

Draegan heard a trumpet blast and saw the soldiers turn to face him. In his wrath he had carved a path into the center of a ten thousand strong regiment and was now surrounded. He brandished his whip and cracked it at the nearest warriors, who fell and were instantly replaced by those who stood behind.

"They know no fear," Draegan shouted. "But soon they will."

Once more Draegan charged forward, lashing out with the coils of red flame as he was met by a charging throng of armored warriors pushing forward with spears lowered. Draegan spun and snapped the Burning Chains, creating a fiery wheel of death around him that felled all who stepped within the Artifact's reach.

For hours Draegan fought, his arm never tiring as the soldiers pressed forward, never relenting. Bodies piled in heaps around him so that before long he had created a small hill of armor that he stood upon, affording him a better view of the basin as his attackers were forced to mount the small rise in order to strike at him.

Ahead he saw the great metal disk with Vangen at its center. Lightning struck about him as the green vapor rose and coiled around his body. Above him the clouds swirled and pressed in on each other, forming a sort of vortex of black in the crimson sky. But ahead of Draegan, between his position and Vangen was a sea of helms, pikes, spears, and banners, pushed in tightly against each other. He stood on a small island swallowed in a sea of iron plate and ringed mail.

"I shall never get to Vangen in time," he said, cracking the tongues of flame around him and adding another handful of bodies to the growing pile of dead that lay at his boots. Draegan set his feet and leapt into the press of unliving soldiers, tearing through them with a hateful ferocity. As the dead fell more warriors stepped in, filling the void as soon as it was created and forcing Draegan back up the hillock of fallen where he stood atop their collection of iron plates.

"For all his tiresome rhetoric, now I would truly appreciate the company of Isarn and his blades," Draegan said as he cracked the whip about him, adding more iron to the growing mound.

Chapter 35: Pyr the Red Scourge

Isarn felt the world close in on him, the darkness filling his vision as all sounds were closed off from his ears. The ground pitched and heaved as he felt a coldness move through his blood. As quickly as the shadows swallowed him, they spat him out onto red earth near a large boulder. Isarn scrambled to his hands and knees and quickly pulled himself into the shadow of the rock.

Isarn looked about him and saw he was in a great basin of reddish earth with a large range of mountains behind him. Across the level plain were great channels carved in the earth and filled with magma that flowed toward a great red keep in the distance. Isarn marveled at the sheer size of the walls that soared into the ruddy sky. Colossal rocks joined with great bands of iron, lending the wall a terrifying aspect as he saw clouds of black smoke issue forth from behind the stones and rise into the red sky. Behind the outer wall and beyond the red towers that stood atop the inner wall he saw an obelisk of red iron suspended above the Keep and bound at each corner by four immense chains.

"I come for you Pyr," Isarn whispered and sprinted from the boulder across the red plain as he drove directly toward the open gate. He followed a channel carrying magma for some distance then leapt over it and continued inward toward the center of the basin and the gate. The heat from the flowing magma was oppressive but he pushed on, always vigilant and searching for hidden perils.

As he neared the outer wall he instinctively pulled the daggers from their sheath and crossed over the threshold of the entrance, his eyes darting about, searching for lurking danger as he ran up the wide road that took him past the inner wall and into the courtyard beneath the obelisk.

Ahead of him he saw a raised series of steps that led to a throne carved of red stone that sat beneath the suspended obelisk. He searched the corners of the courtyard for any signs of movement and looked again at the gargantuan pillar stretching to the sky. Isarn steadied himself as the ground rumbled.

"You are not Vangen, though I do not like the feel of your blades any more than I like the stench of that coward," a booming voice echoed through the keep. "Make yourself known to me."

"I would tell you Pyr the Red Scourge, but you will soon find me more disagreeable than Vangen. I should rather have you cursing his name instead of my own as I speed you on your way to oblivion."

The ground quaked again, causing Isarn to pitch to one knee. As he rose he saw the iron pillar had become a glowing red shard of crystal and housed within he saw a black vapor churning madly as if driven by some violent wind. It paused for a moment, assuming a vaguely human form before swirling away again.

"I waste time with you, Blade of Darkness, and time is precious even in this land," Isarn said as he sheathed his blades. He planted his legs and braced himself as he lifted his hands over his head and brought them down in a violent motion. The obelisk obeyed his movements and crashed into the throne, crushing it and burying its heavy base deep into the dais. The force of the impact shook the Keep and nearly knocked Isarn over as a cloud of red dust billowed past him and pushed through the gate and down the street. He ran through the rubble leaping from rock to rock as he climbed toward the sunken obelisk. His hands slipped into his robe and he drew the Vaghat in one swift motion as he made a final vault toward the pillar, launching himself up and over a large boulder. As he descended he thrust the blades deep into the crystal using his momentum to sink them to the hilt.

The chaotic mass of shadow that swirled in the crystal racked back and forth, throwing itself into the shard in a futile attempt to escape, shaking the entire Keep in its fury. Great cries of pain pierced the sky while Isarn stood firm and held the daggers in place until at last the pillar began to shake. Isarn scowled and leaned into the obelisk, holding the daggers tight as the crystal exploded with a deafening boom that reverberated across the basin. Fragments of crystal shot through the air and rained down in a deadly hail that slashed Isarn in several places.

When the pieces of the obelisk had settled to the ground, Isarn sheathed his blades. He pulled a fragment of the red iron crystal from his forearm and tossed it onto the pile of rubble. "Now to return to Draegan," he said and closed his eyes, recalling the symbol Draegan had shown him. He thought the words of the spell and instantly was engulfed in shadow. Again the ground heaved and he was lost in blackness.

Chapter 36: Return to the Front

Isarn grabbed at the boulder to stop himself from pitching forward. He took a gulp of air as the black mist that surrounded him thinned and evaporated into the air. His vision swam and he felt sick at the stench of the vapor and feel of the cloak, but he pushed his thoughts aside and shaking his head, looked around.

He was back on the small rise, crouching behind the boulder where Draegan had drawn the rune. Looking down into the basin he saw the great metal disk with Vangen standing alone beneath the maelstrom that raged above in the crimson sky. He noticed that the ranks of soldiers that had been so orderly the last time were now pressing in toward a single figure wreathed in flame. As he watched he noticed the throngs of warriors marching ever forward, closing in on the man from all sides as the figure wheeled and lashed out at them with a whip of flame.

"Draegan has taken the fight to Vangen's forces," Isarn said as his hands moved to his back. "But it appears for all his might he is outmatched." Isarn pulled the blades from their scabbard and rose, stepping out from behind the rock before he sprinted down the slope and toward the fray. "I will even the odds for the old man."

***

Draegan lunged forward, snapping the tongues of flame about him and wheeled around with incredible speed, sending the coils of fire in a wide arc that burned through all those within reach of the deadly Artifact. Upon contact the warriors burst into flame and crumpled to the ground, their armor and weapons clattering onto the pile of dead to add to its ever growing size. The fine powdery ash of their bodies rose in the gusting wind of Vangen's storm as was carried off, past the obelisks and into the Ashen Wastes.

"I tire of this, but am unable to take my fight to Vangen. His men choke me, though I turn them to dust," Draegan lamented between lashes of the Burning Chains. "Is there no end to his legions?"

Draegan drew his arm back for a mighty strike when the ground seized and pitched him forward to his knees. The handful of soldiers climbing the pile of empty armor to get to Draegan fell prostrate as the earth trembled. As Draegan picked himself up he heard a crack that was unlike the rumbling thunder in the sky behind him. Looking ahead he saw fissures appear in the colossal obelisk, encircling the base of the pillar. Before he could react, the base of the obelisk exploded, sending shards and razor sharp fragments rocketing through the air, spraying the distant ranks of Vangen's forces with needles of iron.

Several soldiers fell but still they pushed forward relentlessly, nearly trampling each other in their frenzied rush to attack Draegan. As he stood, Draegan watched in wonder as the obelisk slipped on its base and began to fall, the upper reaches of the pillar howling as it began to speed through the air in its deadly descent. Draegan snapped the whip before him and carved a path through the soldiers as the obelisk continued its tumble toward to the basin floor. He dove as the immense pillar of iron slammed to the ground where he had been standing moments ago, crushing the pile of armor and a thousand soldiers as well. The shock of the impact flattened tens of thousands of warriors, knocking them to the ground, though the obelisk fell short of the metal disk Vangen stood upon.

Draegan leapt up and raced through the clearing created by the falling pillar, heading as fast as he could for the edge of the basin.

"Isarn has done well," he said as he sped past the recovering throngs of soldiers. Ahead of him the warriors had begun to rise and once again pressed in toward him. Draegan sprinted to the base of the fallen pillar, its rune-filled iron on his left acting as a defensive wall. To his right the legions had regained their wits and pushed in after him, closing off his escape ahead. Draegan lashed out with the whip but the flames sputtered.

"Isarn has done too well," Draegan said and threw the handle of the Burning Chains ahead of him into the onrushing throng of soldiers that charged forward, spears lowered. The handle of the Artifact exploded and the coils of flame sprayed out, spinning into the ranks of warriors. Draegan continued to press forward, reaching behind him to unfasten the buckles that held the World Render.

"I shall soon see if this Artifact favors me as it did Gron," he said, taking the axe in both his hands as he ran. A flash of light burst from the pillar, blinding Draegan and causing him stop and cover his eyes. He felt a great wind pull on him, sucking him closer to the downed obelisk and then the force reversed, blowing out with such fury it sent Draegan tumbling. He rolled forward, holding tight to the axe and when he sprung to his feet he saw that the obelisk and the red armored soldiers of Pyr were gone.

A great empty plain stretched out before Draegan to the lip of the basin. Every trace of the multitudes that had been closing in on him was gone and now his path to the edge of the basin was clear. But only for a moment. A sea of warriors crashed in to fill the empty space, howling and brandishing their weapons. They clashed together ahead of Draegan, cutting off his escape and rushed toward him. Behind more warriors poured in to the empty space and forced him forward.

He came near a group of soldiers and brought the mighty axe down with tremendous force. The ground fractured, heaving up and tossing a handful of soldiers into the air. Draegan slowed and pulled the bit of the blade from the earth and prepared for another strike when he saw the soldiers stop. He was surrounded on all sides, the soldiers forming a circle thousands deep around him, their pikes and swords brandished at him, frozen, as if they were locked by a binding spell. Near the edge of the basin a few hundred yards away where the fractured base of the obelisk rose he saw soldiers begin to fall in place, and he heard their bodies crash to the ground. "What magic is this?"

"Will you stand there like some befuddled ox, or will you make use of the time I bought you?"

Draegan heard Isarn's voice rise above the howling wind and knew the source of the falling warriors. Smiling he grabbed the World Render and charged forward, knocking bodies into the air and cleaving through the less fortunate as he pressed for the edge of the basin.

With a devastating strike, Draegan felled a handful of soldiers and saw Isarn standing in a clearing of bodies before him. Behind he saw a clear path carved to the edge of the basin.

"Thank you for your help, Isarn," Draegan said as he rushed by him, swinging the axe at the frozen soldiers that lined the edge of the clearing.

"Thank me when you have the time," Isarn panted. "My spell unravels even as we speak, and I do not know how much longer I can maintain it."

"Come then, sheath your blades and leave first. I will stand and secure your exit."

Isarn did as he was bid and shot past Draegan who followed after him. They were less than a hundred feet from the edge base of the fallen obelisk when Isarn yelled and the soldiers rushed in, the spell broken. Isarn dove out of the basin and drew his blades as he turned to push back in. Behind him he saw various limbs and helmed heads flying above the fray. Moments later the ground heaved and tossed a hundred soldiers in the air. Draegan pushed down the cleared path and ran to Isarn.

"Back to the hill," he said and sprinted by him.

Isarn looked behind him as he ran up the small hill and saw the warriors had stopped their pursuit at the edge of the basin. When the two collapsed behind the rock they peered out and saw the warriors reforming their ranks within the great bowl they had escaped.

"They give no chase," Draegan said. "Why not, when they have us on the run?"

"You and your friend have proven quite a nuisance, but now I require the utmost concentration to complete my spell," Vangen said, his voice echoing through the sky. "I prefer that you watch from a distance and allow my forces the time they need to restore their numbers."

Isarn and Draegan watched as a thin green ring glowed softly around the lip of the basin, encircling the three remaining obelisks and all within. Small green embers began to rise from the ring and float on a gentle current nearly to the top of the obelisks.

"A light wall," Isarn whispered. "A powerful shield, and difficult to unweave, even for me. He may well have bought himself the time he needs."

Draegan nodded. "But there, look at his ranks," he said gesturing below. "They form again but their numbers have dwindled. They are now half as many." He turned to face Isarn. "Destroying the Blades of Darkness truly reduces his legions. Though they are able to regenerate if killed, if the master they were bound to is banished, so too are they."

Isarn scanned the legions as they spread around the metal disk. "What you say is true. But even at half his strength, Vangen's army is more than a match for the combined forces of Fyrian."

"I wish that we had time to find the other three Blades of Darkness," Draegan said. "But Vangen nears the end of his spell and prepares to march his hosts through the portal."

Isarn thought for a moment and exclaimed. "When I was thrown to this realm from across the abyss I descended a cliff and entered a burned forest. I felt a great evil when I passed, though then I knew not what it could be. Having encountered the others, now I know it to be a Blade of Darkness I sensed. When I was there I made a mark that could allow me to revisit that place."

Draegan looked at Isarn. "You can Shadow Walk without the use of the cloak?"

"It is a different spell altogether. And one that would be hindered by this foul garment," Isarn said and removed the cloak, tossing it to Draegan. "Though considering the way time flows in this realm it will be nearly as instantaneous as your dark version."

"Then go with haste. I will assail his wall from without, hoping to harry him while you hunt another Blade," Draegan said and stood, turning to face the glowing green wall of light that shimmered in the distance.

Isarn nodded and crossed his legs where he sat in the dust. He drew a great sigil around him and paused, gathering his thoughts. He closed his eyes and breathed slowly, his hands resting in his lap. Draegan watched as Isarn began to tremble and beads of sweat formed on his brow. A tremor shook the hill and Draegan turned to the swirling clouds gathered above Vangen. When he turned back to Isarn he saw nothing but a shimmer of light where he once sat.

"He has command of powerful magic indeed. I would not like to face him in a fair fight," he said and turned once more to the basin, charging down the slope to the glowing shield of light.

Chapter 37: Malthier the Hideous

Isarn watched the gray earth streak by him as the sky blurred to a smear of crimson. He blinked and when he opened his eyes he saw a twisted black mass blocking his view. He locked his legs and stepped back as the world came into focus and he saw the charred forest rise before him.

"Once more into this dark wood," Isarn said and shot off, plunging past the leafless branches of the burned trees. He pushed through the forest, ducking twisting branches that raked at him, threatening to tear the flesh from his bones at the incredible speed with which he was moving past them. He leapt over the curling roots and kept his footing as he headed deeper into the forest, the twining branches choking out the crimson sky above.

After hours of running Isarn paused and turned to look over his shoulder. "There, I sense the baleful hate of a Blade in this direction," he said and turned, charging forward, slipping through the seared branches that clawed at him.

He continued on, noticing the forest beginning to thin as he ran, watching the streaks of red through the tangled canopy of charred branches. A tremor shook the ground, knocking limbs and branches loose from the burnt trunks that held them. It seemed as if the forest was collapsing in a shower of black ice, for when the limbs struck the earth they shattered into razor-sharp pieces. Isarn jumped close to a large tree trunk and pressed against it, making himself as small a target as possible for the falling branches.

He listened for the sound of breaking branches to dwindle before he pushed off from the tree and headed toward the edge of the forest. As the trees thinned he saw further across the plain to a single hill that rose into the sky directly ahead of him. Atop the large motte stood the ruin of a single tower, broken and piled in a heap, and chained above that, a black obelisk floated gently, framed against the crimson sky.

Isarn left the charred forest behind and scrambled up a small rise to get a clear view of the fortress that lay ahead.

"A solitary tower, and it lies in ruins" he said. "This should prove easier than the Red Keep."

As Isarn spoke, a cold wind lifted his robes and caused him to look to the sky in wonder. He saw no indication of the source of the wind, for the clouds here hung lifeless above him. It seemed the source was the broken tower that lay before him. "Your tricks will not save you from your ruin, Blade of Darkness. You are mine to hunt," Isarn said and ran ahead, crossing the plain.

The biting wind howled across the open expanse as Isarn struggled to move forward against it. The air chilled him as he pushed forward to the hill, changing its direction at will and buffeting him from all sides. His robes wrapped around him and proved a great hindrance.

"This realm is beyond reason," Isarn said, tugging at his garment. "I burn in one valley and freeze in another."

He took his robe and threw it off. The wind caught it and lifted it high into the air. Beneath his white and scarlet robe he wore the gray leather breeches and woolen tunic of a disciple of the Rookery. His black boots had become covered in the gray dust of the wastes giving him a monochromatic appearance.

"The priest has shed his skin and a Raven lies within," a cold voice hissed on the biting wind. Isarn felt the air coil about him, wrapping him in cold. "What would a fledgling crow seek in this dead land?"

Isarn shivered more at the tone of the voice than the chill in the air. "I am no Raven. I am Isarn of the Clade and I seek you, Blade. I am your bane."

The voice let out a laugh that sent shivers up Isarn's spine. "You are less than Vangen, and even he struggled to best Malthier, child. You are no match for me even in this state."

Isarn drew his blades and ran forward crossing the remaining distance of the plain as he pushed toward the ruined tower. He slipped by wagon-sized remnants of the black ashlar that once faced the broken tower and pushed up the hill, wending his way through the rubble with considerable speed.

He heard a hiss from the obelisk as he approached and looked up to see the black iron had turned a translucent green. Inside the crystal he saw the black vapors swirling and coiling throughout the massive pillar. "You bring a foul magic to my door, crow," Malthier hissed as a driving wind bit into Isarn, pushing him back as he covered his face from the stinging chill. "I will relieve you of those unkind knives and you will crawl before me, begging for release."

Within a hundred feet of the obelisk the piles of rocks shifted and Isarn fell, swallowed in blackness as the ground gave way beneath his feet. He plunged down a brick-lined shaft through the earth and smashed onto the ground, losing his grip on the blades. Immediately he rose to chase after the blades that clattered ahead of him and again he tumbled, sprawling forward, head over heels as he descended through darkness until at last he smashed his shoulder into a wall and fell back against a solid wall.

Above him he heard the wind howling and then a mechanical thump cut off all sound. All was silent and black as pitch as he placed his hand against the damp rock of the wall he sat against. He tried to stand and fell, his leg twisting under him as his foot rolled at an odd angle. A bolt of pain shot up his leg.

"I have no medicine or cloth to bind my ankle," he said and winced as he reached forward to remove his boot. His left shoulder popped as he moved toward his ankle. He ground his teeth and inhaled sharply as his arm fell slack in his lap. "This will add to the challenge," he said and reached across his chest with his right hand. Grabbing his shoulder he lifted his disjointed arm and pressed it against the wall, leaning into it until it cracked back into place.

He slumped against the wall and drew several breaths, trying to stay the pain and keep from blacking out. When he regained his composure he leaned forward and tucked his legs under him, wincing slightly before he folded his hands in his lap. He closed his eyes out of habit although the chamber he lay in was completely dark. He cast a *topos* spell and sat in silence, etching the results of the enchantment into this memory.

"A labyrinth of twisting tunnels and hidden chambers. This will be more challenging than the Rookery, even without my current injury." He leaned against the wall and pushed up, keeping all his weight off his bad foot. "The Vaghat calls to me from several floors above, though getting to them will prove no small task."

He hobbled down the corridor, with his hand against the cold stones and his good leg bearing all his weight as he hopped forward. He made it to the staircase at the end of the hall and groped in the darkness for a rail. Finding none he clambered up the stairs on his hands and knees until he came to a landing where he pulled himself up against the wall.

"This floor had several exits but none seemed to lead to where my blades lie. The shortest route would be through…" he said and stopped. He felt a thread brush against his hand. He instinctively wiped it away and felt another stick to his cheek. He grabbed at it in the darkness and felt it cling to his hand. "Cobwebs?" he asked, looking about, though he could see nothing. Listening carefully he heard a scrape against the stone floor. It was soft but followed by another then another.

"Something moves here, and I am in no state to deal with it," he said. "It is time to even the odds in my favor." Isarn backed against the wall and sat slowly, taking time to avoid doing further damage to his shoulder and ankle. He drew a series of runes in the air before him and chanted softly under his breath. He felt a fire grow within his body as energy coursed through his veins. The pain in his foot disappeared. He flexed his leg and ankle with ease. His shoulder gave no indication that it had recently slipped from its joint. With his hand he drew a final sign in the air and exhaled. The symbol he had traced with his finger flared to life, casting a red glow through the hall in which he sat.

He jumped to his feet in horror as he looked ahead and saw a hundred unblinking eyes amidst a fanged and hairy head only a few feet from his face. The creature shrieked in the fading red light of the spell and scraping its needle sharp legs across the flagstones fled to an open door in the side of the great hall with surprising speed. Isarn stood frozen as he saw the outline of a giant spider melt into the darkness as the incantation lost its light and returned the chamber to utter blackness.

"If only I had not lost my daggers," he whispered. "I have nothing with which to face this creature, though it seems unaccustomed to light," he said, trying to regain his composure.

He stood still listening intently for any signs of the beast. He heard the slight rasp of the creature's legs upon the stone, though in the cavernous hall the sound echoed, making it difficult to place its position exactly.

"An illumination spell will solve this riddle," he said and raised his hand over his head. Nothing happened. He felt the gossamer thread of webbing wrap around his hand and pulled it back instinctively. "There is not light here with which to draw upon," he said. "Then fire will prove your bane."

Isarn wheeled and flung his hands from his body in an arc, his fists glowing red before they erupted in great jets of flame that curved through the hall, illuminating every corner and crevice. He saw the scale of the great room, with its rows of columns that supported a grand ceiling on sweeping arches. Along the far wall barred doors were sunk between each column except for one entrance where the gate was rusted to the ground. From these inky depths he saw the fading light of the fire spell reflected in a hundred unblinking eyes.

"Do not shy from your fate, creature," Isarn said and ran across the flagstones of the hall in the dimming light. He heard the beast chatter and its many legs scrape against the stone as it slid back into its lair. Isarn pushed through the webs that choked the entrance, the thick strands clinging to his body as he struggled past them. He shouted and held out his hands as a burst of flame burned down the corridor, consuming the thick webs that clung to the walls and clearing a path for him. He saw the shadow of the spider cast upon the far wall as it turned a corner and slipped down the hall.

Isarn tore down the hall and around the corner at top speed and slammed into a net of thick webs that caught him and lifted him off the ground. He thrashed against them, feeling their viscous fibers cling to his body more tightly as he fought. He tried to shout and cast his fire spell, but webbing clung to his jaw and throat, preventing him from speaking.

Isarn closed his eyes and quieted his mind. He heard the excited chittering of the creature closing in on him and felt the slight vibrations as it moved smoothly on its webs. He recalled a spell Isirah had taught him and thinking of the rune traced on the yellowed pages of the dusty tome he opened his eyes, now able to see in the pitch blackness. Before him the arachnid stood, suspended in the corridor on its thick webs. It stepped ever closer, inching toward Isarn's face as it dragged its bulky abdomen over his legs pushing him down deeper into the webbing. He felt the needle-like hairs on the spider's underbelly scratch against the fine mail he wore under his tunic and recoiled in disgust.

The creature hissed, its face inches from Isarn's, spraying droplets of venom across his cheek. Isarn looked up to see the fangs of the beast descending from the creature's hideous maw, rivulets of venom coiling around the curving blades. It pressed its abdomen against Isarn, crushing his chest and pinning his legs as it lifted itself up to strike.

His mind was overtaken with fear and anger as he saw his end. He had come so close to Draegan, only to let him slip away on this fool's quest. The training and teachings of the Clade hammered into him by Isirah had amounted to naught. The beast sat upon his chest, squeezing the air from his lungs, and all Isarn could think of was his failure. Trembling with rage, he drew a breath and tried to devise a way to escape from the foul creature, but his head swam with horror. Here he was, about to meet this end at the fangs of the only living creature in the whole of this cursed, dead land. There was something almost familiar in his despair.

Isarn smiled and looked up at the beast. "Be gone vapor," he said through clenched teeth and exhaled sharply, the air in his lungs forced out by the spider's bulk. Like mist, the spider parted and curled in eddies of dark haze, looping lazily and rising in the stale air of the corridor.

"I know your secret, Malthier," Isarn shouted. "Your artifice is undone and so are you."

Isarn opened his eyes and drew a deep breath of cold air. He stood on the windswept hilltop among the rubble of the fallen tower, the great obelisk suspended against the crimson sky before him. The icy air swirled angrily about him as he bent to pick up the blades of the Vaghat that had fallen at his feet. Malthier howled and shook the crystal, the great chains snapping with the force of his rage.

"You wove a spell within me, and one of great cunning, using my own nightmares against me. But I fear failure more than any beast that haunts the mind or heart, Blade of Darkness. And this you missed when you attempted to trap me within my own terror."

Again the pillar shook and tested the strength of the colossal links that bound it, as Isarn sheathed his blades and raised his hand to the sky. "I will show you mercy as I tear your shade from all existence and send you beyond the abyss." He lowered his hand in a sharp motion, bringing his fist down to his side, the great obelisk obeying his movement as it crashed into the heap of rocks, sending boulders and fragments of stone flying in all directions.

Isarn braced himself as the shock of the obelisk shook the plain, blowing clouds of dust and debris past him. He drew his daggers and walked carefully through the rubble as he approached the green face of the massive crystal, now half buried in the rubble of the broken tower. Malthier hissed and lashed out at Isarn as he drove the blades into the obelisk. Isarn leaned against them for some time as the roiling mass of shadow slammed against the crystal, until at last the pillar exploded in a flash of green light that lit the sky. Pieces of the obelisk rained down for some time, showering the plain with fragments of black iron.

As the last pieces of the pillar fell, Isarn rose and dusted himself off. "Now back to Vangen," he said with a sigh of relief. He sprinted across the gray plain and headed for the burnt forest on the horizon.

Draegan charged at the wall of light, the World Render held high above him. Beyond the shimmering light he saw the filmy outlines of Vangen's forces reforming their ranks around the metal disk. With a yell he brought the axe down with all his strength against the shimmering curtain. The axe struck the wall and bounced back with such force that it sent Draegan flying across the plain. He rolled for nearly a hundred yards, his cloak wrapping around him as his body skipped like a stone, leaving clouds of dust in his wake.

Draegan groaned and picked himself off the ground, spitting the dust from his mouth as he rose. "This is proving a challenge," he said, limping through the ash in search of his axe. It lay a few feet from the wall in the soft powder, its intricate carvings highlighted in the green glow of the barrier. He bent to pick the weapon and felt its weight in his hand. His shoulder groaned in protest as he lifted the heavy dual blades from the earth.

High above the curtain of light the storm roared and thunder cracked as the clouds boiled over each other. "His incantation nears its end," Draegan said as he hefted the mighty axe over his shoulder. "I must redouble my efforts."

The ground quaked, throwing Draegan to his knees. A peal of thunder ripped through the sky, deafening him as he rose, though he noticed it left a metallic ring in his ears rather than the low threatening tones of the storm. Looking across the basin he saw an obelisk flash before it burst into a thousand pieces at the base, the top teetering unsteadily. A moment later he bent over in pain. The Black Horn, slung over his hip, had exploded, burying fragments of itself into his ribs. He dropped the axe and steadied his breathing before he began pulling shards of the horn from his body. He felt the earth shake again and saw the obelisk had slammed into the ground.

The wall of light had deadened the sound of its fall, though as he watched he saw the obelisk pulse before it vanished, taking a hundred thousand of Vangen's soldiers with it into the ether.

"Isarn has done well, and acted more quickly than I imagined," he said, gingerly extracting the last piece of the Black Horn from his side and tossing it to the earth. Draegan grasped the handle of the World Render and charged once more at the wall of light. When he was within range he stopped, planted his feet wide and swung the bit of the blade directly at the glowing wall. The sound of thunder tore through the basin and Draegan recoiled from the force of the blow. He stumbled back, catching himself and using the axe to stop from toppling over. His ears rang and it took a moment for his eyes to focus, but when he again looked at the barrier he saw it shining as perfectly as before he had struck. Inside the curtain Vangen's legions had reformed, their orderly regiments facing in toward the metal disk as they encircled the platform.

"This barrier is more than a match for the World Render. I have failed to delay Vangen. Already his forces are prepared to march through the portal and here I stand outside the barrier, useless," Draegan said as he leaned on the axe. "While Isarn finds success in destroying the obelisks outside the barrier, perhaps I will find better luck within." He cracked his back and hefted the mighty axe from the ground. "It is time to try another tactic."

He took the axe and backing up a few steps, charged once more at the wall but when he neared it, he stopped short and drove the World Render deep into the earth. Cracks and fissures spread from the buried blade like a spider's web as they coursed under the wall, fracturing the ground and casting large masses of earth up into the air. Soldiers fell as the ground shook from the force of his blow, but soon they had righted themselves and were standing again in perfect formation.

"I do little more than annoy them in there, like tapping on a fish bowl," Draegan said, "while out here I am bested by a barrier spell though I wield the mountain-splitting World Render. Gron would be ashamed of my performance. If only I had learned to channel the berserker rage that aided him in the use of this Artifact." He turned the handle of the mighty axe slowly in his hands. "Perhaps it requires something of me before it unleashes its power. If it desires hate and fury, then I shall drown it."

Draegan stared past the small embers of green light that rose lazily from the glowing ring before him and beyond the legions of soldiers that stood at attention near the great metal disk in the center of the basin and focused on Vangen. He felt a hatred grow within him as he saw his brother amidst the host of warriors, his arms outstretched beneath the churning black clouds that spread across the crimson sky. Draegan set his jaw and ground his teeth while he watched lightning strike the metal plate, knowing the incantation was nearing its completion and his time for ending Vangen was drawing to a close.

"He has taken everything from me, my father, my mother, my king, my wife and child. And now he would have my people," he hissed through clenched teeth. "If there is justice in this world then let it fall to me to bring it to him," he whispered, his hands squeezing the handle of the axe so tightly as he spoke that the carven images began to dig into his palms. He felt a movement in his hands and looked down to see the serpents that were fashioned on the grip begin to coil slowly around his wrists, wrapping up his forearms. The keen edge of the blades began to pulse and glow a fiery red.

"Today you will know my wrath," Draegan shouted as he lifted the axe, feeling how light it had become. The twining serpents that had coiled around his forearms now sunk their arrow-like heads deep into his flesh, binding the Artifact to him. Draegan's head swam as his vision blurred, the only point of focus being the lone figure standing on the metal disk. He ran forward, slowly gaining speed as he went until he was charging the wall at a full sprint, the World Render aflame as he drove the blade into the smoldering green barrier.

With a thunderous crack the blade sank into the wall of light. Instantly a web of fissures spread from the point of impact and ran across the curtain of light. Draegan growled with animal ferocity and wrenched the axe out of the wall, its flaming blades searing the air around him as he pulled the World Render behind him for another strike. He spread his feet and locked his legs, driving the axe into the wall once again.

The wall shattered as if it were made of glass. The ground shook as shards of green light fell in a rain around Draegan, evaporating with a small hiss of curling green smoke as they touched the gray ash of the wastes. He stood still, letting the fragments of shimmering light fall around him, the blade of the axe resting on the ground as he held the handle tightly.

With a roar he sprang forward and charged toward Vangen, pushing through the formations of unliving soldiers as he ran. He swung the axe with a possessed fury, felling those warriors around him in a flaming path of destruction as he marched toward the metal disk. He wielded the axe with animal savagery, throwing all caution aside as he hacked his way through the frozen ranks, the sounds of his axe cleaving through metal drowning out the thunder that echoed in the sky.

He looked up to see a thin strand of emerald light pierce the raging storm and strike his brother who stood in the center of the disk. Vangen clapped his hands and shouted. Instantly the clouds parted, dissolving into the sky as if carried off by an unseen wind. Draegan stopped his mad onslaught and an eerie hush fell over the basin. For a moment there was no sound, and even Draegan held his breath. Then all was thunder as a great pillar of green flame erupted from the entire surface of the disk, consuming Vangen and launching straight into the sky. The once crimson canopy that stretched over Draegan and the entire shadow realm began to turn a bilious green as the great flame issued forth into the heavens.

Then, as quickly as it began, the pillars of flame died out, leaving a thin trail of embers that lifted gently toward the sky before they lost their momentum and floated softly back to rest on the metal disk. Vangen was crouched in the center of the disk, his cloak spread over him as he rested on one knee.

"You have arrived too late, brother. The spell is complete," Vangen said between labored breaths. He rose slowly, and when he was firmly upright, he straightened his robes and took a deep breath. "However you are in time to see my final triumph."

Draegan saw that the runes carved in the disk now throbbed with an ethereal green light. From his position near the edge of the basin he could see down toward the center of the depression where the first ranks of soldiers marched forward and stepped up upon the circle. His heart froze as he saw them disappear as soon as they made contact with the disk.

"The portal is open and my legions march through Athar." Vangen's laugh filled the valley. "I have bridged the worlds and undone the work of the Elder Gods, brother. I am beyond them in my power."

The legions of warriors pressed forward slowly, their massive numbers making it difficult to move with any speed toward the disk. With another shout, Draegan tore into the throngs once more, the World Render carving a fiery swath through the soldiers. They did not fight against him. They only moved forward one step at a time as each forward rank stood upon the disk and disappeared, the next rank moving forward to follow suit.

"You cannot kill them any faster than I can give them life again," Vangen yelled as another rank of soldiers stepped upon the disk and vanished. "Lay down your arms and come to peace with your failure." Vangen lowered his arms and shifted is weight, staying in the middle of the rune filled disk. "You gave good sport, but you cannot hope to defeat a god."

"You are hardly a god, Vangen. Have you in your conceit not noticed that only two of your pillars remain? You are trapped in this realm with me and I will end you this day."

Vangen smoothed his cloak and looked toward Draegan. "I suppose I must commend you for your achievements, though I think my admiration belongs more to your young friend in white. But I see he is not here, so I must assume he sprints across the Wastes, searching for the two remaining obelisks in a vain attempt to destroy them." Vangen smiled. "You have caused me to consider alternative measures for crossing the portal, but I have limitless time in this realm to devise another plan. You, however do not."

Vangen lifted his hands to the sky and brought them back down. Green bolts of lightning seared through the air and struck the ground within inches of Draegan, flinging soldiers into the air. Draegan ducked as the empty shells of armor fell back to the ground, lifting clouds of gray ash as they struck the earth.

"Am I such a threat that you would kill your own men in an attempt to get at me, Vangen?" Draegan sped forward, crushing rows of warriors with the World Render as he pushed toward the glowing disk.

Again lightning fell from the sky, decimating scores of troops as Draegan carved through the ranks. He noticed a slight delay between Vangen casting the spell and the green light crashing to the ground. Taking advantage of this brief pause he shifted directions each time Vangen dropped his arms. Planting his feet, the coiled muscles in his legs propelled him at a hard angle from the direction he was running, safely launching him clear of the devastating lightning.

"You prove more a nuisance than a threat," Vangen said, his voice rising as he spoke. "You are wasting your time. If you seek to delay me while your friend hurries to destroy the remaining obelisks then your effort is wasted." Vangen spread his arms wide, gesturing to his legions of soldiers. "As you hack your way through them they continue to step through the portal, entering Athar and laying waste to those who you claim to protect."

Draegan lashed out with the axe, an arc of flame cleaving through a hundred warriors. Their bodies crumpled to the ground, leaving Draegan standing alone in a clearing of empty armor. "A thousand or more soldiers may march through to Athar by the time I've dealt with you, Vangen, but the armies of the Fyrian Empire will prove more than their match."

Vangen laughed, his voice filling the basin as yet another row of soldiers stepped upon the disk and glowed briefly before they vanished.

"How quickly you forget, Draegan." Vangen shook his head. "Through your sense of duty you have secured Athar's downfall. Or is it vengeance?" Vangen lifted his gaze to the once crimson sky which now glowed green. "When you came here with the Artifacts you took the one hope the people of Fyrian had of stopping my army. You disarmed my prey and took away their fangs, turning wolves to sheep. And now my legions will slaughter them like lambs." Vangen looked across the basin toward Draegan. "Their blood is on your hands, for your hatred of me is what drove you here with the Artifacts to seek my life."

"Ceredyn devised a way to stop your reavers," Draegan yelled. "Those in the Rookery will craft yet another that doesn't rely of the Artifacts."

Vangen smiled. "These are not reavers. They will not fall to your petty sorcery. They are deathless souls that I have returned to life, and if they should fall they return here to these Ashen Wastes, where I press their shades into service once again. You cannot hope for victory."

Draegan shouted in anger and sunk the axe into the ground, rupturing the gray earth before him for several hundred yards. Great fissures opened, swallowing scores of soldiers as the cracks filled with fire that poured from Draegan's axe.

"I should thank you, brother. You disguised your lust for vengeance as a noble deed for the greater good and came here with the six Dark Artifacts. And now they are two." Vangen laughed. "By some comedy of ignorance you have even discovered a way to rid the realms of their power, a feat not even the Sages could claim."

Draegan roared and launched himself forward, pushing toward the metal disk and the ranks of soldiers that pressed toward it as another hundred stepped upon the raised circle and vanished.

"There will always be a way. There will always be hope," he said charging into a throng of soldiers and laying them low with a ferocious swipe of his great fiery axe.

Vangen snapped his fingers and Draegan fell to the earth, catching himself on his knees. The World Render dropped from his grasp and settled in the powdery ash. "You shall bow before me, brother."

Draegan struggled to stand, but was pinned by a binding spell. The serpents that had coiled around his arms moments before now withdrew into the handle of the World Render, which lay inches before him but entirely out of his reach.

"You labor under a delusion that I would cure you of," Vangen said. "You think me mortal. Here I stand before you, while you grovel upon the ground, not unlike our prior meeting in my old study. My forces now march across the abyss and into Athar. I have unwoven the barrier that held this realm in the shadows. Not only have I undone the work of the Elder Gods, but I have added to my accomplishments by crafting another spell that allows my legions to pour like a raging river into your kingdoms to drown them in a flood of death."

Vangen clasped his hands behind him as he looked across the metal disk, its glowing runes casting a green light upon him, accentuating the pallor of his face. "As I said before when you stood beneath me in the Red Keep, I have moved beyond life and death. I split my soul long ago in my study in Dullahan. Now I stand outside the circle of life and death, able to see it for what it really is, able to grasp and manipulate it, able to bend and shape it as I will."

"You're nothing more than the sickly, loathsome child of a disappointed father," Draegan said, trying to keep the bonds of the spell from crushing his chest as he spoke. "No matter what you gain you will always hunger for more to fill the emptiness in your heart. The emptiness that came from being second to me in Leon's eyes."

Vangen lifted his hand and Draegan fell flat to the ground, his mouth filling with ash as he struggled against the great invisible weight that pressed him into to the earth. His breath became labored as he felt the blood rush to his head, unable to move his hands or fingers. The World Render was inches beyond his grasp, but every muscle in his body was frozen.

"You speak as one who knows the end is near and has nothing to offer but incensed words," Vangen snarled. He narrowed his eyes as he looked toward Draegan lying in the dirt. He drew a breath and a wry smile spread across his face. "I shall have you watch as every soldier walks across the disk and into your kingdoms. I shall show you the dead that litter your fields and choke your rivers as my warriors sweep across your land like a plague. And when Athar is wiped clean of life I will bring this realm across the abyss and rejoin the two halves. You will watch as your kingdoms are swallowed by the sea and the sky rains fire upon your home."

Draegan managed to turn his eyes to the side. He could see across the basin and out to the two obelisks that stood around the perimeter of the depression. He smiled and choked out a laugh before the shackles that bound him tightened and he winced in pain.

"Soon you will meet you limit, Vangen," Draegan hissed between his teeth.

Vangen's eyes opened wide. Raising his arm he lifted Draegan high into the air, several feet above heads of the legions of soldiers that continued to march onto the metal disk. He hung suspended in the air, bound as if in chains though he struggled with all his might.

"I remember now," Vangen said, a cruel smile spreading across his ashen face. "I had a message to relay to you." With his left hand raised in the air and keeping Draegan held above the throngs of soldiers, he slid his right hand to his side and drew the blade he carried there. "This sword was to serve as a reminder of my tale and I had nearly forgotten with all the preparations."

Draegan lifted his chin toward the bilious sky and stretched his body against the invisible cords that bound him. "The story of your blade holds no interest for me. Loosen my bonds and I will have the World Render sing you a song of destruction that will drown out your tired tale."

Draegan choked back a scream as he felt the chains of the spell tighten around him and dig into his flesh. He heard a ringing in his ears and his vision blurred, the green sky becoming a smear of light as his eyes rolled in their sockets. He felt the fetters loosen and he took a breath, reorienting himself.

Vangen drew the sword from its scabbard and held it in the green light emanating from the sigils carved in the metal disk. "The story of this blade should interest you above all others, for it involves you, or rather, one close to you."

Vangen swung the sword through the air, admiring the green light that coruscated along its length. He kept his left hand raised high in the air, keeping Draegan suspended above the soldiers that continued their slow march forward, each rank stepping upon the platform, glowing for an instant and then vanishing.

"It seems like ages ago, and trying to recall the exact proceedings is like walking through a fog, but I can still piece together the events." Vangen looked from the blade up to Draegan. "You once had a betrothed, a young woman from Vatn, as was the tradition of our fathers. When you left her shortly after your wedding ceremony to lay waste to villages throughout the Empire, she grew weary of life in Dullahan and your continued absence and eventually left you, did she not?" Vangen chuckled as he looked at Draegan struggling against the spell. "When she abandoned you she returned to Vatn. But several months later I happened upon her as I walked the dim corridors outside my study. Issa was her name."

Vangen's smile twisted on his face and his thin lips parted revealing his yellow teeth and forked black tongue. "She had returned, hoping to find you and make amends, for she had news to share with you. But of course you were gone, lost somewhere in the north, no doubt killing villagers at my request. I told her this which seemed to dismay her. I guess you had not shared our secret with her, but alas, now that she knew I had but no choice to run this blade through her heart."

Draegan screamed and flailed against the invisible bands that held him in the air, choking on his rage as the spell tightened and threatened to constrict the life from him.

"Calm yourself, brother. The story does not end there. As she fell and lay dying in my arms she whispered the most curious thing in my ear. Death has a way of loosening even the most stubborn tongues and as the darkness closed in around her she told me of her child on Vatn. Her child with you." Vangen narrowed his eyes as he looked at Draegan. "I could hardly believe such a thing. You, a father? How preposterous. I took her soul and her blood and hammered her being into this weapon, trapping her forever within the metal and keeping her always by my side. You know I had always admired her. She was quite pleasant to look at. I never understood why father picked her for you and not me. Not that I really wanted her, but I suppose it was the principle of the matter that offended me the most. That and seeing you happy."

Vangen dropped his left hand and Draegan fell with a thud into the ash covered ground. He took a breath and began to rise, grabbing the World Render that lay before him. He was about to launch himself at Vangen when he felt a hand on his shoulder.

"Stay your rage, father. He is mine to kill."

Chapter 39: The Confrontation

Draegan turned and saw Isarn at his shoulder, looking past him at Vangen upon the raised platform.

Vangen spat. "So the priest has shed his vestments and returns to his friend in the feathers of Corvus. I must say the pure white of Vatn lent an air of somber piety that the drab gray of Corvus lacks. You look quite dull, boy."

Isarn drew the second blade from its scabbard and stepped in front of Draegan. "I am neither of Vatn nor Corvus nor any kingdom. I was forged by the Clade and carry the Vaghat of Greydin Vir, the bane of the Sages, and now your doom, Vangen."

"You presume too much, fledgling." Vangen lifted his hand and curled his fingers into a fist. Green ropes of light burst from the ground and coiled about Isarn's legs like ethereal snakes. As quickly as they twined about him they fell off, like dead leaves from a tree, vanishing as they hit the ground.

Isarn kept walking slowly forward, his eyes fixed on Vangen, the blades pulsing by his side. "I never knew my mother other than her name and a handful of stories people would offer out of sympathy toward me that spoke of her generous heart. But for your actions twenty years ago I would have simply been another acolyte of Vatn, withdrawn from the world and peacefully whiling away my days in the gardens and library." Isarn set his jaw and smiled dryly as he walked toward the platform. "But by your hand you sent me, an orphaned infant, on a path that led me to the Clade. There, I was shaped to be the sole instrument of Draegan's death. I was fashioned in the fires of the secret sect and honed by trials so cruel they would break all but the hardest of men. Now the curtain has been drawn back and I see that it is you who will slake the thirst of my blades and quench my rage, not my father. And I will rid the world of your malevolence and restore order to the kingdoms once again."

"You are the son of Draegan and Issa?" Vangen burst with laughter then collected himself as he looked at Isarn. "To see father and son reunited at my feet brings joy even to my hardened heart. I had always wondered what became of the babe Issa left on Vatn but never thought the child would come seeking me. And now here you both stand, walking to your doom together, just as I send Athar to its own." He shook his head and laughed again.

"Your magic is undone and so are you, Vangen," Isarn said. "For the honor of my mother and all of Athar and I will have your heart in my hand," he said as he walked forward, the blades glowing in his hand. Vangen sheathed his sword and raised his hands to the sky, parting the clouds and summoning a great mass of lightning.

Isarn kept walking forward, holding the blades by his side, which throbbed with ethereal energy. Several strikes of lightning hit him as he approached the disk but they bent inches above his head and fell to his side, tearing into the marching soldiers.

Draegan rolled as lightning fell from the sky striking the ground where he had just stood. He rose, and taking the World Render, charged toward the metal circle, the axe carving a red path through the throngs of soldiers. As Draegan continued along his deadly path, Isarn kept his slow methodical pace, the daggers beginning to crackle with energy as he approached the disk.

Vangen sneered and stepped back drawing his hands to his sides. "My legions will be reborn. You, however, will not," he said as he shot his fists forward. Around him the air hissed and a great unseen force exploded outward from him in all directions, driving out from the center of the disk and spreading across the valley, smashing into his soldiers and sending their broken bodies flying as if driven by a gale.

Isarn stood untouched and folded his arms over his chest, crossing the blades of the Vaghat. The thundering energy slipped by him as harmlessly as a gentle breeze, while around him the soldiers turned to ash. Their armor and helms shattered and spears splintered from the force.

Draegan saw a tidal wave of fallen soldiers rise up before him and slammed the axe into the ground, heaving a great wall of earth up in front of him. He ducked behind it as swords and spears and shields flew by him and he heard the sickening thud of bodies smash into the earthen bulwark. A moment later the strange force Vangen had unleashed tore by, completely destroying the bodies of the soldiers before it slammed into the slab of earth and smashed it to pieces.

The force sent Draegan flying back a hundred feet. He slammed into the ground and rolled, knocking the World Render from his grip. He sprung to his feet unharmed and rushed to his axe, lifting it in one smooth motion as he sprinted ahead, finding his footing among the piles of scattered armor and weapons. It was if a great storm had leveled a field of ripe grain. Shadows of bodies were etched on the ashen ground, which was littered with fragments of armor and rent helms. He looked ahead as he ran and saw that the entirety of Vangen's forces were gone. A lone figure in gray stood at the base of the platform.

"You are a curious child, indeed," Vangen said from the center of the disk as he watched Isarn approach the platform. "I have attempted to blast your soul into the abyss twice and yet you still stand before me. When I try to bind you my chains slip from you as if they were water." Vangen furrowed his brow. "I have poured through the archives of Vatn and the banished tomes of Iss, but never have I read of a power quite like yours in all the histories. I shall enjoy pulling your secrets from you, boy."

Isarn put one foot up on the platform, keeping the other planted firmly in the gray ash. Instantly the glowing runes incised on the edge of the disk faded, their green glow softening before going cold. Isarn stepped forward onto the disk and smiled as he approached Vangen.

"There is no need to pull them from me, Vangen. I offer my secret freely that you may know the depths of your folly." Isarn took another slow step forward and another ribbon of runes pulsed and faded. "There is another library, deep beneath a small island off the coast of Vatn that gets very few visitors, for only membership in the Clade gains one entrance. It contains the unadulterated truth of the history of Athar and the Fall of the Sages, of Greydin Vir and the founding of the Clade. In these buried books, locked deep within the tomb of rock where I was raised you will encounter the tale of these, the Vaghat." Isarn turned the blades of his knives slowly in his hand as he walked closer to Vangen. "But I shall give you a personal introduction to Bhel and Asai, rather than a tedious lecture," he said and sprung at Vangen, his blades crackling with energy that left a trail of deep blue and red light as he slashed at his enemy.

Vangen drew his sword and parried the whirling daggers that struck at him with blinding speed. He was forced back, the pressure from Isarn too great for him to mount an offensive. Vangen raised his hand and clenched his fist as spectral chains rose from the disk and twined about Isarn. The chains fell to the metal plate, slack and lifeless, and then disappeared. Vangen raised his arm again and shouted, bringing it down to his side in one swift motion. The sky rumbled and flashed with a hideous green light, but as it descended on Isarn it sputtered and died before it struck him, vanishing into the air.

"How do you unweave my spells so adroitly?" Vangen asked as he jumped back, dodging another ferocious swipe of Isarn's blades. "You neither form signs nor utter incantations."

Isarn stopped his attack and looked at Vangen, a cold fire in his eyes. "The Vaghat is the final gift of the Elder God Helian to mankind. It is our salvation from a world riddled with evil and corrupted by hate." Isarn looked at the blades burning with an ethereal fire. "These were forged by Greydin Vir, the consort of Sage Vatn from a piece of the heavens that fell from the sky when the Elder Gods sundered the world. Helian had heard Greydin's cries and sent this power to him to be used in his repentance for his wrongdoing." Isarn looked at Vangen and clenched his jaw. "They contain a magic neither of this realm nor of Athar, and were used by Greydin to slay the Sages. Now I will pay his penance by ending you."

Isarn leapt at Vangen with both blades held high and brought them down with tremendous force at Vangen's chest, seeking to plunge them through his breast. Vangen wheeled and caught the falling daggers with his sword. Turning, he moved to Isarn's side and holding out his palm at Isarn's face uttered a series of foul words in rapid succession, his black, forked tongue rolling out over his thin lips as he hissed the spell. A green light congealed in Vangen's palm and wavered for a moment before it guttered and went out.

Isarn rolled out of the way and coiling himself, sprung at Vangen once again. Isarn slipped under the downward strike of Vangen's sword as he drove his shoulder into Vangen's chest and sent him sprawling onto the disk.

Isarn waited while Vangen collected himself. "Rise monster, that you may face your death on your feet and die with some dignity."

"So it is those blades that unweave my magic and not any skill you possess." Vangen picked up his sword and laughed. "To think that in some forgotten corner of Athar there exists a weapon more powerful than the Artifacts. A weapon that can unravel the most powerful of spells without the thought or effort of the wielder. It is most peculiar that such a treasure was kept from all knowledge for so many thousands of years."

"The Clade is uninterested in power or the affairs of man," Isarn replied. "We are tasked with using these blades only to guard the Artifacts and prevent them from reentering the six kingdoms."

"Then I must say you have done poorly in your charge, for Draegan has brought the six Artifacts of Darkness here, unchecked by you. And if Draegan is able to best you even with those daggers, then you will prove of little consequence to me."

Isarn and Vangen ran at each other when a violent tremor shook the ground. Both men stumbled and when Isarn regained his footing he looked past Vangen to see Draegan rushing toward the edge of the disk with the World Render held high above his head. Isarn watched as Draegan sunk the blade deep into the platform causing the metal to crack. The force of the impact dropped Vangen to one knee and Isarn used the moment to launch himself into the air bringing the blue and red fire of the Vaghat over his head in a sweeping arc as he plunged the blades toward Vangen's neck.

Vangen rolled as Isarn slammed into the platform, his terrible strength driving the daggers to the hilt into the metal. As he set his feet and pulled hard on the handles, desperately trying to remove the blades from the platform, Vangen rose and pulling back his sword drove it at Isarn's chest.

Isarn ducked and wheeled, springing from a crouch and using his momentum to pull the daggers from their hold. As he turned he saw the silver blade of the sword that would have passed through him plunge into Draegan's chest. Draegan grunted and grabbed the blade, pulling himself down its length and toward Vangen, forcing a smile as he did so. The blade slid out through his back and under his shoulder as he took a step forward. He grabbed Vangen in a great embrace pinning his arms to his side as he pulled him closer, driving the blade deeper into this chest.

"End him now, Isarn," Draegan said between racking breaths.

Isarn saw Draegan and Vangen locked together. The silver-white blade protruded from his father's back as Vangen struggled against Draegan's hold. Isarn walked forward and then stopped, his daggers crackling with the intensity of lightning.

"If I come closer, Bhel and Asai will undo the magic that lives in your Talisman of Light. The Great Aegis you wear pinned at your neck will become nothing more than lifeless silver and your wound will become fatal."

"Do not think of me," Draegan replied. "My life is nothing when weighed against those in Athar. You must act now and strike while I still hold him."

"In your hesitation you have lost all," Vangen said as he threw his head back to the sky, mouth open as black veins began to crawl up his neck. His eyes turned a milky white as his body racked in Draegan's grasp.

Isarn sheathed his blades and sprinted toward the pair, closing the distance with incredible speed. He shoved Draegan away from Vangen as hard as he could, sending his father sprawling onto the metal disk, the sword stuck in his chest scraping against the metal as he fell to the ground. As Draegan collapsed, Vangen reached out and clasped his hands around Isarn's neck. In a flash of light, two blades sliced through the air, leaving shimmering arcs of azure and scarlet light in their wake. Isarn plunged the glowing steel into Vangen's chest, buried to the hilt.

"It is you who have lost all," Isarn said through clenched teeth as he felt Vangen's hands loosen on his neck. "You are undone."

Vangen laughed and once more tightened his grip on Isarn, dropping him to his knees as Isarn wrestled against the iron grip of his enemy. "I have crossed the threshold between the mortal and immortal, child. Your moment is lost, your life forfeit. You placed you faith in weapons of steel and iron, but I am beyond anything of this world." Isarn's vision began to swim as Vangen's hold relentlessly choked out his life. In his final moments, Isarn realized that the years of training and sacrifice he had gone through had been wasted. Regret that he had spent his time hunting his father instead of trying to understand him clouded his last moments of consciousness.

Suddenly, with a painful burn in his throat, he was once more sucking in air. Isarn heard a hissing gasp from Vangen. Wrenching himself from the weakened grip of Vangen's hands, Isarn stumbled back, and as his vision returned, he saw above him a silver white blade drive clean through Vangen's mouth. All at once, Vangen was still, the blade that held Issa's soul protruding from the base of his skull. Draegan appeared as a shadow in the periphery of Isarn's watery vision and pulled the blade from Vangen's face. Draegan and Vangen both collapsed to their knees on the disk. Isarn stood, gathering himself and clearing his mind.

Pulling Bhel and Asai from Vangen's body, Isarn drove them once again into Vangen's chest and watched as a thin web of frost grew from the wound Asai had inflicted, and spread over Vangen's body until he was covered in powdery white crystals. A flame erupted from Bhel, buried in Vangen's heart, and raced over Vangen's body, consuming him in a fire that burned brightly, but without heat. Vangen crumpled to the ground, frozen in place, his mouth agape and eyes unblinking as black bile poured down his chest, hissing as it came in contact with the flame.

"My blades do not only unweave magic. They are capable, through my practiced hand, of unraveling the gossamer threads of a soul, pulling each strand from the tapestry of life and sending it beyond the abyss and out of all existence. With the help of my mother Issa's soul I have taken yours Vangen. Now you are truly undone."

Vangen's charred body lay still on the cold metal disk. Isarn sheathed his daggers and turned to lift Draegan. "Your wound is grievous, and though I have no supplies with me to treat it, I know many healing spells and can staunch the bleeding. I will need to remove your cloak…"

Draegan waved his hand, and tried to push Isarn away. "It's too late for me. The Talisman of Light that had guarded my life until now was weakened by your blades when I came too close. Now I pay the price." Isarn began to object, but Draegan continued. "Take the Aegis from me and return to Athar. Take my place as Emperor and do what must be done to save the people that still live. End the curse of Vangen. Destroy the deathless soldiers who walked across the portal, but Isarn, you must leave me here to die. My soul will buy you passage."

Isarn began to object.

"You do not listen," Draegan said, his voice gentle but firm. "Vangen's forces march on my people, on your people, Isarn, as you sit here and linger over a dying old man." Draegan grabbed Isarn's hand. "I will show you how to open the gate and teach you the words, but you will need a soul to pay the price. We are the only two living beings left in this cursed realm so I shall pay the toll."

"There must be another way," Isarn stammered, looking around in desperation.

Draegan rolled to his side and coughed. "There is not. You must do as I say. Take the Aegis from me and return to our homeland. Unite the people again, and free them from the tyranny of Vangen."

"I am no leader of men, Draegan. I was forged by the…"

"Yes I know Isarn," Draegan said, smiling weakly. "You were forged by the Clade to kill me. But here I lay dying so it is time you took on a higher purpose." Draegan paused to catch his breath which had become labored. "I left the world on the brink of war. The kingdom of Skeldus had fallen and the Tribe of Docga was no more. I cannot imagine what has transpired in the time we've been here, but if people still walk within the five kingdoms then it is your duty to lead them, protect them, and restore order to their world. Your work here is done. The Artifacts are no more, save the two that will be forever trapped in this world when you cross over. It is time you assume your birthright."

Isarn looked at Draegan with pity in his eyes. He watched as Draegan struggled to breathe, a puddle of foaming blood gathering under Draegan's shoulder and spreading slowly out, pooling in the carved runes of the platform on which he lay. Behind him the charred corpse of Vangen lay twisted and frozen, the few remaining flames slowly dying out. A soft breeze blew through the basin, scattering the white ashes of Vangen across the platform, some swirling up into the air before they fell slowly, a soft snow upon the gray wastes.

Isarn looked toward the endless horizon of the dead land, lost in thought. After a moment he turned again to Draegan. "I will return to Athar and rid the land of the unliving scourge. But I can promise no more. I am not a creature of your world, trained and raised by a king. I lived for twenty years beneath the ground, training for one purpose alone. Now it seems there is little more I can to offer. What you ask is more than I can bear alone."

Draegan looked up and gave Isarn a pained smile. "A good king does not bear his burdens alone. Seek out Gron, if he still lives. He has taken the white of Vatn, but once fought by my side. He is a good man and will guide you well."

Isarn frowned. "What of the cloak and the axe? I will not take them with me, nor do I dare leave them here. If they still exist, even in this world, I fear another may rise and seek them."

Draegan lay silent for a moment, his breathing slow and shallow. He looked up at Isarn who kneeled over him. "I will show you how to open the gate. You may use that dark knowledge however you wish and if you choose, you may return here to destroy the two remaining Blades of Darkness, and their Artifacts." Draegan blinked slowly and fought to keep his eyes open. "But you need a soul to pay passage to leave, so if you come here again, you will be trapped."

"Time grows short for us both, father. Show me the sign and teach me the words. I will return to Athar and do what is asked of me."

Draegan smiled and closed his eyes. "Bring me Vangen's sword. I should like to be near Issa when I pass."

Isarn grabbed the sword and flung the black bile from blade, spraying it on the metal disk. It shed the viscous liquid easily and shone silver-white again even under the green sky that cast a sickly pallor across the land. Draegan winced in pain as he struggled to sit up, taking the sword and laying it in his lap. He showed Isarn the runes and taught him the words, watching as he marked the circle on the platform.

"When you take the Aegis from me, I won't have much time left, so you must move quickly. Know before you take your leave how much I regret the decisions that have brought us here. I wish I hadn't been so blind to Vangen's ploys, so easily led where he would have me go. I wish too that I hadn't left Issa and that we could have been a family. But I was a fool. Now I place my failures and my burden upon you that some small good may come of my sins."

Isarn stepped into the circle he had drawn around Draegan. "By your actions you have ended the greatest evil Athar has ever known and have rid the land of four of the Dark Artifacts. I do not know how history will judge you, but in this short time I have spent with you, I know that you only sought what was the greater good, and will remember you for that. And I will remember that we fought together, side by side, at the end." He leaned close to Draegan's face and took the silver pin of Skeldus from his neck.

"And now I take my leave father. May the Gods grant forgiveness for your soul. You already have mine." Isarn rested his hand gently on his father's shoulder for a moment before letting the spell take him.

Draegan slumped as the circle around him flared to life, the red flames turning black as they hungrily climbed up Isarn, swallowing him until, in a flash, he was gone.

The body of Draegan sat motionless in the dying fire, its head bowed and shoulders hunched forward. Pale silver light flashed through the sword and then went out, and the blade turned a dull gray.

Chapter 40: The Council at Dullahan

"Enter and make yourself known." The old voice echoed across the chamber.

Silently the great doors of the council chamber swung inward, the larger than life-sized figures carved into the stone still moving slowly as the doors parted. The sun that bathed the white marble of the chamber in a soft glow poured out into the darkened hall and spilled over the figure standing between the massive doors. The light struck his scarlet and red cloak, and fell over his shoulders and giving him an otherworldly appearance.

"I am Isskai, the Holy Radiance, forged in the fires of the Clade and second heir to the White Throne after my father, Israis, the Holy Light, Grand Warden of the Four Cardinal Gates and Keeper of the Keys, first heir to the White Throne after Isarn, the Holy Iron, Servant of the Empire, Keeper of the Realm and beloved grandfather."

Isskai stepped past the doors as they began to shut behind him. He circled the great black obsidian table that sat in the center of the council chamber and took a seat across from his father and next to Isarn. He pulled the scarlet hood back and let it fall over his broad shoulders, the evening sun streaming through the room, making his white blonde hair appear even lighter. He nodded to his father and smiled at Isarn.

"What would you have of us, all gathered here so late in the day? I was led to believe we would receive the noblemen tomorrow. Have they arrived this night?"

Israis leaned forward and stroked his black beard as he looked at Isarn. "As much as I enjoy the company of family, father, I too am curious why you would call away my son from his bedchamber so soon after his marriage. Less than a month ago he completed his training with the Clade and returned here to be married. Soon he will leave us once again to train with the Night Watch. His time is nearly as limited as my own."

Isarn took a deep breath, his frail shoulders rising and falling beneath his white robes which swallowed his bent and shrunken form.

"And my time is more limited than both of yours," he said looking at each in turn, a fire burning in his eyes. "You speak of precious time, but are still at the dawn of all your days," Isarn said waving a gnarled old hand at his grandson Isskai. "And you are King of the Free People of Fyrian, a lion in his prime, the sun upon your shoulders," he said jabbing a bony finger in the air toward Israis. He sighed and slumped back into his chair. "But I am nearly ninety six years old, and the sun begins to set for me."

"Nonsense, grandfather," Isskai began but held his tongue when Isarn raised his hand.

"But I did not call you here to bemoan my fate. I grasped full well the implications of this forty five years ago when I stepped across the void and returned to Athar, three decades lost in an instant. Thirty years of pain and suffering endured by the people of Fyrian while I pursued Draegan across the void." He sighed and continued.

"When I returned from Iss, Athar was on the verge of collapse. Skeldus was a barren shell, not unlike the wastes of the shadow realm. Docga had been razed to the ground, a cursed land with not a living soul dwelling in its charred forests. Stanrocc had devoured itself for lack of leadership while the Clan of the Iron Mountains and the House of Corvus threatened to annihilate each other in bloody combat. And into this troubled world came thousands upon thousands of deathless soldiers and one middle-aged warrior chasing after them with grand hopes of peace."

Isskai smiled to himself at the familiar story told so often by his grandfather.

Isarn laughed dryly and shook his head. "It took considerable effort and no small amount of luck to end the threat of the unliving army that savaged the land and to unite our people. But we have enjoyed a tenuous peace since I ended the curse and rebuilt Dullahan." Isskai and Israis smiled indulgently at the old man's pride. "I struggled for years to abolish the imagined boundaries of the five kingdoms, ceding land and granting charters until the lines on the map had become so blurred the people themselves were unsure of their own heritage. Sending their children here to Dullahan be educated is a great sacrifice our people make, but with each successive generation the old hatreds lessen and the past hostilities and ancient feuds are left in the history books, rather than the border towns."

"And we are all familiar with the history books, father," Israis said. "Your exploits are well known by every man, woman and child in the Empire. The Chronicle of Fire tells of your deeds and every student that comes to us is made to recount your tale." He opened his hands and shrugged his shoulders. "But you did not call us here to have us bask in the light of your glory. You always frowned upon such conceit."

Isarn nodded his head and stood, rising slowly from his chair, his robes hanging slack from his thin frame.

"You see that the council floor has been scrubbed clean of the old lion of Skeldus," he said pointing to the area around the great black table. "There are no more kingdoms, but the old ways of thinking still exist in many minds. It is much easier to remove symbols than it is to change hearts and minds. I began the process but you must continue to uphold it. You must continue to train your children in the ways of the Clade as each generation succeeds the previous. The priests and priestesses of Vatn teach temperance and compassion in our school and these ideas plant themselves in the minds of our youth to flower when they return home. But this system needs constant gardening. You must be always vigilant to guard against hate. Keep teaching of the old ways so that we may learn not to repeat the mistakes of the past, and not be slaves to tradition."

Isarn circled the table and headed toward the massive doors. He turned and faced the table, looking over it to the far end of the hall where a single scarlet banner hung between two white marble columns that stretched to the domed roof. The sunlight streamed through the oculus and seemed to light the banner on fire. In the center of the scarlet silk, billowing gently in the soft breeze was a single, white circle.

"The empty circle," Isarn mumbled, transfixed by the brilliance of the banner and the glowing room. "The history books tell only part of the story and I have shared only some of the truth with you. You both know I worked tirelessly to remove all traces of Iss from our Empire. I have scoured the archives of Vatn and poured through the Rookery and sought even here any lingering traces of the shadow realm. I have destroyed not only its warriors but also its knowledge. I have sought to remove any chance of history repeating in the form of another Draegan."

He reached to his neck and touched the silver pin that clasped his robes. "But still traces of the old days persist."

"The Aegis and the Vaghat are tools for good, grandfather," Isskai said, rising as he spoke. "Surely you can't mean to take them from us?"

"Indeed I do, my grandchild," Isarn said. "The circle must be complete and it must be empty. When I stepped across the portal those many years ago, I made a promise that I would return. Two great evils still exist in the shadow realm and before my time comes to a close I will return there to end them."

Israis ran his hands through his jet black hair and then folded his powerful arms across his chest. "You are ninety-five years old father. How do you intend to kill the last two Blades of Darkness at your age?" he asked turning to face Isarn. "There is only one way to cross over. It requires the souls of the dead and blood magic, father. I cannot allow that in my Empire and cannot make an exception, even for you."

Isarn smiled. "There is another way, one known only to me and I will take this secret knowledge with me so that none may follow. I will end the remaining Blades of Darkness with the Vaghat and destroy the two Artifacts, sealing the shadow realm in the void where I will stand warden for eternity, a deathless king in a dead land."

"I would never presume to question your actions, for you have given me little cause to doubt you in the past, grandfather. But this seems ill-conceived. Why should you suddenly make to leave us, with a moment's notice and return to the shadow realm? You would be sealed there forever, within the curse erected by the Elder Gods. We are not threatened by the cataclysm any longer. The Dark Artifacts are gone from our lands and the Aegis and Vaghat are our strongest tools, should any evil rise again. Do not take them from us." Isskai softened his face as he smiled weakly at Isarn. "It would be folly for you to leave us as well grandfather. The people love you. You are a hero, a living legend. You must reconsider."

Isarn bowed his head with a sigh, and then turned to face Isskai. "The cataclysm was not undone, only delayed. I must act now if I am to stop it." Isarn waved his hand dismissively at his son and grandson, who gawked at the implications of his words. "But you will understand in time. In my study is the full account of what I know from my time at the Clade, and several of the hidden truths I unveiled when I scoured the land in the hopes of destroying every remnant of Iss. It will explain more than I ever could. Read this if you seek answers. Then you will know the truth of the events that led to the salvation of Athar, and will understand why I must leave."

Isarn reached through his loose sleeves and pulled the twin daggers from within his robes. He placed them upon the polished surface of the black table. The metal lay lifeless and dull, though the sun shone directly on them, the bright light washing out the intricate etchings on each blade.

"They were not always named Bhel and Asai, Flame and Frost. Before they fell from the sky on the night Athar was sundered by the Elder Gods, the metal they were forged from was originally called Dalus and Dalthyd, named for the twin sons of Greydin and Vatn. In fact their very souls have slept in this metal for three thousand years. But now they cry for release. I will give it to them and set them free."

Isarn motioned for them both to rise. He walked to each and embraced them for a moment before taking the blades from the table and slipping them under his sleeves.

"When I have left you, read what I have written and know the truths I have kept hidden. In time this knowledge should become part of the common wisdom, added to the Chronicle of Fire."

"I must agree with my son," Israis protested. "This is most unlike you father. You have gathered us here to tell us you are taking leave this very night, never to return. You take with you the Great Aegis and Vaghat, the only means we have of protecting the people of the Empire, should another evil arise." He folded his hands across his chest and stared at his father.

Isarn smiled patiently. "I am sorry for not preparing you sooner my son, but my time is limited and only recently have I finished the tasks I came here to do. My next lies beyond this realm." Isarn looked at both men and bowed his head. "Tomorrow with the rising sun, go to my study and all will be revealed. To say more now would only confuse the point." He smiled and looked up.

"Goodbye my children. I leave the White Throne and this world in your capable hands," he said and turned to the great doors. "Open for Isarn Ferus, Holy Emperor of Fyrian, Servant of the Empire and Keeper of the Realm." He turned and faced the two men, standing in helpless silence. "I will take my leave of Athar this day before the sun sets. Isskai, I shall not be here to see your son come into this world. Would you pay me a kindness and name the child Draegan? It would make my heart glad to think that as I leave this land his name would return to it."

Isarn turned and stepped through the massive doors and into the dark corridor without looking back. Israis and Isskai stood in stunned silence as they watched him walk away.

***

The study door locked shut behind Isarn, bolts and bars clicking into place as he stepped into the circular room and headed for the large oak desk. The room was spare and orderly. A desk and chair were the only furniture, and a scarlet banner embroidered with a simple white circle hanging on the wall behind the chair was the sole ornamentation. The single window let the rays of the setting sun spill into the room, giving it a warm red glow.

Isarn shuffled toward the desk and nodded. The great flagstone in the center of the room began to groan as it slid open, revealing a staircase that spiraled down into darkness. He sighed and ran his hand over the smooth leather cover of the single tome that lay on the polished surface of the desk. He took one last look out the window at the fiery sky and descended the steps, the flagstone grinding closed behind him and sealing him in darkness forever.

Outside the study several swallows darted past the window, their shadows racing across the desk. The light of the setting sun caught the tooling of the leather bound book illuminating each letter of the title which read: *The Fall and Rise of Draegan Ferus, Savior of Athar, as recounted by his son, Isarn.*

In the distance, the songs of the swallows could be heard as they rose through the air in playful flight over the gentle green fields of Athar far below.

Other works by T. R. Edwards

What happens next? If you'd like to be the first to know when more stories from the Dark Artifacts are published, please sign up for our mailing list here: http://eepurl.com/bF4-lz

I thank you for reading this book. If you enjoyed it, please take a moment to tell others by leaving a review.

If you're interested in reading more about the world of Athar and the characters in it, please take a look at these other books:

The Rise of Draegan (Book 1 of The Dark Artifacts)

About the Author

T. R. Edwards is a life-long fantasy fanatic. He is a web-designer with a degree in the visual arts. Mr. Edwards lives with his wife and two kids in a small village outside of Philadelphia. The bucolic hamlet has yet to suffer a single orc invasion.

www.ingramcontent.com/pod-product-compliance
Lightning Source LLC
Chambersburg PA
CBHW070657180626
46817CB00006B/2405